Prisms, Veils

I0611645

"Limpid and strange, teasing and discomforting, enlightening and mysterious, *Prisms, Veils* is a wholly captivating sequence that probes at the very form of fiction. David Bentley Hart reminds us that not all fables offer themselves up to be reassuringly decoded, to instruct, let alone to moralize. In his hands they leave us less, not more, certain—and the richer for it."

— China Miéville, author of *The City & The City* and *A Spectre, Haunting*

"With perfect pitch for nature's colors and tones, equally successful speaking as man, woman, faery, or bard, these mesmerizing tales all manage to become love stories in the shadow of capricious gods. Again David Bentley Hart reveals himself as a wondrous hybrid of creative writer, theologian, and channeler of world cultures. Gorgeous learning experiences for body and spirit."

— Caryl Emerson, author of *All the Same the Words Don't Go Away*

"David Bentley Hart is one of the finest writers now writing in English. Hart's mastery is evident not only in the conception and shape of a given story but in the gorgeous sentences that lead us unerringly to its denouement. Though the veil of mystery he weaves is never entirely lifted, there is at the same time a passion for clarity that, in satisfying us aesthetically, enables us to probe ever more deeply."

— Henry Weinfield, author of *An Alphabet* and translator of *The Labyrinth of Love*

"This collection of philosophical parables, modern day myths and metaphysical yarns, infused with a passion for humanity and love of nature, celebrates the moments when our lives are ennobled by something we were not looking for but should have known was there. In a manner reminiscent of Borges, but with the confidence that divine mystery can (at least in part) be known to us, David Bentley Hart demonstrates that while reality can fall short of the visions of perfection it inspires in us, the answers to its most precious and elusive riddles are gloriously manifest in our own lives."

— Tariq Goddard, author of *High John the Conqueror*

"This collection is a treasure trove of gems: sparkling, amusing, thought-provoking, unnerving, but always entertaining and profound. I spent some time trying to come up with a comparable short storyist and found myself somewhat flummoxed. Sometimes it is Tolstoy that comes to mind; sometimes it is Saki. There are stories by E. M. Forster, particularly those with a classical theme, that offered comparison. The closest I can suggest are two of my own favorite writers, Sylvia Townsend Warner and Jorge Luis Borges."

—Salley Vickers, author of *The Other Side of You* and *The Gardener*

"Whether he's adding a satyr-play to the end of *The Tempest* or wandering through labyrinths, David Bentley Hart reminds one of Borges, but a Borges who has read Borges and found him to have been rather too influenced by Pierre Menard. Which is to say that *Prisms, Veils* is up to date in its belatedness, a vast memory palace stocked with madeleines, 'Gothic here, Byzantine there, Baroque somewhere else.' Don't bother dropping bread crumbs as you peruse these fables—you don't want to find your way back out."

—Michael Robbins, author of *Walkman*

"Written by moonlight with quicksilver ink, these fables (some might call them parables, or simply tales) of David Bentley Hart may remind the reader of Wilde and Stevenson, of Kafka and Borges. They have a luxurious grace and leisurely pace that would satisfy a nineteenth-century aesthete, and yet they are deeply satisfying to an anxious twenty-first century sensibility, which, sometimes in secret, sometimes openly, longs to immerse itself in what we can simply call magical language. Hart is a sorcerer. He is a devotee of Eros. He is an architect of alternate realities. He is a prodigious scholar. But above all, he is a visionary writer of breathtakingly beautiful sentences. Come in, reader. A feast awaits you."

—Norman Finkelstein, author of *In a Broken Star* and *Further Adventures*

"Hart is our Borges, our chronicler of the liminal and crepuscular, our game theorist, our puzzle-maker. There seems to be nothing he hasn't read or hasn't hidden in these curiously maximalist miniatures. Pay careful attention as their winds blow out to sea; there are far more than spiders riding on them."

—Trent Pomplun, author of *Jesuit on the Roof of the World*

Prisms, Veils

PRISMS,
Veils

A Book of Fables

DAVID BENTLEY HART

University of Notre Dame Press

Notre Dame, Indiana

Published by the University of Notre Dame Press
Notre Dame, Indiana 46556
www.undpress.nd.edu

Manufactured in the United States of America

Library of Congress Control Number: 2024937286

ISBN: 978-0-268-20845-5 (Hardback)
ISBN: 978-0-268-20844-8 (Paperback)
ISBN: 978-0-268-20846-2 (WebPDF)
ISBN: 978-0-268-20843-1 (Epub3)

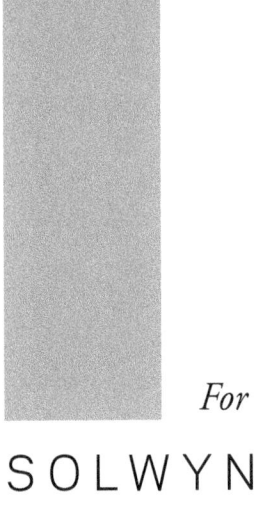

For

SOLWYN

and

PATRICK

Je suis peut-être un imbécile, mais je ne peux croire que ce que je crois. . . .

Ce n'est pas le monde réel. C'est tout au plus un rêve que nous avons rêvé

dans l'ombre de la réalité. C'est un fantôme qui se fond toujours dans

notre étreinte. Et entre ce monde spectral et le monde réel qu'il reflète

faiblement, se trouve la distance de notre exil. Parfois cet intervalle est un

prisme, admettant la lumière pure de l'au-delà, mais seulement dispersée

en éclats brillants de sa beauté. Parfois, c'est un voile qui cache

complètement cette beauté à nos yeux. La vocation de l'artiste est

«vatique»—si tu me pardonnes d'avoir inventé un tel mot. Sa vocation

est de ramasser ces irisations éparses . . . de percer ce voile. . . . Peux-tu

comprendre cela?

—*Aimé Foinpré,*

Letter to his sister Sophie,

12 May 1878

Contents

1   The True Helen

Having been stricken blind, he believed, for his poetic defamations of Helen—whom the Laconians of his day adored as a goddess—Stesichorus regained his sight by composing an expiatory "Palinode," in which he proclaimed that the Spartan queen had never really eloped with Paris, that the Achaeans and the Trojans had fought their great war over a phantom, and that the true Helen (who had remained ever virtuous) had gone instead to Egypt to live under the protection of the Pharaoh Proteus. Euripides later elaborated upon the tale, claiming that Paris had abducted a mere "*eidolon*" fashioned from aether by Hera while Hermes had carried the true Helen away to Memphis. And Herodotus recorded a somewhat less fanciful variant of the story. But the legend is of far more ancient provenance.

It was known in Sparta even when Menelaus and Helen still reigned, and had begun to spread along the Eurotas valley before Troy fell, and was the common lore of Lacedaemonian artisans and peasants before the ship bearing their king and queen sailed into the dark purple waters of the port of Gytheion. Helen herself heard of it the day after reaching harbor, from one of the Helot girls given to her as handmaidens for the triumphal procession to Therapne; and it provided her a few moments of amusement to think how foolish it made Menelaus look to suggest that he had returned from the war not with his truant wife, but only with a dream of a woman. But for the next few days she gave the tale no thought. In the following weeks, however, as the hideously gradual and circuitous royal progress crept across the alluvial plains stretching between the looming gray ridges of Taygetus and Parnon, and wound along the edges of dry ravines strewn with rocks, skirting farms and villages and olive groves, often accompanied by the discordant songs of the local rustics, Helen reflected upon the story more and more frequently, with an ever deeper fascination. Sometimes at night, after Menelaus had exhausted his carnal importunities of her and fallen asleep, she would leave her tent and look toward the far rises where distant shepherds' fires gleamed in the darkness like stars floating above the ocean, as if this land she despised had melted altogether away, and she allowed herself the fantasy that, rather than the dreary hovels of Sparta or the pale argillaceous foothills to the north or the prospect of the grim Dorian citadel awaiting her, the morning would reveal a fabulous land of sparkling sands, vast temples, emerald river basins . . .

How thoroughly she had forgotten Sparta's squalor, she often thought to herself during that journey. And already how remote seemed her memories of Troy's great golden walls, the opulence of Priam's palace, the high bright houses of the city. Now she must return to this rude, hard people she had never cared for, with their sullen satisfaction in their own terseness and their impatience with subtlety. She had loved the Trojans' oriental delight in periphrasis and elegant bombast, and their insatiable appetite for everything splendid, intricate, and oblique, and had delighted even in the languid postures and inhuman aspects of their gods—like that hauntingly terrific image of Poseidon on Tenedos. But perhaps, she thought, it really was all an illusion. Or perhaps she was the illusion, and her memories only the dreams of a phantom. True, she recalled it all. Above all she recalled, with an aching tenderness, how that lissome youth, with his long perfumed locks and his almost epicene beauty, had borne her away at night and lain with her for the first time among the fragrant grasses of the island of Kranai, while soft salt breezes poured over them from a sea made violet and sapphire in the morning twilight. Yet now even that seemed as if it had hardly ever happened. This was not an entirely new feeling. Among her own people, after all, she had been half a myth from childhood: among those who had seen her loveliness, and even more among those who had only heard of it—all those rapturous whispers that her father was not really Tyndareus but Zeus, or her mother not Leda but Nemesis. At times, she had almost found the tales more credible than her own recollections. Even as a young girl, she had occasionally suspected that the world she knew was somehow false, that it was not her true home, that she was not who she seemed to be (even to herself). And now she found it almost plausible that every man who had embraced her, from that night on Kranai onward, had been like Ixion coupling with Nephele, and that she had all along been only her own phantom, and that her true self had been—and still was—somewhere else, very far away.

In the long years after her return to Sparta, Helen often dreamed that she was standing on the high walls of Troy, looking down to where the Scamander glittered among dark grasses and bone-white rocks as it flowed down to the blue and silver sea. But occasionally, and far more vividly, she dreamed that she was wandering at evening in the porches of a great temple built in a strange style, among immense statues of bulls and of gods with the faces of beasts—cats and crocodiles—and that far off she could see a verdant river plain, and still further off a sea of golden sand stretching to the horizon, shimmering beneath a sky of deep translucent blue and a moon that shone like burning glass.

When the Samaritan sorcerer Simon had found her in a brothel in Tyre, Helen had been barely more than a girl, though she had practiced her trade for seven years. Her uncommon beauty had made her a favorite of the house's clientele of merchants and sailors, as well as a source of considerable profits, and so she was astonished when she learned that this odd and troubling stranger, who it seemed made his living as some kind of itinerant holy man, had possessed the wherewithal to buy her away from her owners. At first she was afraid of him, though there was also something about him she found compelling: something in the entrancing limpidity of his dark eyes, and in the strangely melodious intonations of his voice (despite the harsh Levantine accent of his Greek), and in the guileless earnestness with which he disclosed to her his secret teachings about himself—and about her.

The same night in which he led her away from the brothel he sat with her on a low harbor wall, and, as they gazed out at a brilliant moon shining upon the sea, he told her that he was God incarnate, who had descended from a divine Fullness, a realm of eternal light, to find her and deliver her from captivity, and through her to bring salvation to all the lost. She was, he told her, the divine *Epinoia*, the first emanation of the divine mind, who had languished in bondage to malign angels age upon age, passing through countless lives of degradation, again and again, fettered in flesh and forgetfulness. Most of what he said she found incomprehensible. But he went on for hours, telling her of the divine All, of *Nous* and again of *Epinoia*, of the Hebrew Demiurge, of the Archons and Angels who had created the world and then enviously imprisoned her, their mother, in matter; he recounted how in each age she had been a cause of contention among the angels, and so also among men, and how as Helen of Troy she had been fought over by gods and nations . . .

Here, at least, was a name she recognized. A few years before, a young tutor of wealthy merchants' sons had made surreptitious use of her services on several occasions, and on account of her name had related to her the story of the Trojan War more than once; and she, starved for any diversion, had taken it in and had held fast to the memory. She could not help, therefore, but take some pleasure in the thought that she had once been the most beautiful and famous of women, the object of every man's desire. But she found the Samaritan's words preposterous.

In the year that followed, she traveled as his consort, spoke the words he gave her to speak, watched him perform marvels, and hid her boredom well during the long discourses with which he enchanted his followers. And sometimes she allowed herself to wonder whether indeed he had not, amid the nonsense of his elaborate mythologies, touched upon the truth about her, or upon some portion of the truth. Ever since childhood, and certainly ever since she had been made a prostitute by those who owned her, she had known moments when she had felt as if it were all a terrible dream, an illusion visited upon her by some invisible but redoubtable power of spite, and as if she were not truly there at all, and as if this world were not her true home. And even now she could not avoid sometimes feeling that perhaps her true self had always been—and still was—somewhere else, in a place of light, far away.

At night, she often dreamed of the brothel and of her misery there, and would sometimes wake in tears. Occasionally, though, and more vividly, she dreamed she was gazing from high city walls upon a shining river flowing across a plain of white rocks and dark grasses, down toward a pale strand where black ships were drawn up upon the sands, and then out into a vast glittering silver bay. And on very rare occasions, far more vividly still, she dreamed that she lay with a beautiful youth in the morning twilight, among fragrant island grasses stirred by soft breezes, fresh with salt, blowing in from a violet and sapphire sea.

2   The Scholar
and the Nymph

As he stood alone in the immense library of his college a week after Michaelmas term, mourning the arrival of his sixty-fifth birthday and contemplating the mild, pristine, white light pouring in through the high arched windows, the senior scholar reflected that over the years he had perhaps added no accomplishments at all to those his father had instilled in him as a child. And these had been few enough: mastery of classical languages, knowledge of antique literature, and skill in the hybridization of phalaenopses. Moreover, he thought, closing the volume of Statius that had lain open on the table before him at no particular page for ten minutes, in none of these spheres had he ever equaled, let alone surpassed, that saturnine, perpetually weary man, whose image he could now summon up in memory only as a spectrally pallid face casting a disappointed gaze over the top of milky spectacles. Then again, he mused, he *had* finally succeeded, as his father had repeatedly failed to do, in producing a durable orchid from two seemingly incommiscible breeds: one a small ruby lithophyte—rupestrine, riparian, originally plucked from granite scree winding in a sleek purple ribbon along the banks of a Chinese mountain river—the other a cream-white epiphyte—sciophilous, with petals of almost carnal lushness, roused long ago from a moist mossy bed among the blue shadows of a Malaysian forest. And the issue of that unlikely exogamy had been truly lovely, reminiscent of a *Phalaenopsis aphrodite* but somewhat more delicate, with an elusive peach patina misted by faint red stippling, most concentrated at the blossom's center and wholly dissipating just short of its petals' edges, leaving a thin satiny hem of flawless white. It was a feat of natural magic before which his father might have felt, and even deigned to express, real admiration; but by then the old man was long dead.

The scholar sighed, lifted the book from the table, turned about, replaced it on its shelf at the end of the nearest case, and idly ran his finger down its lustrous red leather spine. As a classicist, he thought, he certainly had made no contributions comparable to his father's. His entire scholarly and literary posterity would consist in one tedious monograph on philological reconstructions of Attic pronunciations, a critical edition of Appian, a few boringly recherché articles, a translation of Nonnus's verse rendering of John's Gospel, and the one volume he had written that had achieved a small measure of popular success (but that his colleagues mostly regarded as a frivolity): his book on the classification of nymphs. Perhaps this was his father's real legacy to him, he thought. The old man had rarely betrayed any hint of a suppler, more poetic nature hiding behind the starched curtains of his prosaic demeanor; but his love of Greek myth at its most Arcadian, like his fascination with exotic flowers, suggested depths of imagination belied by the stilted aridity of his manner. There was, after all, that single mysterious utterance he had allowed to escape in one unguarded moment, in reaction to twenty lines of Latin verse his son had composed at school and brought home at the Christmas recess: "In one's life, one may know only one moment when perfect beauty is within reach; and then the rest of one's life means nothing." But he had never elaborated upon the remark—or, for that matter, said what he thought of his son's poem.

That book on the nymphs, though—the only book he had ever really wanted to write—but for his father . . .

He moved further down the stacks, to another shelf, and removed—he had no need to search for it—a large, black, handsomely bound copy of Golding's translation of Ovid: the same edition that his father had kept in his study and to which as a boy he had often repaired not so much for the text as for the exquisite and tastefully salacious ink illustrations. He took it back to the reading table and opened it with a practiced hand; he had to turn only three pages to find what he sought. It was a plate depicting Lotis running from Priapus, before being turned into the flower bearing her name. Framed by vine-leaf illuminations was a full-length image of the fleeing nymph, viewed from behind, and the figure of her pursuer, from the waist upward, looming in the fore-ground: she outstretched in flight, unclad except for a diaphanous wisp of raiment irrelevantly flung over one shoulder and billowing out be-hind her, all her dorsal loveliness fully revealed, her face turned back in three-quarter profile with an expression of pure terror, her hair a wild tumult of hyacinthine locks more appropriate to one of the Anthousai than to a Nereid; he a shadowy mass of brute sinew, with one grasping arm outstretched like a warped oak branch. The scholar closed his eyes after a moment. That image had delighted him when he was a boy; the figure and face of Lotis had so perfectly accorded with—or formed—his ideal of feminine beauty that he had repaired to it continually during certain crucial years. And still, he thought, after all this time . . .

Something stirred beside him, at his shoulder; there was a soft, high sound of breath taken in, surely a woman's, and the sound of bare feet gently falling on the hardwood floor. But it took him a few seconds to wake from his thoughts, open his eyes, turn, and glimpse a woman's naked hip, shoulder, and calf, disappearing around the edge of a row of stacks, trailing a tangle of hyacinthine black tresses and a wisp of filmy white fabric. He caught his breath, trembled violently, and then heard himself—before he was aware of speaking—calling out in a strained voice, "Wait, please!" Then, scarcely aware of what he was doing, he was running, unsteadily, and in a moment had come to the end of the row, already out of breath. There she stood, halfway along the length of the stacks, turned sideways, gazing at him with a gorgeously enigmatic smile, her near leg drawn up and delicately crooked, her arms gathered in, her fingers at her lips, in a pose that seemed—despite her nudity—impeccably demure. "Oh," he said softly, and then began slowly to

\,

approach her. She watched him, without any change of expression, until he was only five feet away; then she turned with a high bell-like laugh and dashed away and in an instant had disappeared again around the row's far end. "Oh, please," he called again, beginning to run once more, and from the other side of the books her laughter rose in a rippling glissando, somehow both innocent and wanton. "Please!"

Now, as he came around the end of the row, he was nearly staggering; and there she was, halfway along the stacks again but now slowly backing away from him, still smiling, beckoning him to follow with her fingers. "*Devte! Devte!*" she called out in a voice of extraordinary sweetness. At this, for a moment he hesitated, slightly confused by the almost liturgical impersonality of the plural imperative; he glanced about to see if perhaps someone else were in the library with them, but there was no one there. When he turned back to her again, however, it seemed that her expression had grown tenderer and that her glistening dark eyes were fixed more intently upon his own. "*Devro,*" she called, more quietly, more gently. But then, as he started forward again, she turned and ran once more, and was gone. Now he began to feel something like despair growing in him, but he followed even so, at scarcely more than a shamble. And, on coming to the end of the row, he had to reach out and support himself on the nearest shelf, and he bowed his head with eyes closed. But then a thrill of warmth passed from his hand along his arm, and he opened his eyes again to see her standing before him, her hand laid upon his; and, as he gazed wordlessly at her impossibly lovely smile, she suddenly leaned forward and pressed her lips against his. There was something like the taste of honey, the fragrance of nameless flowers, the softness of a gentle rain—something delicious, something heartbreakingly intangible—and then a feeling of delirium. He shut his eyes once more, felt himself gently sinking down against the shelves, and again that musical laughter rang out, and faded overhead.

He must have lost consciousness for a time; something, at least—perhaps the altered angle of the daylight coming through the windows—told him so when he opened his eyes; but he had no recollection of it. And he knew she was gone.

It was several moments before he was able to rise to his feet (laboriously as a man of sixty-five must) and return to the reading table. It was several moments more before he was able to detach his gaze from the image of Lotis—in part because the longing it had always provoked in him now seemed subtly displaced by something like happiness, and in part because the expression on her face now seemed to him less one of terror and more one of mirth—and to return the book to its shelf. And then it was half an hour more before he felt composed enough to leave the library for home, reflecting as he walked through the doorway that perhaps he had surpassed his father after all, and at something of the greatest importance. At least, he knew something now that the old man had not known: there may indeed come only one such moment in a man's life, but when it comes it does not reduce the rest of life to meaninglessness; quite the reverse, in fact.

3 Twilight

There were things, it all at once occurred to him, far more terrible in their holiness than all the mysteries of religion taken together—more ominous than any prophecy, more forbidding than any secret initiation, more tantalizingly impenetrable than any sacrament, more dreadful than any ritual slaughter. The vast silences, for instance, dwelling behind an ashen twilight over a dying city. Shadows deepening among deserted streets and derelict buildings. Deteriorating brick and black iron tenements, dark from burnt coke and powdered bitumen, awaiting demolition. The loneliness of a cool, early autumn evening descending upon a colorless world of stone and concrete and asphalt. A single tenuous ribbon of smoke in the distance, unfurled against a softly glowing silver sky. A desolate sense of vanished futures. These, he thought, were the true traces of the sacred. These were the true signs of any gods that might actually exist. Detached gazes, amused indifference, casual malice.

He could not have said why the thought had come to him just at this moment—unbidden but, for one stark instant, suddenly piercing—but he certainly knew he could not say anything about it aloud just now. Not only would there have been no purpose in doing so; it would have been an act of unpardonable cruelty. It could only have increased her sadness. Even unspoken, however, it had all at once rendered him unable to offer her the solace she wanted. He had known her too long not to be perfectly aware of what she hoped for from him, of course—what he was supposed to say next, what comforting words he had spoken to her many times before—and they had performed this scene together so often over the years. She was waiting patiently for him to discharge his accustomed part; but now he could not provide what she was seeking. She had wiped the tears from her cheeks several times as she sat there on the wide concrete rim of a square brick planter full of long-barren soil, which stood like an uncovered well at the center of the small brick courtyard. Her voice, subdued and lachrymose, had maintained its perfectly pitched cadence for better than an hour now, lapsing into poignant silences at only the most affecting intervals. She had kept her side turned to him nearly the entire time—a pose of inviting physical and emotional obliqueness, tacitly understood by both of them—and had been staring away for several minutes toward the far end of the broad, open alley between the rows of apartment blocks, where a chain-link fence with a missing gate marked the near boundary of the boulevard beyond. About her feet, placed so precisely together, a few bleak sprays of etiolated grass rose from the disintegrating mortar. Her long straight hair, normally a light brown verging on dark gold, had a hue like brushed steel in the waning day's empty glow. Her clothes too—a thin, limp cardigan, an undyed cotton blouse, a short woolen skirt, opaque serge hosiery—had lost their already muted colors and become just so many shades of gray and charcoal. Her wire-rimmed glasses glinted liquidly in the hand she was resting in her lap while her other hand played idly with the uppermost button of her blouse. The lines of that exquisitely delicate profile of hers, scarcely changed since the days when they had been children living two houses apart, had acquired an almost abstract purity in this ambiguous light, like smooth alabaster or white jade. And, as he looked at her, that familiar, hopeless tenderness that she alone had ever been able to induce in him gathered in his chest once more. But still he could not speak.

So he leaned back against the brick wall, a few feet away from the open door that led directly into his ground-floor apartment—the last inhabited room in this once-crowded building—sinking further into the latticed tracery of shadows from the fire escape balcony overhead. He wanted a cigarette but had none with him; at her insistence he had given the habit up three years before. He knew that he could not refuse to answer her indefinitely, and knew also that she would not cease waiting. But this sudden sense of the immensity of that impersonal scrutiny—that invisible divine malignity—had left him incapable of emollient banalities. Yes, he reflected, he loved her deeply, and it hurt him to see her reduced to weeping yet again by an unworthy lover, and he wanted keenly to ease her sorrow. And yet how strangely trivial— how tediously predictable, in fact—the occasion of her tears seemed to him at this moment. As so often before, she had thrown herself with utter abandon into a new romance, had for a time been nearly delirious with the same guileless happiness that had betrayed her so many times in the past, and had then discovered with the same shattering disillusionment as in every previous case that she had been deceiving herself. From the start, he had thought her foolish to imagine that the selfish if vapidly charming man she had taken up with had merited so much as her attention, let alone her devotion or hopes. He had known all along that the affair would come to nothing and that she would be injured once more and that it would fall to him yet again, as her oldest and closest friend, to keep her company among the ruins, and to wash and bind her wounds. She had done something similar for him often enough, admittedly, when his various dalliances had come to their inevitable rancorous endings; but he had never really expected any of his love affairs to last, whereas she had never learned to expect anything else. More was always required of him than he had ever needed to ask from her. Not that he resented this. In a very real sense, he took a kind of pleasure in it. For once, however, he simply could not oblige her.

Instead, after failing to reply to the last remark she had left dangling between them for nearly three minutes, he abruptly told her that she was an idiot, in as hard and impassive a voice as he could contrive. The word clearly startled her, and she turned her eyes to him, questioningly, her brow furrowed, her lips parted. At once, his resolve began to waver. He tried to persist anyway. He sighed wearily, maybe somewhat too theatrically, and added that he was tired of seeing her give her heart repeatedly to detestable men. As he spoke, though, the forced note of vehemence quickly dwindled away into a haplessly gentle, unmistakably fond whisper. At that, her expression of surprise changed into something like a meek smile, and she turned her gaze away from him again, back toward the distant fence. She quietly said that of course she knew he was right. Still more faintly, in little more than a murmur, she reproached herself for always making the same mistakes. Then he saw her lips tremble, in a way he knew very well, and heard a quaver in her voice that portended further tears as she said that she had been certain that this time she had found someone who . . . There, however, he interrupted her. He told her he was well aware what she had thought, since it was what she always thought, because in her mind it was always going to be different *this time*, even though it never really was. Again, he tried to sound very stern; and, again, he could not sustain the effort all the way to the end of a sentence. She told him that she knew that everything he said was true and that she did not understand why she never learned from past mistakes. He saw, as he knew he would, another tear descend her cheek.

He felt about for the pack of cigarettes that had been absent from his pockets for three years. "I suppose I should kiss you on the head," he said dryly, "and put my arm around you, and tell you that everything will be all right . . . and make you dinner, and keep you up talking till dawn . . . "

"I wish you would," she replied, now turning her gaze down toward her feet.

He closed his eyes and breathed deeply. "I will," he said after a few seconds. "You know I will. I'll look after you. I just wish . . . " He opened his eyes again. She was still staring at her feet, almost primly motionless, like a child waiting to be rebuked. And now the familiar ache of desperate affection intensified, and filled him beyond his capacity to contain it. "It *will* be all right, you know," he said, audibly yielding to the rising surge of tenderness. "You're safe with me. You know that. Just . . . just stay here tonight."

He would never not be there to catch her (as he thought of it). He had to be there. Far more than a mere long friendship united them. There was also that abiding, tremulous bond they both felt whenever they were together and no one else was about: that deeper, nameless love, at once disconcertingly erotic and soothingly familial, always almost romantic but also always hesitant and perplexed, pervaded by too many mundane recollections, many of them from early childhood, some of them quite absurd. She had provided him his first and still deepest experience of intimacy with a woman—of a shared understanding whose emotional and physical expressions were infinitely more moving than any connections he could ever forge with his male friends. He and she had even, on two occasions in the past, when both had happened to be otherwise romantically unattached at the same time, become lovers; but each time they had soon drawn apart again, conscious of a sentimental dissonance neither of them could quite modulate away—perhaps a recognition that sexual love was somehow inadequate to what truly kept them together, or perhaps the invincible reserve of two souls too deeply acquainted to surrender to one another with the necessary degree of ingenuousness or credulity. The first time had been after her return from her year in Paris as an undergraduate; her enthusiasm for everything French, especially French literature, had been a constant since her middle school years, she spoke the language with an all but impeccable Parisian accent, and she had set off for France in an effervescence of eager expectation; but while there she had become involved in one of the earliest of her many doomed romances. The second time had come five years or so later, when he had been in a state of listless depression over a disastrous liaison of his own, and she just happened to be available, and her sympathy for him briefly carried them both further than they anticipated. On both occasions, the sexual excitement had come and gone in a few days, only to be succeeded by a guarded awkwardness; but the love tying them to one another had remained unchanged, apart perhaps from the addition of a new, vaguely whimsical dimension. Still, even so, he also knew that there had always been, at least once they had grown out of childhood, an undeniable element of erotic longing in his feelings for her, and (he was quite certain) in hers for him. There was something far more selfish than mere sympathy in the anguish he felt when he saw her grieve over other men, just as there was something more enthralling than mere temperamental preference in his tendency to look for her in other women and always to be bitterly disappointed when he failed to find her. Then, too, when she turned to him for solace it was clear that she was seeking something far more encompassing and replenishing than mere friendship. But there also seemed to be an implicit agreement between them that these things should not be spoken of, or even wordlessly acknowledged by more than the most restrained of gestures.

Until now, perhaps. At just this moment—just here, under this pale, glassy, colorless, mildly gleaming sky, spread overhead like a vast mirror in which somehow nothing was reflected—something all at once seemed to him to have changed. He began to sense that perhaps the terms of this honorable silence no longer bound him. Precisely why, he did not know. Maybe it was because of the smoke in the twilit air. Or maybe the grimly imposing cinder and quicksilver shapes of the apartment towers. Rough lines drawn in coal and chalk. Fine lines etched in burnished lead. Pearl against ebony. Deepening shadows. The cool, faintly moist air. A landscape emptied of life. The cold, clandestine, insouciant gods haunting this chiaroscuro world. All of it together, perhaps. Whatever the cause, though, a sense of resignation was now stealing over him, but with it came a burgeoning sense of respite, of liberation from past inhibitions. Perhaps an incipient resolve to resist the tyranny of those watching presences. A feeling of fatigue but also of relief. He tried to make sense of it for a few seconds but then decided it was imponderable. Instead he simply raised a hand and held it out toward her. She failed at first to notice, as her eyes were still fixed on the ground before her, so he resorted to the old signal they had used with one another since childhood and softly whistled three descending notes. She looked toward him, tilted her head quizzically, and narrowed her eyes. Then a restrained, morosely bemused smile appeared on her lips, but she remained seated and said nothing. He continued to hold his hand out, however—imperiously, imploringly, both—and after many seconds her smile became somehow shy but also quite calm. She rose to her feet, put on her glasses, swept her hair back over her shoulders, smoothed her skirt over her hips, briefly arched her brows, and began to walk toward him. As she came, he remarked that, dressed and bespectacled like that, she looked like an extremely studious schoolgirl; but his attempted tone of levity was a failure, and his voice clearly revealed how much the sight of her touched him. She took his hand in hers and reminded him that he had in fact chosen this style of her glasses for her, when he had accompanied her to the optician's office the year before and she had been unable to make up her mind. Then their eyes met, directly, candidly. An understanding passed between them, though doubtless neither of them would have been able to put it into words. The subtle pink of her lipstick, he noticed, had also disappeared in this light—only a pale, pretty hint of glossiness remained—as had that soft flush her cheeks always bore (whether naturally or as the effect of very deftly applied rouge he could never quite tell). He stood up straight, stepped away from the wall, and bent forward to draw her into his embrace. His lips inadvertently brushed a damp cheek, and that fragrance of jasmine she liked to wear rose up around him. She rested her head against his chest and laid her hands lightly on his shoulders. He held her close to himself and, for a few moments, rocked gently from side to side. Then he became still, and they remained like this for some time.

At last, she began to detach herself from him, at more or less the moment at which both of them would normally have known to release one another. But he did not let go. Rather, his embrace became tighter. For several moments, she said nothing, apparently waiting for him to explain himself, her hands half gripping his shoulders and half pushing them away. Then she asked, in a voice more fragile than inquisitive, "What are you doing?"

"Holding on to someone I love," he replied.

A few seconds passed, and then the pressure of her hands on his shoulders relented. After a few seconds more, she rested her head against him again, more languidly this time. She asked him if he was quite sure this was wise, and if he knew what he was doing.

It was several moments before he answered, and then only with questions of his own. He asked her whether it was not perhaps time they tried again—time they ceased searching elsewhere for what no one else could give them—and whether she was as tired of this interminable pathetic dance of theirs as he was.

A day earlier, he probably would not have uttered those words. But now, holding her like this, in this light, under this menacingly vacant sky, everything that had seemed unimaginable until only a few hours ago now seemed not only possible, but inevitable. And this was confirmed for him when he felt the slight nodding of her head against him and heard her simple whispered, "Yes." He pressed his lips against the top of her head, breathed in that jasmine perfume more deeply, and then bent down, caught her legs up with one arm, lifted her from her feet, and cradled her against his chest. She responded with a quiet gasp of surprise that terminated in an even quieter laugh, and as he took her into the apartment she whispered some witticism about how unexpectedly old-fashioned it was of him to want to carry her over the threshold. Without replying, he set her on her feet, took her glasses and placed them atop his dresser, closed the door to the apartment, and turned back to kiss her. They could scarcely see one another's faces in the vanishing light, but they did not switch on any of the lamps. He simply began to help her undress, gently sweeping the cardigan from her shoulders so that it fell to the carpet, unfastening the buttons of her blouse as she slipped off her skirt and leggings, kissing and caressing her flesh as she gracefully emerged from the last of her clothing. For a time she allowed herself to luxuriate in his attentions, and he could feel her body growing more and more yielding in his hands and against his lips. When at last she pulled gently away and slid under the sheet and coverlet of his bed, darkness had almost entirely engulfed the room. He saw her head sinking down into his pillows as only a silhouette among shadows. When he too had undressed and had joined her and they drew together, and he felt the warmth of her flesh against his, he could tell that neither of them felt the sort of astringent self-consciousness that had interposed itself between them so insurmountably on earlier occasions. And there was now no need to rush. Everything was flowing naturally toward the emotional consummation whose elusiveness in the past had rendered the previous fitful episodes of mere physical consummation so painfully unsatisfying. He felt the old ineffable tenderness, the nameless understanding always there between them, the love whose depths they could never fully sound; but he felt it with greater intensity than ever before, and he wanted nothing more, ever, than to be here with her.

The unseen presences on high were still watching, of course, out there where a world of shadows was succumbing to the night. Of this he had no doubt. But he was certain also that their cold, pitiless gazes could never penetrate this very different darkness that he and she had drawn around themselves, safe in one another's arms. The world out there, in fact, had as far as he was concerned already dissolved into nothingness. Why, really, had either of them ever even wanted anything from it? Why had they imagined they could find any real happiness out among its forsaken streets and desolate buildings and empty lots, or anywhere at all for that matter other than in this better world that existed only between them, when they were alone together, hidden from the eyes that watched from behind the sky—hidden from that dispassionate prurience and idle cruelty?

Some time later, when they had exhausted their desires and she had fallen asleep next to him, it occurred to him that this too—this protected, secluded, blessedly carnal refuge they had at last been able to take in one another—was something holier than any of religion's morbid consolations. And, in this case, it was something far more beautiful as well. If only this night could be the final scene they would ever again need to play to its end. He kissed her lips and eyes and cheeks. She stirred but did not wake. Then he enfolded her more closely in an embrace that he now knew contained all he ever truly wished to cling to in this life. There were no other mysteries worth seeking to understand. He knew everything—*everything*—about her, better than he knew himself, and he loved all that he knew. More than that, he realized, he knew himself best only in and through her, and had no desire to know more of himself than she could give him. And there was a bliss in this unlike any other joy he could ever find.

When, not long afterward, he woke from his dream, in his bedroom on the second floor of the small suburban house where he lived alone, he was aware at first only of the golden morning light pouring through his uncurtained window, spilling across his crimson bedspread, and glowing on the cream-colored walls. Then, far more acutely, he became conscious of the overwhelming, consuming, wholly inexpressible, all but intolerable ache of longing that he had carried with him from that world into this. It took him a few moments to remember who he was not, and then to remember who he was, and at that point a wave of pure pain passed over and through him. He wrapped his arms around himself, moaned once or twice quietly, bit his lower lip, and did not rise from his bed for some considerable time.

When at last he regained control of himself, he strove also to calm himself, and made a concerted effort to resist every impulse toward anger or dejection. He knew he had to do so. He was desperate to relinquish nothing of the intensely palpable sense of her that still haunted him . . . of that darkened room that had sheltered them . . . of their retreat together into the inviolable secrecy of their love. He did not want to relinquish even the feeling of grief that now accompanied it. He knew that to surrender any part of it would be to inaugurate the process of losing it all—of letting it all slowly dissipate in the ordinariness of waking consciousness. He had had some experience in this matter, as it happened, in the past. He had occasionally before known this sudden shock of exile on waking from a dream, this traumatic expulsion from a life that, so long as he dreamed it, seemed far more true and substantial than the quotidian life that was always waiting while he slept to reclaim him for itself. The gods he so hated—or whatever one might call those sublime, faceless presences who watched him with such implacable malevolence from the other side of all phenomenal forms—had played this monstrous trick on him in the past. Although, in fact, he had come to believe that perhaps it was not entirely their game that was being played. Maybe, on this occasion as in the past, someone from beyond their dominion had somehow reached out momentarily to touch him in his sleep, attempting to rouse him from their sorcery, and they in a panic had had once more to tear him away from her before she could free him from their power. Gods are notoriously jealous beings, he recalled. "Now, lest he put forth his hand, and take also of the tree of life, and eat . . . " He knew precisely how precious this lingering, gorgeous, indefinable combination of delight and torment was to him but also how transitory and fugitive it would prove if he could not sustain it until night came again.

After perhaps fifteen minutes, he moved his covers aside and got to his feet—carefully, deliberately, with as little thought as possible—resolved to do nothing more than he must in the hours of daylight that lay before him. Those hours would be long. Curiously, he still felt the desire for a cigarette, though he had never smoked one in his entire life; but perhaps this too, it occurred to him, was a detail of the dream—of its enveloping atmosphere—that he must take care not to let fade.

A half hour or so after that, holding his coffee in one hand, he went to the double window of his dining room, pressed the fingers of his other hand against the glass, and looked out at his back garden—or at what would have been a garden had he not so long neglected it. There was a slight but constant breeze blowing outside, he could see. The sunlight sparkled in the leaves of the untended oleander bushes. The shadows of the oak branches overhanging the garden's back wall quivered and writhed in the fallow flowerbeds. A goldfinch, its yellow breast brilliant in the sun, alighted atop the back gate and briefly ruffled its pinion feathers. The deep porphyry blossoms of the crêpe myrtle near the western wall of the house flickered like flames. A monarch butterfly floated across the garden on outspread ochre wings, a few feet above the grass. And over everything the high dome of the sky, in which a few stray, mother-of-pearl clouds were drifting past, was a dazzling cerulean.

He stayed there for a long time, until his coffee was only just warm enough to be still potable, staring through the glass but barely registering anything he saw. He was trying to fix in his mind again the image of her profile in the silver twilight, and the image of her crossing the small, dilapidated brick courtyard toward him, and the image of her faintly melancholy smile as she took his hand in hers, and all the other images of her that he could recall from his dream. True, he did not know who she was, or how she had entered so effortlessly into his deepest feelings, or how she had incited that profound and frantic affection in him. His dreaming mind, now that he thought of it, had not so much as given her a name (maybe because to have done so would have shattered the spell). But, whatever the case, he knew he must not let go of her now. He had understood her so perfectly there, during those moments. She could not have been only a phantom of his imagination, he reassured himself, or just a creature of his unexpressed longings, or some ephemeral figment born out of the womb of his loneliness. If only he could preserve the peculiar ambience of the dream in his mind until he slept again, and of all those details and nuances that had made her seem so immediate and real and familiar to him—the predictability of her tears, the memories of memories, the fragrance of jasmine, the taste of her lips, the feeling of her body against his, the tenderness and the jealousy and the bliss—he might, he thought, just be able to make his way back into the world that held her and find her there once more, still waiting for him in the darkness. Surely, after all, a love so penetrating, so rich and deep, so full of delicacy and pain and delight, could not possibly be only an illusion. Surely.

4 Zalmoxis

The tale reaches us only at the end of a long but narrow historical corridor, and even then apparently as a message passed from hand to hand so many times that no one can be certain of the original author's true identity. Its sole appearance is in a document of dubious authenticity, a substantial fragment of a letter allegedly written by John Tzetzes between 1169 and his death in 1180, rescued from a library burned by Western Crusaders during the sack of Constantinople in 1204, subsequently transported to Alexandria by a Coptic merchant along with a small collection of other salvaged codices and unbound papers, then discovered in a private library by Constantin von Tischendorf in 1859 while *en route* to the Monastery of St. Catherine at Sinai, then either purchased or purloined that same year by a Russian dealer in antiquities, then sold by his son in 1882 to the British Museum, and there promptly submerged in an ocean of avidly hoarded but never properly curated documents and artifacts. It came to light again only at the turn of the twenty-first century. Some scholars have argued, credibly but not necessarily convincingly, that it is a forgery. Even among the small coterie of palaeographers and Byzantinists who know it and regard it as genuine, its dating and its attribution to Tzetzes are issues of some contention, being based as they are only on two excruciatingly oblique references in the text to the historical situation in the city at the time of its composition and on one elliptical, disingenuously self-effacing mention by its author of his own considerable achievements in the writing of histories.

Even if the fragment is authentic, moreover, the tale is recounted only thirdhand, and itself may have been derived from an earlier forgery or pseudonymous document. Tzetzes (if he was indeed the letter's author) reports reading the story in a treatise composed by the great Neoplatonist Iamblichus at some time in the early fourth century; but he supplies no title for the text, and if it ever existed it is now no longer extant (perhaps as a result of those same Crusaders' fires). Supposedly, it contained Iamblichus's extended reflections on the gods and sacred mysteries of the Illyrians and Thracians, including the eccentric monotheistic cultus, peculiar to the Getes and Dacians, of the god Zalmoxis (or Salmoxis). According to the letter—and this at least corresponds to what we know from the philosopher's surviving works—Iamblichus believed (along with many others) that the real Zalmoxis had been a mere man, a disciple of Pythagoras in fact, but that the Dacians had so revered him as their first lawgiver that they had eventually elevated him to the status of a god, and in time to the lonely station of the one and only god there is. But the letter also adds the detail that, in the course of his exposition, Iamblichus provides an extended epitome of an unfinished memoir supposedly written by Pausanias late in life, near the end of the reign of Marcus Aurelius, but otherwise unattested by any other author of late antiquity.

This, incidentally, is the chief arraignment brought by skeptical scholars against the letter's authenticity: all the evidence suggests that Pausanias's *Hellados Periēgēsis* was little regarded and scarcely known in the centuries following its author's death, and it seems very unlikely that a vestige of a later, abortive work by the same hand, even had it somehow been preserved from the ravages of time, would have attracted the notice of a figure as eminent as the great Neoplatonist. Even so, the story may be true, and, if it is, it grants us our only glimpse of the Zalmoxian cult, at least in one of its marginal expressions, as it still existed in the late second century of the Christian era, on the eve of its final extinction and inevitable supersession by the new religion.

Pausanias—so the account goes—conceived a desire late in life to journey through the lands of the Illyrians and Thracians. He had traveled far in his time: all over Greece and Macedonia, through Egypt and Campania and parts of Asia Minor; he had seen Jerusalem, Antioch, Joppa, and Rome; he had visited the ruins of Troy and ventured as far as Alexandrian Troas; he had made pilgrimages to Delphi and Olympia and had sojourned in Mycenae. But those wilder territories that stretched from the northern shores of the Aegean and Marmara to the western shores of the Black Sea had never much excited his interest, given their poor reputation for the things that most interested him— civic and sacred architecture and art—and in his earlier years he had made only rare and hesitant expeditions across the northeastern boundary of the Peloponnese and into the Thracian frontier. On the other hand, he was also a collector of myths and sacred lore and local theologies, and he had seen the urn that supposedly contained the bones of Orpheus the Thracian, set upon a pillar in Dion, below the slopes of Olympus. Perhaps in his last years the gods of Thrace summoned him to their altars and groves, and the call proved irresistible. Certainly the material recorded by Iamblichus is exclusively concerned with religious practices and traditions, and it seems that Pausanias spent a good portion of his peregrinations attempting to compile a complete mythology of the Phrygian and Thracian god Sabazius, the divine horseman who rode through the sky bearing a staff or spear of celestial power. Pausanias speculated, it seems, that Sabazius might really be Dionysus, or perhaps the Thracian Zeus, or even perhaps Apollo. Like Dionysus, he was in some accounts a god of ecstasy, and on occasion his staff was depicted as a thyrsus. Like Zeus, he was said by some to wield the fire of heaven. Like Apollo, he had slain a chthonian serpent. Pausanias also, it seems, described at some length the peculiar iconography associated with the god's worship: the strange copper or bronze figures of a hand or gauntlet raised in apparent benediction and densely festooned with esoteric devices—reptiles, intertwining serpents, turtles, toads, pinecones, branches barren of leaves, caducei, balances, eagles, rams, urns, women suckling babes, lightning bolts, mounted hunters, hounds, lions, and so forth. He also described statues of the god that he had seen in three temples, each of which depicted Sabazius as a brawny figure with thick hyacinthine locks and a heavy, ringleted beard, standing with one foot placed upon the head of a ram and holding a scepter tipped by one of those same mysterious benedictive hands. He also repeated rumors of some ancient enmity between this god and the Anatolian Great Mother, Cybele. If, however, he reached any particular conclusions regarding the god's identity, either Iamblichus or Tzetzes neglected to record them.

Pausanias apparently penetrated quite far into the Thracian hinterlands, moreover. Tzetzes's letter tells us that he had been only a day's journey or so from the Black Sea when he learned that the region's other famous cultus—the antique faith of the Getes and Dacians—still existed in some version in the mountainous regions to the north. At this point in his memoir, it seems, Pausanias interpolated the account of the Zalmoxian religion written down by Herodotus some six centuries before. There Herodotus had reported that the Getes, who were the fiercest and bravest of the Thracians, believed in and worshipped one god and one god only, whom they called Zalmoxis or Gebeleizis. They believed as well that they themselves were immortal and would each of them, upon his or her death, join their god in his heavenly demesne. Furthermore, so the story went, it was their practice every five years to dispatch an embassy to the god in the form of a sacrificial victim. This fortunate soul was flung by his hands and feet onto the heads of three sacred spears; if he died as a result, this was taken as a sign that the god had looked with favor upon their oblation and would turn an attentive ear upon their impetrations; if, however, the chosen victim had the impertinence to survive his own slaughter, he would on the instant be adjudged a wicked man whom Zalmoxis had found repugnant, and another emissary would be sent in his place. When menaced by great storms, Herodotus had also reported, the Getes would menace Zalmoxis in return (at least, this is how he interpreted their actions) by loosing arrows into the clouds. Then he had noted that the Greeks of the Hellespont and Black Sea region were of the opinion that the original Zalmoxis had been a slave of Pythagoras and an initiate in the Eleusinian Mysteries who had become a prophet or teacher among the Thracians, had built a great banquet hall where he had often hosted the

Thracian chieftains and taught them that they and their descendants would enjoy eternal life, and had then retreated to a secret subterranean chamber and hidden himself away for three years, so that his reappearance in the fourth year might be accounted a miracle. (Herodotus, of course—a detail neglected by Pausanias or Iamblichus or Tzetzes—was also convinced that Zalmoxis had been merely a man, though one who had lived well before the days of Pythagoras.)

In any event, it seems Pausanias turned his journey to the north and ventured into the mountains, traveling for many days with only two slaves and an Illyrian guide, finding the country progressively wilder, the people increasingly more uncouth, and the quality of the spoken *koinē* Greek ever more deplorable as he went. After almost two weeks among remote villages and stony passes and jagged crags and shadowy woods, he came at last to a village of the Dacians where indeed Zalmoxis was still adored as the one and only god dwelling on high. Only one of the villagers was able to communicate with Pausanias or his slaves in a tolerably fluent Greek. This man agreed to act as an interpreter for a small fee, and even provide lodging for the visitors. Pausanias stayed for nearly two weeks, having learned on the day of his arrival that, quite by chance, the villagers would soon be observing the greatest and rarest of their sacred mysteries, the same quinquennial embassy to the heavenly court reported by Herodotus—or, at any rate, a version of it. It was to be celebrated over a course of days, at the base of the high, lone escarpment overshadowing the village, within which there was a cave supposedly containing a fissure in the rock from which intoxicating fumes and the voices of holy daemons often emanated. Just as Herodotus had reported, a victim was chosen from among the villagers as envoy to the god. And the rite, again in keeping with Herodotus's account, involved three spears, though employed in a different manner.

On the first day of the festival, amid a cacophony of pounding drums and clashing cymbals and blaring horns, the entire village processed along a somewhat narrow ridge that rose from the village to a clearing before the cave's mouth. There fires of green pine, from which thick smoke issued, were already burning in large braziers on tripods. The victim—on this occasion, a young man of extraordinary comeliness—drank three goblets of wine infused with some potent nepenthe and then, after several litanies had been recited and several hymns sung, was stripped naked and laid upon the ground with arms outspread.

With the first spear, a priest in robes of solemn gray pierced each of his palms. With the second, another priest pierced the soles of his feet (and, even in his drugged condition, the young man could not refrain from crying out at this). And, with the third, yet another priest carefully opened the flesh just below his right ribs, all the way to his loins. A small patera was used to collect blood from each of the wounds, then oil and wine were applied to them, and then a salve of some kind, and finally clean linen bandages. Then some men of the village lifted him from the ground, placed him upon a simple bier, and covered his body with a dark brocaded cloth. He lay for some time in a stupor as more hymns were sung and as women from the village scattered handfuls of small white wildflowers that grew in profusion on the rocky slopes over his recumbent form. (From this detail, we may deduce the ceremony was celebrated in the spring.) In time, four priests bore the bier into the cave and out of sight, amid dense clouds of resinous smoke, followed by a fifth priest reverently holding the blood-filled patera before him, above the level of his downcast eyes.

For three days, the people waited. There was a constant traffic between the village and the clearing above, and at no time, day or night, did the sound either of discordant music or of hymns and litanies cease. Pausanias learned that the purpose of the rite was not, as reported by Herodotus, that the sacrificial emissary should simply die, so that his soul might bear the people's entreaties before Zalmoxis, but rather that he should enter a liminal state between life and death and, while suspended there, address questions to the god and obtain oracles to bring back to the faithful. Most of the prayers offered up during those days, in fact, included petitions for the victim's survival of the ordeal—at least, for now. It was unclear to Pausanias whether the victim was still expected to die at some later point, as the price claimed by the god in exchange for those vatic deliverances; but he could not imagine that, even in a place so remote, anyone would dare defy imperial proscriptions on human sacrifice. On the morning of the third day, the whole village gathered again before the cave's mouth and, to the sound of a single drum's continuous beat, punctuated by a single horn's occasional blast, the young man was brought out again, still alive but very pale and clearly weak. In addition to the priests carrying the bier, he was accompanied by a woman in a black robe, her head covered by a mantle that left nothing of her face visible except her lips and chin. Pausanias described her as a kind of Sibyl or Pythia. The villagers now fell absolutely silent. The drums and cymbals and horns were all laid aside. The priests placed the bier upon the ground in the center of the clearing and then retreated some distance away, leaving only the woman at the young man's side. She knelt down by the bier and spoke words into his ear that no one but she and he could hear, and then inclined her head so that her ear was just inches from his mouth. She remained in this attitude for several minutes, listening intently until he grew faint and turned his face aside. At this, the woman rose to her feet, drawing back her mantle and uncovering her head. She did not appear particularly old, as Pausanias had expected she would; her hair, in fact—in which she wore a braided chaplet of laurel leaves—was dark without a trace of gray. She spread her arms out to either side and closed her eyes, and in doing so revealed other eyes, with enormous dark irises, painted in thick white and black pigments on her eyelids. These appeared to stare outward blankly, vastly, at everything and nothing. The effect was uncanny enough for the usually blandly dispassionate Pausanias to confess to a shiver of horror or awe. Then she uttered—or, rather, loudly intoned—the oracles that the young man had supposedly brought back from the throne of Zalmoxis. Pausanias described her voice as harsh, savage, unearthly. Not knowing the Dacian tongue, however, he could not tell what she was saying. He knew only that her ecstatic cries continued to ring out for many minutes until at last, depleted, she fell silent and dropped weakly to her knees in an apparent swoon. All at once, an ecstatic shout went up on all sides of the clearing. The drums and cymbals and horns roared out again, more loudly than before. A great din of laughter and delighted cries swelled around Pausanias, then a thunderous but rhythmic clapping of hands, and finally a great chorus of voices singing an obviously joyous song (albeit with a barbarous melody). Apart from a few women who went to kneel beside the bier—probably his mother and other women of his family, Pausanias at first assumed—all the locals were soon dancing and singing, and shaking rattles and beating drums, and were beginning as one to flow down again from the clearing, along the ridge and toward the village, where further celebrations were evidently yet to come.

Impatient to learn for himself what had elicited the crowd's exultation, Pausanias sought out his host and asked what the "Sibyl" had said. Effusively, the man informed him that Zalmoxis had told them that the life of mortal men is brief, like the flower that blossoms and withers in a day, or like the flame of a candle caught in a rising wind, and that beyond the grave lies no happiness for anyone born of woman. At most, the dead linger on briefly as dreams among dreams, or as shadows wandering in shadowy places, lasting only so long as the living retain some memory of them. Then they fade like smoke against the sky. And the god had also revealed that, well before any of them might die, all the loves that made the world a home to them would fade, all their hopes would be extinguished, and all their joys would be exposed as illusions. It had been better for them never to have been born.

Pausanias, needless to say, was amazed. It was quite the opposite of what Herodotus's account had led him to expect. More to the point, he could not imagine how tidings of that kind had moved the villagers to such exuberant and obviously sincere elation. Surely, he said to his interpreter, these oracles must be an appalling disappointment. His host laughed, however, and replied that the message was always the same, and had been delivered in like fashion for centuries, and no one could possibly be surprised, much less disappointed, to learn what everyone already knew. But why then, persisted Pausanias, did they rejoice at the message? What comfort could anyone take from it? To this, the man responded with a certain incredulity of his own. Surely Pausanias must know, he protested, that the great god of all, Zalmoxis, dwells very far from the habitations of men, and that his words must travel a great distance to reach the waiting ears of those who adore him. What could be more delightful than to hear his voice? What rarer or higher favor could he bestow upon his worshippers, and what higher honor could mortals know? The god speaks only truth, after all; but truth directly from the lips of the god is purest nectar to the devout, sweeter than honey from the honeycomb. What could possibly be more precious? What gift could be more worth treasuring in the secret places of the heart?

There is a lacuna in the text at this point where what appear to be a dozen words or so have been almost wholly effaced, with only an "and"—a *kai*—still unambiguously legible among them. Where the narrative resumes, it records that Pausanias now noticed that the women kneeling beside the young man were not attending to his wounds or giving him water to drink or in fact moving at all. And then he saw that, while none of them had brought bandages or salve or water or a wineskin to the bier, at least two of them had apparently brought long bronze knives, which were lying in the grass beside them, and another had brought what looked like a butcher's cleaver with a concave lunate edge, which was resting in her lap.

Here, however—curtailed either by Pausanias's death or by an omission on the part of either Iamblichus or Tzetzes—the story abruptly halts.

5   *Dramatis Personae* I

"I'll tell you how the story ends," he said, "and then you supply its beginning for me. I don't quite know where to start, you see, even though I'm certain where I'll finish. But if you can provide me with the first scene—or just the initial moments of the first scene—I'm sure the rest of the story will unfold naturally between its two fixed poles. I know the final scene will conclude with him watching her from his window as she walks away and gradually vanishes in the falling snow. He realizes he'll never see her again, and it would be futile to try to call her back yet one more time. I know also that the setting is a city street, an older residential area with venerable Greystone edifices, but laid out along a broad, slightly downward sloping avenue beyond the end of which, in more clement weather, one can see thoroughfares crowded with pedestrians and the headlamps of traffic and the windows of tall commercial buildings. The scene's lighting is important of course—crepuscular, that is . . . the evening rapidly falling. The streaming snowflakes crown the streetlights with violet halos. Through the darkening twilight and the glitter of the snow, the stony façades of the homes across the street seem to waver in hue between silvery pink and moonstone blue. The windows above the pavements are all slowly becoming oblongs of glowing gold or ruddy bronze. Farther away, beyond her retreating form, the headlamps of passing taxis gutter like candle flames through the slow, steady downpour. Soon her charcoal gray coat and open umbrella merge with the color of the falling snow, and then she briefly becomes a fading shadow, and then she's gone. He continues staring for a long time, however, as the darkness outside deepens, until all at once he realizes that he's looking only at his own reflection in the glass, illuminated by the lamp on his desk, and on seeing this he turns away bitterly."

"It seems to me," she said after only a moment, "that the best beginning is the most obvious. The story should start with him before a mirror, early in the morning, precisely adjusting an exquisite silk tie or combing his hair to perfection. He's in a hotel room in the countryside, in the springtime, an expensive one with opulently appointed rooms and a sort of absurd, ostentatious, orientalist grandeur about it. A hotel a little out of its time, perhaps. Something like a spa for a vanishing aristocracy, maybe. He turns his eyes from the mirror to look through his second-story window at the slender ornamental cherry trees of the hotel gardens below, which are all in full blossom on the other side of a low, unmortared stone wall. And there he sees her for the first time, like a miraculous apparition. A breeze is blowing, you see, and the sunlight and shadows of the trees are dancing all around, and just as he looks down she walks out of the garden, emerging—practically materializing—from the clouds of descending cherry blossom petals. At once, he's seized by a fascination with her—with her great loveliness, and the elegant ease of her bearing, and the expression of innocent pleasure on her face, and of course with the sheer magic of her sudden appearance out of that dainty little tempest of beauty. I know it could all be rather trite—the artificial, chiastic symmetry of the two scenes, I mean—but a writer of your gifts should be able to avoid all the treacherous reefs along the sea-lanes. But I think the images would have to be *full* inversions of one another to be effective: the direct contrast of morning and evening, spring and winter, garden and city . . . the image of her emerging from a shimmering cloud of new blossom petals and the image of her disappearing into a shimmering haze of ice . . . Most important, it seems to me, is the inversion of actions: the initial image of him turning from the self-absorption of his mirror to the suddenly wider prospect of her otherness, out there, abruptly invading his existence; and then the final image of her retreating into an outer world rapidly contracting into nothingness, leaving him once again with only his own reflection, imprisoned in himself—the petty enchantment of the mirror becoming the bright enchantment of her gracious arrival in his life, then the dark disenchantment of her fated departure becoming the hellish disenchantment of his loneliness. Mind you, a touch of foreshadowing would also help, I suppose, just to make the obvious counterpoint of vernal and hiemal imagery a little subtler: you know, an echo of the pink of the blossoms in the pink and violet of the cityscape that swallows her up—some splashes of Monet at the edges of the canvas—but also a premonitory hint of the bleak gray of the granite façades of those older, urban homes in the gray of the garden's stone wall—a few strokes of Corot, maybe. And I imagine that the figural inversion would need to extend across the entire length of the narrative and all its episodes, so that the story as a whole has a kind of palindromic structure. Again, of course, I'm assuming that your gifts are more than equal to the challenge of avoiding too mechanical a set of correspondences. I'm also assuming you won't become too exquisitely Henry James about it all. Still, there has to be a kind of pivot at the very center, a peripety . . . a dividing line, like the surface of a mirror, a precise instant where the inversion of the story occurs . . . where the two characters' convergence toward one another is no sooner consummated than their subsequent divergence commences, so that it's clear that that one evanescent moment of perfect harmony has exhausted all the possibilities of pure happiness between them."

"Yes," he said, "yes, I like that. And it's all quite correct. The shape is obvious to me now. It's ingenious, really, and I think it would be very lovely. Tell me, though, if you were to write it, how much time would pass between the first and last episodes? And do you imagine that the failure of their love is his fault, or hers, or the fault of both, or of neither? I know what I want to do with the tale. But I'm curious as to how you would go about it."

"I really have no idea," she replied. "As for how much time should elapse, it seems to me that it could be as many as twenty years or as few as two. It all depends on how one orchestrates the events, or manages the tempo and the syncopations, so that the symmetry between episodes feels natural. I think maybe seven years would have a certain classic appropriateness to it, and would leave more than enough room for all possible dramatic and emotional developments. As for the question of fault—I don't have any opinion or inclination there. I shouldn't think it would matter whether it's his fault or hers, or just the result of any number of external circumstances—material, social, emotional, what have you. I don't even think it would matter to me whether one of them is particularly good or particularly bad, or whether they're both good or bad or neither, so long as all the episodes are well crafted and follow plausibly upon one another, and any foreshadowings or recurrent symbols are deftly constructed and convincingly rendered. I tend to think the contents of plot details are secondary to their larger aesthetic function. They should provide the occasion for the text's necessary symmetry, and not the reverse."

"I might have guessed that would be your answer," he said, smiling wryly. "Yours is a colder eye than mine. I find it as much a moral as an artistic difficulty to subordinate character and emotion and action to a preordained pattern. For me, at least, it would involve a touch of . . . cruelty, I suppose."

"I expect you're right about me," she replied with a quiet sigh. "I'm afraid it's my nature. I don't believe in moral truth, either in life or in art. There are only the moral illusions we cultivate, collectively and privately, and try to preserve so that we won't perish from reality's pitilessness and moral meaninglessness. But I wouldn't be able to abide the hypocrisy—hypocrisy *for me*, that is, not for anyone else—of letting that need corrupt my art."

"You're a nihilist," he remarked fondly.

"No," she said. "I may not believe in moral truth, but I do believe in aesthetic truth, which I think applies as much to life as to art. And I'm quite sure that character is a fixed property—or at least a fixed destiny—in all of us. Even our seemingly free choices are determined by circumstances, past contingencies, physiological and psychological attributes we can't amend, material necessities, personal limitations . . .

But, all that being granted, I'm still able to take solace from the thought that perhaps we're only figures within some greater work, and that it's a work of art, whose concinnity and complexity and beauty are all apparent from some vantage forever denied to us. I know, if nothing else, that such a vantage exists somewhere, from some . . . exalted position, at an oblique angle to the narrative flow—some place from which a synoptic view is possible—if only as a logically possible, and so logically real, world. I doubt there's anyone there to enjoy it, admittedly, but it's there as an objective fact. Just knowing that—well, I think that's what Spinoza meant by the 'rational love of God.'"

At this, he uttered a single terse laugh. "How terrible for us, then," he remarked, "who must live out the empty days in between those fixed moments of aesthetic order, imagining the events of our lives to be meaningful and significant in themselves."

"Again," she answered, "I don't believe in moral truth, so the scandal is invisible to me. But that's also why I'm not a nihilist, as you suggest I am. My belief in aesthetic truth is genuine, deep, and devout. It's a very real piety on my part to accept that the tale isn't told for our benefit, or acted out for our pleasure. We aren't the spectators of the drama. At most, we're its motifs."

6   Dialogue on an Island

[On the strand, ARIEL and CALIBAN: the former seated atop a milk-white boulder with knees drawn up beneath his chin and wings folded behind him, the air about him stained with a mild prismatic splendor; the latter crouching in the surf with one hand shielding his eyes from the sun and his thick purple tongue grotesquely thrust out before him to taste the spray rising from the softly surging foam. Both are gazing out over the water to the far, glistening green horizon, where the tip of the departing ship's masthead is just now melting away, fading between azure sea and sapphire sky like the last pale flicker of a candle's dying flame.]

ARIEL. [*Speaking mostly to himself.*] I shall miss him, however much I relish the loosing of the . . . gentle bonds his magic held me in . . . even those that constrained my tongue to speak in verse . . .

CALIBAN. [*With a disdainful hiss*:] I don't mourn the loss of my yoke. He wouldn't have struck it off at all if he hadn't gone. [*He lowers his hand and his eyes, then runs two finny fingers thoughtfully along his scaly jaw.*] He was cruel, and tireless in his demands of me; he drove me to my tasks with ten thousand pinches. He didn't cosset and caress me as he did you.

ARIEL. I never attempted carnal outrages against his daughter—and when she was just a child—to people this isle with my own kind.

CALIBAN. I was a child too . . . at least in apprehension . . . wild as this sweet desert. It was a natural impulse only. I knew only my lovely hunger . . . my delight in the delicate vision that had descended on these shores . . . that beauty . . . and no one had yet taught me to speak my joy. I knew only to grasp at it. Anyway, how could you understand? Are you even man or woman, you dainty sprite?

ARIEL. [*Laughing*:] How now, you impudent monster. Are you man or fish?

CALIBAN. I am as Setebos framed me, in his wisdom, when he twisted together fibers of flame and sea and air to make me.

ARIEL. Then he was a very incompetent craftsman indeed. No, you are as your father sired you: a mooncalf . . . an incondite cambion. Those misshapen limbs, that hide both hirsute and squamous, that brutish brow, those pendulous lips and ears, that shambling gait—no, even a doltish sublunary daemon like old Setebos couldn't err that egregiously. You are what you are because your vile dam coupled with an incubus whom she had summoned down with goetic art from the sphere of fire. You are the deformed issue of an abominable congress, an atrocious mingling of two natures equally vicious but mutually repugnant.

CALIBAN. [*Pressing his fists against his bowed head*:] You mock me so cruelly only because you know I can't catch you. Revile my god, if you wish; but it's cruel to speak so of my mother. I still dream of her. She was tender to me . . . stroked my head and limbs, and sang to me . . . fed me with sweet snails and berries and syrups of boiled flowers . . . loved me.

ARIEL. Do not, I pray you, extol Sycorax to me. Twelve years I was imprisoned in agony in that cloven pine.

CALIBAN. I speak . . . [*But, opening his eyes, he pauses, moans in eager glee, and snatches a small mussel from the sand where a receding wave has just deposited it. At once he cracks it with his teeth, greedily sucks out the meat, swallows, then sighs contentedly. Tossing the fragments of shell aside and brushing the sand from his lips:*] Tender. Sweet.

ARIEL. [*Smiling in amusement:*] Very well. So, then, what will you do with your freedom? Is there any notable difference between liberty and servitude for you?

CALIBAN. [*Raising his eyes to the horizon again:*] Why do you need to ask? Everything is freedom. I'll sleep amid the grasses blown by the salt winds till evening comes and the shoals' waters shimmer with the little dancing fires of the sea. Or I'll wander in the woods and sip honey from the heavy combs of golden bees, then lie down to sleep high in the hills, sunk among the billows of red flowers that grow there, and see the stars above me like shining gems that I might almost touch. Or I'll dine on cool succulent fish plucked from silver streams that run amid smooth stones and twisting roots, listen to the strange music that drops from the air everywhere upon this island, grow drunken on the fragrant breezes, drowse . . .

ARIEL. [*With a look of genuine admiration:*] My, my, monster—how can so wretched a brute conceive such lovely dreams? And what will you do tomorrow, then?

CALIBAN. The same. Or something else. But how can so thin and insubstantial a sprite understand my dreams? You're just a . . . a luminous shadow. How can you know the gorgeous heaviness of things, their wondrous firmness and thickness, the scent and taste, the joy of stroking and chewing and . . . ?

ARIEL. [*Somewhat irate now:*] Your temerity astounds me. Can you really compare your delights to mine? I can swim among the aethers above the moon or dive into the emerald depths of the ocean to alight upon the spires of coral palaces. I can grow so small as to slip between blades of grass like a deer coursing through a forest, or float in the crystal pools the rains leave gleaming in the rocks. I can grow so great as to dance upon the cloudy floor of heaven, or upon the rainbow's peak. I can spring to the heights of the burning meridian and descend again in an instant. I am as fleet as thought—and as free.

CALIBAN. I'm as wild as sense—and as free.

ARIEL. [*Pausing, looking up to the sky, then smiling again:*] Perhaps that's true. Very well, you prodigy. Perhaps each of us is complete in his own measure, and there's a just proportion between us . . . so long as each remains in his right sphere. [*He laughs again.*] Each nature fulfills its proper end if left to itself, and in this way great Nature herself achieves her plenitude. Yes, that seems right. The appetites of flesh, the ecstasies of spirit . . . mortal pathos, immortal contemplation . . . I wonder, though. Perhaps the only thing truly unnatural is the thing that transgresses the division between the two.

CALIBAN. Why do you babble so?

ARIEL. I mean to say, it seems quite right—quite harmonious, in a cosmic sense—that you down there should be you, slouching through the spindrift, and that I up here should be I. But, then, perhaps the true monstrosity—the true chimaera—is that very being who has just now abandoned us . . . our dear master. Really, when I think of it, how hideously terrible it seems—to be at once both brute and angel. To be bound to pain and death and yet to long for eternal things . . . to be tormented by bestial appetites every bit as coarse as yours at their most imbecile and yet also enthralled by spiritual aspirations every bit as exquisite as mine at their most radiant and rapturous. You know, I once asked him whether knowing he must die made all the hidden things of his studies—all the beautiful mysteries—seem vain. He said it made them all the sweeter; and then, after a moment, said it made them all the bitterer too. [*His face growing grave:*] How tragic . . . and mad. My poor master.

CALIBAN. You pity him? He seemed a god to me.

ARIEL. But he was also an animal. Do you not see the horror in that? Really, I am glad he's gone. I loved him, but I would not wish to see him age and die, and all that glory turn to dust. Yes, I pity him. You should too.

CALIBAN. [*Practically howling:*] You should pity me. I must die too.

ARIEL. Oh, that . . . [*He waves a hand insouciantly.*] Evanescence suits you. Think nothing of it. Sensual pleasure without a natural term would become mere repetition, and satisfaction would become impossible. But, you see, what exists in us severally, as a natural division, cruelly combines in him as an unnatural unity. That is truly pitiable. Are you not happy, after all?

CALIBAN. [*Scowling pensively, shrugging.*] When sweet things tremble on my lips . . . and sweet sounds fill my ears . . . and sweet fragrances fill my nostrils and throat . . . and the cold moon shines in the dark blue sky . . . I'm happy then, yes.

ARIEL. Quite. But he can never be—not truly, not for long. Do you not see that? So, no, I cannot pity you. But I cannot fail to pity him—and all his fellow monsters. Ah, well. [*After a pause of many seconds and a final prolonged glance at the horizon, he rises, stretches his limbs, and unfurls his gossamer wings in a bright fan of glittering opalescence.*] I fly. Farewell. [*He leaps gracefully from the boulder and into the wind, and in an instant is gone.*]

CALIBAN. [*Gazing for some moments to where the spirit has vanished, then turning his eyes back down to the surf.*] I'm hungry.

7   The Memory Palace

There was a time when I took peculiar pride not only in having rescued a grand and ancient art from its final nocturnal eclipse but also in having brought it to a level of sophistication it had never known even at its meridian. The achievement had, you see, given my life a kind of meaning. Before I conceived the idea of reviving the practice of mnemotechnics—the system of precise and compendious memorization used by ancient, mediaeval, and early modern rhetoricians—I was only an uninspired classicist, teaching Greek and Latin to undergraduates. And such I would have remained had I not quite by chance been invited to deliver a paper at a conference on Graeco-Roman rhetoric in Vienna, concentrating on any aspect of the topic that I liked, just when I happened to have been reading a mildly interesting article on ancient mnemonic techniques. I love Vienna, and all I needed to do to justify my airfare, meals, lodgings, and honorarium was gather up some easily researched historical details, select a few textual exemplars, and venture a few platitudinous observations. I had long been aware, of course, of the technique of the "memory journey" or "memory palace"—or what I had learned from Frances Yates to call the "method of *loci*"—but had always thought of it merely as a practical device, rather like a string tied around one's little finger, only far more cumbersome. In the days when writing materials were rare and costly, after all, and writing itself a slow and exacting labor, the cultivation of a capacious and organized power of recollection was a necessity for any person of intellectual ambition; and this was doubly so for rhetoricians, who were expected to be able to deliver orations on any occasion of unassailable authority and impeccable eloquence out of a mental archive at least as vast as any Homeric rhapsode's. What I could not have guessed, though, was how thoroughly transfiguring that psychic technology could be if employed with sufficient tact and inventiveness. I had not understood that it was nothing less than a means for enlarging one's inner life—the territory of one's soul, one might say—by incalculable orders of magnitude.

I should have had some inkling of this, to be honest, if only because ancient culture had valued the technique highly enough to devise a genetic myth for it, as though it were a gift from the gods. As Cicero tells the tale, the poet Simonides of Keios, who lived in the late sixth and early fifth centuries BCE, was commissioned by a Thessalian noble named Scopas, who was planning a grand banquet, to compose a panegyric in his honor for the occasion. When, however, the night arrived and Simonides declaimed the poem to the assembled guests, Scopas was indignant to find that it lavished at least as much praise upon Castor and Pollux as it did upon him, and so he declared that he would pay only half the agreed fee, leaving the rest to be discharged by the heavenly twins whom the poet evidently esteemed far more than his patron. Just then Simonides was called away by word of two nameless young men outside requesting his presence; and he had no sooner left the hall and found no one at all waiting for him than the roof collapsed, killing all the banqueters and crushing their bodies beyond recognition. The Dioscuri, it seems, had visited their wrath on the impious Scopas but had spared Simonides as a reward for his devotion. Thus it fell to the poet to reconstruct the scene of the banquet in memory, using whatever visual associations he could to recall where each guest had been seated, so that the bereaved families could accord their dead proper sepulture. In this way, allegedly, was mnemotechnics born.

Even if I had not known the legend, however, I had myself had some small experience of the technique, which should have taught me something. When I was about fifteen, my father taught me a way of quickly memorizing a long list of unrelated objects, and in precise order. It consisted simply in taking a leisurely de Maistrean voyage about my room, list in hand, pausing frequently to imagine as vividly as possible each item in turn as placed on *this* end table or installed in *that* niche or standing between *those* chairs; then, when called upon to recite the list from memory, I needed only retrace my steps to find that, in my imagination, each item was still firmly fixed in place. But I had thought it little more than a charming party trick at the time, and I had never once reflected on its greater significance (which was rather obtuse of me).

What feature of memory is more mysterious, after all, than our tendency to forge durable recollections out of purely accidental associations and juxtapositions? I am not speaking of the naturally explicable connections that exist between certain discrete experiences. It is easy enough to understand how, if I bite into a madeleine dipped in lime blossom tea, the taste might summon up remembrances of times past when I had eaten other madeleines similarly baptized—or how catching a trace of a certain fragrance might remind me of some otherwise forgotten episode when the same fragrance was present, in the way that the odor of peonies always recalls to my mind a lovely statuette of the Buddha that I once saw standing next to a glass vase full of those very flowers in full and redolent blossom. Nor am I even speaking of experiences joined purely by contiguity, such as my recollection of sitting on a certain municipal bench years ago and my recollection of a trivial fragment of conversation I overheard from some women passing by while I was there, neither of which I can now summon up from the depths of memory without the other floating to the surface at its side, and both of which I might long ago have entirely forgotten but for this wholly happenstantial connection between them. I mean, rather, seemingly wholly unrelated reminiscences, from entirely removed moments in one's life, that have become bound to one another by some subliminal sequence of chance relations that one could not possibly reconstruct—say, a glimpse I caught when I was four of an oriole in flight, brightly flashing through the air between an oak and a sycamore, and the mournful beauty of a viola cadenza by Michael Kugel that I heard for the first time when I was perhaps thirty. Who can possibly guess what subtle ties of sensibility—so tenuous as to be utterly invisible and yet so strong as to be utterly unbreakable—unite the two experiences? Perhaps it requires too great a labor of intentionality to isolate and preserve each single memory for which the mind has a use as a discrete item, but perhaps conscious intentionality can be outwitted and seduced by an unconscious grammar of occult associations and sympathies. Maybe it is the very randomness of such connections, as far as reason can discern, that makes so indelible an impression on the mind. Whatever the case, ancient mnemotechnics was nothing but this inexplicable oddity of human neurology or psychology translated into a practical science.

In any event, I began my research for the Vienna conference by going to the earliest extant sources that discuss the technique: the anonymous *Rhetorica ad Herennium*, Cicero's *De Oratore*, and Quintilian's *Institutio Oratoria*. From the last, I gained my first truly clear picture of the method as it appears to have been taught in late antiquity. According to Quintilian, an orator who wishes to fix an oration in memory should plan an itinerary through a large imaginary building, all of whose rooms and galleries, courtyards and corridors, statuary and adornments are as clearly limned as possible, and should then follow that itinerary, distributing a series of images along the way—say, a sword or an anchor—each of which symbolizes a particular topic in his oration; then, when the time comes to speak, he can retrace his journey, allowing each image to remind him of the next passage in his oration. Merely from reading this, I have to say, I naturally assumed that such a method was more likely to complicate than to simplify the process of memorization; but, out of curiosity, I undertook a few private experiments and discovered that it did in fact produce the desired results. And I decided, just out of caprice, that I would enliven my presentation in Vienna with a practical demonstration.

At first, my feats of inner architecture were necessarily tentative and unassuming in scale. There was nothing as yet especially palatial about the little Attic temple I erected in my mind, with its simple forecourt and altar, its elementary shrine and sanctuary, the large but hardly colossal statue of Apollo sheltered within it, the plain unassuming gable of its pediment, its stout Doric columns, and so forth. It was large enough, however, to allow me to conclude my lecture in Vienna by reciting fifty lines from *Paradise Lost* that one of my colleagues had chosen for me to commit to memory only the day before. It was a notable success. Given how dull academic conferences are, that small performance set my paper resplendently apart from all the others. And at that point I had progressed no further in my studies of the technique's history than Martianus Capella's discussion of "artificial memory" in *De nuptiis Philologiae et Mercurii*. But I knew on that day that I had found my true vocation.

I soon realized also that I had discovered the sole sphere in which I could plausibly credit myself with a degree of genius—even if only I would ever be able to appreciate the full range of its accomplishments. In this outer world, my scholarship on the history of mnemonic techniques progressed apace. I spoke on the topic with ever greater frequency, and my repeated but ever varying exhibitions of the technique's efficacy became something of a small sensation, at least in the dainty, enclosed gardens of academe. My greatest performance before an audience of my colleagues took place about two years after the Vienna conference, when I was able to recite two hundred lines of the *Aeneid* committed to memory only that very morning (little did any of my audience know that inwardly I was strolling through a long, brightly lit gallery, gazing at a succession of exquisitely sculpted images of Aphrodite, many of them tastefully salacious, upon the bases of which the memorized passage had been inscribed in gold intaglio, four lines to each statue, and that at the very moment I concluded my recitation I was also enjoying a leisurely contemplation of the goddess in her "callipygous" pose, gazing over her own shoulder and lifting her skirt to admire her reflection in the pool at her feet). Peer-reviewed articles were succeeded by two monographs, which were in turn succeeded by a book for a wider readership that sold unexpectedly well, principally because it included a chapter giving precise practical instructions for mastering the art. It was also, if I do say so myself, an entertaining book. Somehow my special enthusiasm for the topic infused even stories others had told many times before—that of Matteo Ricci, for instance, astonishing the Confucian scholars of the Wanli Emperor's court with his mnemonic prowess—with a certain effervescence. I was especially pleased with my treatment of those Christian rhetoricians who tied mnemotechnical method to imaginative tours of the celestial and infernal regions of the world to come. Perhaps the most purely diverting passage in the book was my detailed account of Cosmas Rosellius's opulently ghastly itinerary of hell in his *Thesaurus artificiosae memoriae* of 1579, and my description of his coldly phlegmatic attachment of articles of memorization to horrific images of eternal torment (the descriptions of heaven are equally expansive, admittedly, but nowhere near as spectacularly exotic and depraved). And I can say, without arrogance, that my analyses of Giordano Bruno's numerous treatises on the arts of memory, and of Lambert Schenkel's *De memoria*, and of Robert Fludd's *History of the Two Worlds*, succeeded in capturing both the hermetic obscurity and the aesthetic radiance of the art.

As I say, though, all of that belonged to the outer world. My true and most monumental achievements took place within. As gratifying as my professional life had become, for me it was little more than a shadow of the imaginative life that had opened up in my soul, and had continued to expand. From the completion of my first exercise in mnemonic architectonics—the design and construction of that small, nobly simple, sun-washed temple under a Peloponnesian sky—my ambitions had grown exponentially. At first, I had merely enlarged on the original edifice in a complementary style. But soon its serene, unpretentious Hellenic proportions had been absorbed into an ever more lavish, audacious, and wantonly heterogenous palace compound, which in time came to be surrounded by sprawling grounds, and these were soon converted into gardens and topiary mazes and butterfly meadows and floral terraces, and were then ever more copiously tenanted by statuary from every region and epoch of the terraqueous globe, and by ornamental cherry trees and flowering pear, and by pergolas and bowers and gazebos and Shinto *torii* and Attic *hermai* and Indian *lingams*. I added wings and stories, and set about articulating all of the building's interiors and exteriors with corridors, buttresses, galleries, annexes, catacombs, colonnades, cloisters, towers, verandas, great clock faces, vaults, cupolas, domes, spires, turrets, arches, tympanums, machicolations, and so on, as well as embellishing all of it with every kind of decorative motif I could call to mind, in an increasingly fantastic mélange of architectural and ornamental styles. The classical soon yielded to the late classical, and then to a ramifying diversity of periods and places: Gothic here, Byzantine there, Baroque somewhere else, then Persian, Indian, Chinese, Japanese—ah, you should have seen the exquisitely tasteful teahouse I installed in the western wing's "garden of the camellias"—until what I had built exceeded the most lasciviously syncretistic fantasies that might be dreamed up by the most decadent of cultural tourists. And each step, each addition—from the most heedlessly grandiose to the most demurely restrained—I fixed in memory as I went along, and revisited as often as I could, lingering in admiration of my own handiwork: a fetching corbel arch here, the pleasingly severe cuspidation of a certain door frame there, a floor tessellated in porphyry and white marble, the glossy green roof tiles of a Chinese pagoda on the eastern boundary of the estate, near a shallow river that splashed along banks of white pebbles . . . Oh, but the physical details of the estate are only a small portion of what I achieved there.

In creating my inner palace I was also creating new dimensions of phenomenal consciousness for myself. When I began working at my great design—before, in fact, it was great at all—my memory palace was only a phantom of what it would ultimately become once my sensibility had developed all its native powers. At first, I could explore those spaces in only the indistinct way of our normal imaginings, which rarely achieve even minimal clarity or depth; I was as yet merely wading in the silvery shallows at the edge of my soul's great inner seas, and could not yet enter into my estate as a completely intuited experience, of the sort I could enjoy in this world simply by strolling through a park. But in time I grew adept in the employment of inner senses that until then I had never guessed I possessed. I suspect that my labors had gradually awakened and magnified that same psychological—or perhaps neurological—power of imaginative transport that psychedelics can sometimes activate in us, but that usually lies dormant. I slowly gained the ability to immerse myself fully in that inner reality, to the point that it was no less palpable to my spiritual senses than the ordinary world was to my physical senses. In truth, during my most intense expeditions into that world, the very demarcation between spiritual and physical perception became indiscernible to me. That was when I began to build large libraries in both of the palace's wings, and to fill their shelves with volumes that I was now able to retain in their entirety simply by reading them with great care while wandering imaginatively through those stacks; thereafter, I needed only take down whatever book I wanted to consult again from its shelf to find the whole text waiting for me between its covers. And still my ambitions were unsatisfied.

Johannes Romberch had, in his *Congestorium artificiose memoriae*, envisaged a mnemotechnical system on an altogether unprecedented scale, one capacious enough to allow a single mind securely to contain the entirety of the sciences and arts; but ultimately he had succeeded in producing nothing more than a recapitulation of mnemonic techniques perfected in the past, mystified with a few tantalizing promises of the still greater synthesis yet to be revealed. More depressingly, even had he succeeded in devising the method he envisaged, it would still have amounted only to a system for the storage of brute facts. I, by contrast, soon realized that this was a mean and meager ambition; I had discovered that it was possible to recall *anything*, and even in a sense *everything*: not merely facts, that is, but every aspect of phenomenal and conceptual experience. So I committed myself to accomplishing not only what Romberch had failed to accomplish but also what he had not even dreamed could be accomplished. When I speak of my method, you see—my science, my palace—I am not speaking only of a mechanical power of recollection, of the sort possessed by those rare, neurologically hypertrophied savants who permanently record every incident in their lives, willy-nilly, without being able to exercise any critical discretion over them. Neither am I speaking of something like the mnemonic curse Borges laid upon his poor character Funes, for whom every experience, in all its qualitative dimensions, was equally indelible. I had no desire to turn my memory into a sterile archive where all the moments of conscious life, from the mundane to the miraculous, might be filed away in a series of identical folders. Neither did I wish my soul to become a passive slate on which the world could inscribe its coarse graffiti. I sought instead to become the author of my entire inner world, its architect and curator, and that meant choosing what to remember and how, and with what depth of intuition and tact, as well as what to consign to blessed oblivion in memory's deepest fathoms. And this, I discovered, required the greatest imaginable subtlety, as well as an exquisite delicacy of taste and temperament.

It would be impossible to describe exhaustively all the refinements I added to my art. I can only give examples of what I was able to accomplish, though even then I doubt I can convey either the overflowing richness or the captivating elusiveness of the prodigies I performed. For instance, in the eastern wing of my palace, in a spacious audience hall in an Italian Renaissance style, there was a particularly splendid pendentive framed by groins of dark embossed gold and painted with an allegorical tableau of "the light of reason" (a figure dressed in gold and scarlet reclining against a tree, an open book in the grass beside him, a new star blazing overhead in an indigo firmament), to which I attached the memory of a particularly ineffable feeling that had once come over me on a spring afternoon when I was perhaps twenty-five years old and had caught sight of a yellow lily nodding in the breeze over a shallow pond's mirroring surface. And, again, let me emphasize that I am speaking not merely of the memory of the event itself, and not even merely of its phenomenal ingredients, such as the hazy glow of that bright gold on the wimpling water—all of that constituted only the most superficial stratum of the recollection. What had become inseparably blended in my imagination with the sight of that pendentive was much more essentially the peculiar and singular sentimental atmosphere the event had conjured up in me—that tender, wistful delight in the sheer transience of the experience, which was also a kind of melancholy, and was somehow haunted by traces of some even earlier memory from childhood. All of this had been experienced as a unique and irreducible combination of sensations and reflections, and all of it was now preserved forever by its marriage to that pendentive. I discovered too how marvelously both sides of a wholly accidental juxtaposition of this sort can be improved by the strange alchemy of random association. On the one hand, for instance, the gold of that painted star acquired a gayer, less portentous quality from the brighter, more ethereal yellow of the flower; on the other hand, all those unutterable but absorbing intimations excited in me by the sight of that flower—those ghostly traces of something nearly but not quite recalled from childhood—now acquired an additional depth of mystery from the dark, abyssal blue of that allegorical sky. Perhaps I am failing quite to communicate what I mean, but this was the true magic—the deep sorcery—of the improvements I was able to cultivate in my art: this capacity for encompassing ever subtler, ever more diaphanous layers of association, ever more intricate patterns of interconnection, ever more delicate congruities, and with it a power for recovering and preserving even the most mysterious and

fugitive aspects of a memory. In just such glorious regresses—in the re-
covery of memories in which other memories had lain latent, and still
others in those, and so on and so forth, echoing on and on in nameless
intuitions and affections and perplexities—I was opening up whole vistas of the past that would otherwise have been lost forever, and discovering the hitherto unimaginable vastitude of an inner treasure trove
not only of things recollected, but of resurrected thoughts and inklings
and impressions and states of consciousness. I was discovering—I was
fashioning—my soul. And, as I have said, I took pride in my accomplishments. Before I began my great labor, I had never so much as suspected I might be any kind of artist, let alone a virtuoso who would
revolutionize his medium. Yet within a mere four years of inner invention—no more!—I had brought my art to a pitch of perfection un-
dreamed of by all its previous practitioners.

In the fifth year, however, everything began to fall apart.

The decline—which at first seemed minor, but which I was unable to arrest as it gradually grew into an avalanche—began one autumn
evening when I had retreated into an atrium of my palace, one of the
earliest of the large halls I had installed in the central edifice, and one
from which broad passageways led in every direction. It was open to the
sky at the center of its ceiling, and there was a lovely babbling fountain
pool in the middle of its marble floor where a stream of water ceaselessly
poured from the mouth of an extremely fanciful statue of a dolphin (in
the ancient Greek style) rearing up from the sea. Along the atrium's
walls were various chairs but also a number of small tables with marble
tops, upon each of which I had at one time or another deposited some
item of memory. I had come here on this occasion to retrieve one of
them, the precise image of a pocket-watch that had belonged to my
grandfather and that I had owned for most of my adult life, but that I
had given to my brother two years earlier on account of his interest in
antique timepieces. It bore an inscription on the inside of its hunter-
case that I wanted to recall. I found it where I had left it easily enough,
resting atop a slender table only just large enough to support a large
vase, near the mouth of a corridor leading to the western wing. But no
sooner had I begun to reach for it than I had to snatch my hand away in
shock, because lying next to it was a delicate woman's hair-comb fashioned from what appeared to be mother-of-pearl. For the life of me, I

had no memory of ever having seen this object before, let alone of having placed it beside my grandfather's watch. Admittedly, by that time I had accumulated so vast an argosy of every conceivable kind of memorandum that I was often pleasantly surprised by coming upon something I had forgotten leaving there; but not a single item in that whole vast collection, once I had assigned it a location in my palace, had ever become detached from the environment of associations encompassing it, or had been rendered unrecognizable to me. What would have been the point, after all, if the things stored away in my palace could lose their context entirely? And yet, no matter how long I contemplated this vexingly dissonant object, I could find no other trace of it in memory, or any clue as to how it had got here. For a moment, something like a fit of despair took hold of me. I felt a premonition—of precisely what I could not have said, but something grave and menacing certainly—and for several moments after that a deep despondency settled over me. Then, however, I forced myself to put my presentiments and anxieties aside. No artist creates without the occasional flaw appearing in his work, I told myself. This hair-comb, if it was anything at all, was only a fragment of something fantasized or half-glimpsed long ago that had somehow insinuated itself meaninglessly into the otherwise thoroughly coherent continuum of my anamnestic world. I lifted it from the table—it was so light that it scarcely seemed solid—turned it over a few times in my hand, and then, with resolute finality, took it to an open window in the corridor by which I had come here and tossed it out into the shrubs below the casement. Then, too preoccupied to remember why I had come, I departed the palace again, still trying to comprehend what had just occurred.

It was two days later that I decided to repeat my visit to that atrium, intent this time on opening the watch case and reading that inscription. But, when I went to the table where it lay, there lying beside it was that damnable, inexplicable, immemorial comb again. I seized it up, stared at it indignantly, frantically even, trying to penetrate its mystery. It was scarcely heavier than a feather, and its pearly iridescence somehow made it seem even more insubstantial. No matter how searchingly I gazed at it, I could assign it no meaning, no place—honored or humble—among the treasured objects of recollection stored in my palace, no metonymic association with some text I had committed to memory as Quintilian had prescribed, and certainly no emblematic attachment to some passing mood or state of mind whose feel I had wanted to preserve. It was a wholly alien object, and its impertinent presence here—especially after I had already disposed of it once—felt like the grossest violation of my privacy. Finally, angrily, I closed my hand on it and squeezed until it broke into several pieces. One of its detached teeth even pricked my palm, and when I opened my hand again I saw traces of blood near the base of my thumb. I disposed of the fragments, this time through three separate windows. Then I departed, once again having failed to inspect the watch, but now far too agitated to care. On returning to this world, however, I found myself unable to think about anything other than that comb. I now felt as if I had left the house containing everything I cared about in this life entirely unguarded, and the longer I was away, the more intolerable my fretfulness became. In only little more than a day, I went back to my palace and practically ran to that atrium. When I reached the table, there the comb was again. It had been reassembled and, apparently, glued back together. The fractures were visible and two teeth were now missing, but it was in every other respect the same offensively strange and inexplicable object as before. Now, moreover, it was resting on a rather handsome sheet of cream-colored stationery bearing a letter written in the sort of lovely, fluent cursive script that was once taught in all the schools but that has now for the most part fallen into disuse. It was clearly a woman's hand, and she had obviously used a fountain pen with a fine nib. I slipped it out from under the comb and read:

> Dear Sir—
>
> It seems to me most unmannerly of you to have twice removed my property from the place where I have chosen to keep it, and positively cruel of you to have broken it to pieces on the second occasion. It is not a particularly precious item, I grant you, at least not as such things are commonly reckoned, but it is dear to me for reasons both very private and very deeply felt. You will note that I have displaced nothing among your possessions, much less attempted their destruction. I ask you, therefore, as you are a gentleman, to have some regard for my sentiments in this matter, some respect for my wishes, and perhaps

some decent reverence for my sex, and to leave this comb where I have placed it, and where I hope ever to find it in future. I doubt it can possibly cause you the least indisposition to do so.

    Most Sincerely Yrs.,

    Mme A-R H—

I was, needless to say, astonished. Where in heaven or on earth could this vaguely antique, earnestly aggrieved, and yet primly confident voice have come from? Now my indignation had been replaced by an altogether uncanny feeling, more than a little tinged by apprehension. I replaced the sheet of stationery, looked all around me in a state of mounting dread, and then turned on my heels and ran, and did not cease running till I had passed through the compound's front entrance, crossed the broad gravel courtyard just outside, and made my way into this world again.

I was severely shaken for many days and knew I would be unable to return to my inner estate for some time. Term was out, so I had no classes to teach. And, being a bachelor, I was able to keep to myself undisturbed while I attempted to make sense of this apparently real but—or so, at least, I had thought—logically impossible invasion of my inner demesne. A colleague twice tried to reach me by telephone, but I did not reply to his voice messages, knowing he would assume I was away on a trip. For the first few days, as well as two largely sleepless nights, I began to wonder whether the sheer magnitude of the labors I had undertaken in planning and building my palace had not damaged my sanity. I certainly could not now deceive myself that the offending object was simply some otherwise forgotten item from my past accidentally dredged up out of the murkier sediments of the unconscious— unless, that is, my unconscious mind was likely to address me in the voice and punctilious epistolary etiquette of a well-bred woman from an earlier epoch. I had felt entirely in command of my medium right up to the moment when I had first found that hair-comb; and I still, for all my worry, felt that I was fully in possession of my wits; but it was impossible not to wonder whether the fissure through which this trespasser had gained entry into my private world might not be some unseen rupture within my own psyche. I flirted now and then with a number of other possible explanations. The least plausible of these was demonic possession. I am not a religious man, but neither am I a confirmed materialist. But surely a demon would have caused more disorder and expressed itself with less propriety. The most plausible explanation was metempsychosis; after all, who is one most likely to encounter in the great inner expanses of one's memory if not oneself in an earlier incarnation? Perhaps, in laying the foundations of my memory palace so deep, I had inadvertently penetrated to an earlier stratum of my own soul, and encountered myself under the aspect of someone I had been in another life. But none of these speculations allayed my distress, or convinced me that I might not be slipping into lunacy. Great labors of the soul, after all, often require great expenditures of mental health. To know for certain, however, I would have to conquer my reluctance and venture back into my now corrupted kingdom.

It was fully a week after my last visit that I again made my way to my memory palace. When I arrived, everything seemed at first tranquil and orderly. I did not bother again with the atrium; I knew now—as I should have realized earlier—that the hair-comb would still be there no matter what, because the very logic of mnemotechnics had affixed it immovably to that little tabletop for me. It was an indelible feature of my inner world now, whether I liked it or not. Instead, I took a long and leisurely tour of a variety of rooms and halls and corridors chosen at random, and then an equally leisurely tour of the grounds, seeking to reassure myself that nothing else had been disturbed or moved, and nothing else added to my collections without my knowledge. And, for the better part of several hours, everything seemed quite as it should be. It was only when I was very near to leaving again, as the evening was approaching in both my inner and my outer worlds, that I caught sight of something amiss. I was out in the terraced gardens that rise up on the gradually sloping grounds beyond the palace's eastern wing, and I was just emerging from a cunningly designed little grotto of sorts filled with white and red peonies in full, extravagant, brilliant blossom. There had been rain earlier, and the cool freshness of a wet breeze mingled very pleasantly with the perfume of the flowers; droplets were shaken down everywhere from branches and leaves, and glittered in the air like little evanescent prisms, and softly pattered among the groundcover and in the grass. I breathed in deeply and looked to the west, where the first blush of the sunset was rising from the horizon, fringed in pale green. That was when I noticed a strange liquid shimmer in the air, like the sparkling of a sunlit stream, but hovering just below a slender bough of a deep purple Japanese maple some thirty feet away, on the next terrace down. Perplexed, momentarily hesitant, I went to it and discovered that it was a diamond necklace in a distinctly overwrought antique design that had been draped upon one of the tree's lower branches and that was now dangling in the early evening zephyr, sending out occasional little opalescent flashes. I reached out toward it but then refrained from touching it, and as I was lowering my hand again a woman's voice rang out behind me from some distance away: "You, monsieur!"

I turned fully about. Resolutely striding toward me up from the lower terraces was a woman in a deep blue dress and matching hat, of the sort that would have been worn for ordinary occasions by a lady of refinement and means in the late Victorian or early Edwardian period. As she drew near, I saw that she was young and extremely attractive, with an excellent figure, dark hair, and darker eyes, but also with an expression of icy displeasure on her face. When she was perhaps six feet from me, she came to a halt and stared directly into my eyes for several moments. I found myself at a loss for words; the sight of a stranger in my private world had rendered me utterly stupid. And so finally, obviously growing impatient, she asked me, in an exasperated voice and rather heavy French accent, "Well, monsieur, have you nothing to say? *Quelles mauvaises manières.*"

I gave my head a shake or two, trying to clear my mind. "Excuse me, madame," I said weakly. Then I cleared my throat and spoke a little more firmly. "I'm surprised . . . astonished, really, to find you here. I had thought that no one but myself . . . " My voice trailed away, however, as she arched a single eyebrow scornfully.

After a moment, she sighed. "Rather than 'astonished,'" she remarked, "I would have thought the word 'delighted' or 'pleased' would naturally have occurred to a gentleman."

Now I felt not only confused, but utterly abashed. "Yes, of course, forgive me," I said. "Of course, I meant that it's a *delightful* surprise. I'm simply somewhat taken aback, as I didn't believe anyone else had access to this estate . . . or was even aware of its existence . . . "

At this, she briefly widened her eyes and then assumed a tolerant smirk. "Did you imagine that an architectural monstrosity on this scale"—she waved a hand vaguely in the direction of the palace—"could possibly be inconspicuous?"

For a moment I gazed at the immense structure, with its heterogenous assortment of turrets and domes and pediments and spires rising up against the softly darkening sky, and then merely murmured, "I suppose not, but . . . "

"*Quelle folie—quelle horrible chimère d'une maison!*" she added with a quick glance back over her shoulder, followed by a small shiver of distaste as she returned her eyes to mine. "*Le château de Versailles fit preuve de plus de modestie . . . et de meilleur goût.*" When I failed to respond to this, she sighed again, more deeply, and said, "I trust you've read the note I left you?"

"Yes," I replied, my voice still subdued.

"May I then rely on you in the future to leave my possessions unmolested?"

I stared for a few seconds into her lovely, dark, implacable eyes, wanting to protest but not feeling certain enough of myself to do so. "*Oui, madame,*" I finally said, "*bien sûr.* My apologies for the former . . . misunderstanding."

For several more seconds, she cast an aloofly appraising gaze at me, seemed to reach no conclusion one way or the other, and began to turn away. "Very well, monsieur," she said.

"And this?" I said suddenly, indicating the necklace hanging from its branch. "This is yours as well?"

She turned back again, briefly glanced at the object, and then looked at me with an incredulous frown. "*Cette vulgaire babiole?*" she said. "*Me prenez-vous pour une courtisane, monsieur?*" Then she turned away again and strode off in the direction from which she had come. The last I saw of her, she was entering the palace through a Persian pavilion I had added to the complex only a month before.

I was now far too bewildered to know what to think, or even what to fear. The mystery of the hair-comb had been galling, perplexing, and then eerie; this actual encounter with a seemingly distinct and autonomous personality in the precincts of my lovingly, lavishly created inner world went far beyond anything I could have anticipated, and made my earlier sense of mere violated privacy seem trivial; and then the presence of some other article of recollection apparently belonging neither to me nor to her . . .

Night was falling swiftly now, and all at once I had no desire to find myself here after dark. I ran down the terraced slope, stumbling once or twice, circumvented the eastern wing of the palace, slipped between a garden house and a shady pool bordered by green rushes and filled with ornamental carp, all but careened across the courtyard and through the front gate, and arrived at last back in this dreary but predictable world.

For some time, I had no desire to reenter my memory palace. I truly dreaded what I might find there—what evidences of my own deteriorating sanity or of the permeability of my consciousness to forces from beyond myself. At the same time, I was seized again and again by a deep indignation at having been driven from a home I had built for myself from the foundation up, and a retreat I had fashioned for myself for what I had assumed would be the rest of my life. And, after all, I had professional concerns to take into account. The larger appeal and credibility of my scholarship on mnemotechnics had become inseparably associated with my ability to demonstrate the efficacy of the techniques I was describing. At least, that had become so firmly established a feature of both my academic and my public lectures that I could not possibly now omit it from my "performances." The new semester was approaching, moreover, and with it my calendar of appearances. And so, a little more than two weeks after my meeting with that strange woman, I ventured again into my inner realm. It soon became obvious to me that many things had changed. There had been no revisions of the architecture or decor, and nothing of mine as far as I could discover had been displaced. But I had been back only half an hour when I found the first of various objects that had newly appeared there without my permission: a Meerschaum pipe and a leather pouch of tobacco resting on a mantelpiece in a small parlor on the second floor of the west wing. An hour after that I came upon the text of what I believe was a Chinese poem (it was in ideograms, in any event, arranged in irregular lines) daubed in sleek black ink upon a sheet of rice paper, pinned to an ottoman. And two hours or so thereafter I came upon some enigmatic symbol or ensign—a golden sword piercing a human heart crowned in flames—painted in vivid pigments on a kind of wooden escutcheon that someone had affixed to the wall in a corridor on the ground floor of the east wing (one of those metonymic devices, I assumed, described by Quintilian). I did not encounter the very attractive and very stern young French woman again, or anyone else, but I had already become resigned to the thought that I was no longer sole master of my own inner world.

At this point, I fell into a recurring cycle of emotions: indignation, followed by despair, followed by fear, followed by indignation once more. Still, I was compelled to return to my memory palace again and again. True, my visits became more sporadic, not to mention more fretful, but I had invested too much of myself in my art to surrender entirely to these invasions. And yet they were growing more frequent, more numerous, and more brazen. With each visit, I found the alien objects of memory growing in number by, it seemed, whole orders of magnitude. By my seventh incursion (as I was beginning to think of it) into my inner realm after my meeting with that young woman, I realized that in many quarters of my palace and its adjoining grounds my own memories were becoming lost in the sheer clutter of an incomprehensible midden of gimcracks and gewgaws and esoteric bibelots. I was reluctant to clear any of it away, however, for fear of another unpleasant confrontation with . . . well, I could not say with whom, but that only made my disquiet all the more onerous. When I found that some formerly empty shelves in one of the bookcases of one of my libraries had now been filled with handsome volumes bound in green leather, all of them in Arabic, I realized with an especially keen pang of dismay—verging on panic, to be honest—that I should soon not be able to find the better part of my own memories if this continued.

Initially, I should note, on the first four or five inner expeditions after that unpleasant exchange in the gardens, I neither saw nor heard anyone else. But then came a day when I was wandering the upper stories of the central edifice and distinctly heard voices rising up from the floors below—two men, perhaps three, exchanging unintelligible words in exuberantly cheerful tones of voice, and then a laugh that was obviously a woman's, followed by the louder laughter of the men. I hurried to the stairs and descended as quickly as I could; but by the time I reached the foyer at ground level, from which I was certain the voices had come, no one was there, though a fragrance of good tobacco smoke still hung in the air. Then, on my next visit, as I was making my way to a dining hall where I hoped to recover the text of a letter written by Georg Christoph Lichtenberg, I caught sight of two figures—a man and a woman in more or less contemporary garb, he in linen trousers and a white shirt, she in a short and becoming yellow sundress—at the far end of a hallway, walking away from me. They turned a corner and were lost to view before I could even consider pursuing them. That same day, I heard a little girl singing in the garden outside a window on whose ledge I was resting, though I could not see her through the high rose bushes beyond the sill. And then, on my next visit, I found my home entirely invaded by strangers. Now the rooms rang with voices. Figures in the apparels of various ages and climes sauntered through the corridors and open halls and galleries. Others strolled through the gardens. Now I was growing furious and desperate at once. Noticing two young men, dressed in tweeds of the sort that were common in Britain from the thirties through the early sixties, deep in conversation on one of the lawns, I decided more or less at random to take my complaint to them. I walked purposefully toward them, with as ostentatious an air of authority as I could contrive—firm gait, confident frown, fists clenched at my sides—clearing my throat just as I was drawing near so that they would desist from their discussion and turn to me. Without the least ceremony I began speaking: "Look, this is my home, you know. This whole estate is private property—my special retreat. None of you has any right to be here."

For a moment the two of them stared at me, saying nothing, both wearing the same bemused smile. Then they exchanged glances that suggested they were both attempting not to laugh.

"Well?" I persisted. "Can you explain yourselves?"

After a moment, the one on the left—a handsome fellow with auburn hair, of average stature but apparently quite fit—spoke in a clear Irish accent: "So, then, it's the lord of the manor, is it? Well, I was wondering when his grace would deign to show himself."

"I . . . ?" I was astounded by the sheer impudence of the man's manner. "I'm frequently here. If I've been absent more often than in the past lately, it's because of these unpardonable intrusions . . . "

"Did you think to post notices?" asked the other man in an English accent of the Oxbridge variety—also a fairly handsome fellow, if in a more willowy way, with sandy hair and a trimmed mustache and a slender build. "*No Trespassing* signs and such? I hear they're devilishly effective at discouraging vagrants." And at this he and his companion again exchanged looks of amusement.

"I . . . I . . . " I looked back and forth at the both of them several times as I fought for words. "I shouldn't need to post anything in my own . . . "

"Well, we'd have paid them no mind anyway," said the Irishman. "Neither would anyone else have done."

I took a deep breath and sought to compose myself. "Look," I said after several moments, moderating my tone, "let's be reasonable. This is a private home—one I built myself, at considerable expense . . . spiritual expense, so to . . . "

"Private?" said the Englishman. He looked about him, briefly opened his arms as if to indicate everything around us all at once, and then laughed. "What in God's name does that mean? Did it never occur to you as you were building this . . . *thing* that the constant inflation and aggrandizement of your estate would inevitably cause it to encroach on the habitations of others—and, as happened here, upon their commons? Enclosure is the gravest imaginable injustice against your fellow man, you know. That is"—he lowered his eyes to mine and all at once his expression was harsh and penetrating—"if you're even capable of acknowledging that you're merely one man among others."

"I was more mystified, myself," remarked the Irishman to his companion, "by the word 'built.'" He looked at me, momentarily dropping his eyes to my hands and then raising them again. "For one so industrious, you've a miraculous absence of calluses."

I could make no sense of any of this. "Look," I said, "I don't mean I physically constructed the place. And, anyway, how can I have enclosed anyone's commons? This whole estate—this whole world—it's within me . . . it's my own soul . . . "

"Well," said the Irishman, "if you think your soul's only your own property, and no else's beside, then you're probably too miserly by nature to notice the little allotments you've run roughshod over. But that's how things are with the gentry, I suppose."

"Now, really . . . ," I began.

"Oh, off with you, Squire Avarice," said the Englishman with a dismissive wave of his hand, his manner all at once curt and vexed.

"Shouldn't you be out riding to hounds, or expelling tenants from their farms, or flogging peasant children, or impregnating a maid, or something of the sort?"

The two young men turned their eyes from me, as if to resume their conversation.

"I was raised a New Deal liberal," I faintly protested.

The Irishman cocked an eyebrow and glanced at me sideways. "And perhaps the royal family votes Labour, for all any of us knows, but that doesn't really alter the order of society, now does it?"

And, with that, they both decisively turned their backs on me and walked away.

From that point on, it was clear to me that I had no hope of reclaiming my estate for my exclusive use. But neither had I any hope of continuing to produce work in my chosen academic specialization, let alone of making any further advances in my art, if I merely capitulated to these invading hordes. And hordes they were. I forced myself to return again and again, and each time the crowds proved to be larger, and the items they had distributed throughout my estate more numerous and cumbersome and uncouth, not to mention all too often carelessly heaped atop items of mine, hiding them entirely from sight. Sometimes when I went there in search of some particular article of recollection, I found I had to force my way through a throng of intruders—now composed of persons from every corner of the globe and every century of recorded history—just to get to the prize, and then was forced to look about almost guiltily (as if I had any reason to feel ashamed) before discreetly moving a good quantity of other objects aside until I had found what I was after. Sometimes the crowd so obscured my view of what I was seeking that I had to give up trying to see it at all. How I could have convinced myself that this was an even remotely sustainable situation I cannot say. But what artist is ever prepared to abandon his art? What king is ever eager to abdicate his throne? Still, it was impossible.

The final disaster came on the night of what proved to be my last public lecture on the history and methods of mnemotechnics. I had foolishly consented to conclude my address with a recitation of a text that would be presented to me the evening before—which turned out to be, of all things, a long extract from Browning's *The Ring and the Book*, a work whose verse I had always found about as palatable as a mouthful of thorns and cinders. I managed to gain entry to my palace early enough the next morning—well before dawn, in fact—that almost no one was there to impede me, and it took only a little mental effort to allocate five lines of the passage each to brass banderoles affixed to the frames of a series of oil paintings of the life and labors of Heracles, which hung high up all along the walls of one of my palace's grandest reception halls. It occurred to me that, even if a great number of persons should be milling about in the hall that night, the pictures were so far above floor level that they would still be visible to me. Then, however, the hour arrived. In this world, I was concluding my lecture on stage before a gathering of perhaps a hundred persons and preparing for my recitation. In my inner world, dapperly clad in the same charcoal pinstripe suit I had donned for my lecture, I was hastening toward the doors of that great hall. And there those doors were, standing wide open. But now, for some reason, they were guarded by two very tall, very imposingly muscular men in black ties and dinner jackets. More-over, music was emanating from within—a woman's voice, a soprano of superb beauty and remarkable power, singing what I immediately rec-ognized as Fauré's setting of *Le Parfum imperissable* to the accompani-ment of a piano. A placard stood upon a tripod to one side of the en-trance, giving notice, in printer's cursive, of "A Concert of Schubert's *Lieder* and Fauré's *Melodies*, performed by Mrs. A-R Hadot." I drew closer in a state very nearly of panic, and now through the open doors could see row upon row of a large seated audience of men and women in formal attire, their backs toward me, their faces toward a raised stage at the far end of the hall. There a man in white tie and tails sat at a grand piano (a late nineteenth-century Bösendorfer, if I am not mistaken) playing with admirable delicacy while a woman stood at the front of the boards dressed all in shimmering pearly white and singing with impec-cable timbre and expression. My shock at the scene was enormous, but it took only a moment for it to be surpassed by amazement of another kind. Almost at once, I found myself entranced by the singer's beauty— so much so that I even briefly forgot my anxiety. Then I recognized her. It was the young French woman who had left the hair-comb next to my grandfather's pocket-watch, and who had reproached me in the gardens for having moved and broken it. But, as lovely as she had appeared on our first meeting, she was now incomparably more adorable. In part, no doubt, this was because of the added effect of that truly exquisite voice—as light as gossamer, as powerful as thunder—but it was also because of the lustrous raven tresses that now, having been liberated from the rather ordinary blue hat she had worn during our previous encounter, had been artfully arranged to frame her lovely face and its fair and rosy complexion perfectly. Then too there was her evening gown. Its tastefully intrepid décolletage left her perfect shoulders and a generous portion of her bountiful cleavage deliciously bare, while its fitted contours frankly exhibited what her stiff and flounced skirt on the earlier occasion, with its undergirdings of petticoats, had only hinted at: the wonderful roundedness of her hips and hindquarters—as, in the latter case, became briefly evident when she turned her body toward one side of the audience with expressively open arms. For one warmly rapturous moment, I nearly lost all recollection of why I was there, and began practically to float forward toward her. But then the two large men had interposed themselves between me and that enchanting vision.

"No one is allowed to enter once the concert has begun," said one of them in a quiet but firm voice—a shaved and pomaded blond Viking giant with a midwestern accent.

"I . . . I . . . " I paused and swallowed. All at once, I was excruciatingly conscious that as I had been gazing at that divine creature I had also been suffering a more than merely incipient priapism, and I feared that, if I could not contain it, it would be humiliatingly obvious to those in attendance at my lecture back in this world, since the lectern at which I was standing consisted in only an acrylic reading surface atop a thin, flexible metal column. I strove to gain control of myself. "Listen, it's an emergency," I said, trying not to think about the young woman on the stage. "There's something of mine in there that I absolutely must get to."

Neither of the men moved, and neither altered the impassive expression on his face.

"Look, you don't understand . . . ," I began, beseechingly and fiercely at once.

The second man—even taller than the first, black, broad-shouldered, almost preposterously handsome—silenced me with a raised hand and a cold stare. "No," he said in a Caribbean accent of some kind, "*you* don't understand. No one may be admitted while the concert is in progress. No one. You're not going in." He spoke even more quietly than his companion had done, but with an additional touch of menace in his voice.

"This is my house," I practically hissed. "My home. I never agreed to allow a concert here, and I won't be prevented by one from . . . "

"I'll deal with this," said the second man to the first, taking hold of my bicep with such power that I could only wince submissively as he drew me two dozen or so yards away from the open doors. "Now listen to me," he said, glaring down into my eyes, "we know exactly who you are, and I can assure you that you do yourself no favors by reminding us." He released my arm but then began straightening and brushing down the lapels of my jacket in a way that seemed even more threatening than that crushing grip. "It certainly does not give you license to interrupt a performance by an artist of such transcendent gifts . . . not to mention such manifest charms. If there's anyone here who commands the devotion of everyone in this commune, it is surely and solely that angelic creature—whom, if I'm not much mistaken, you've already wronged once."

"Commune . . . ?" I rasped.

"It might interest you to know," he added, "that just this morning we installed a new monument on the grounds here, down near the bend in the river. A singular sort of monument, as it happens, since it's also a fully functioning mechanical apparatus, and since it's devoted to a particularly terrible goddess. Madame Guillotine, we call it—call *her*."

"Please," I murmured, "I'm only trying . . . "

"I'm not myself a Haitian," he continued, taking no notice of me, "but on my mother's side I'm descended from some of those mighty heroes who rose up under the leadership of Toussaint Louverture to overthrow the tyranny of wretched little landlords and slavers like you. I assure you that your ridiculous, mincingly bombastic claims of proprietary rights have no effect on me other than to tempt me to take you out to the garden, as an offering to our new tutelary deity. It's a keen, bright sword she wields. *Madame Guillotine a toujours soif*, as the saying goes, and it would cost me not a moment's regret to slake a little of that thirst with your blood." He withdrew his hands from my jacket, took a step back, and surveyed me with an expression of candid contempt. "So I think you had better go."

At least the embarrassing tumescence of moments before was gone, having subsided into total flaccidity as he had been speaking to me. That was something of a relief. But still I wanted to protest, to tell him that he did not understand me at all, to abjure formally any ambition as *le seigneur du manoir*, and to ask what I had done to occasion such anger from him or anyone else in this place. But there was a restrained fury in his eyes that I simply did not want to kindle into rage. I tried to stare back at him with some semblance of dignity, but after only a few seconds I dropped my gaze, turned, and left.

I was unable to recite the passage from Browning. I foolishly attempted to do so without the help of my mnemotechnic aids, but was forced after only a few broken lines to abandon the effort. I apologized profusely to my audience, pled fatigue and a recent illness, endured their generous applause, hoped that my momentary indisposition had gone unnoticed, submitted to their kind remarks and congratulations as the evening dwindled away, went to dinner with four of my hosts, affected as much buoyancy of spirit as I could, and resolved never again to lecture on the topic that had obsessed and (until recently) delighted me for half a decade. I concluded that I was like the last Bourbon monarch, having seen my absolute prerogatives seized away with surprising ease; but, unlike him, I had the option of making a prudent retreat into elective exile before the revolution reached its inevitable, horrible denouement. In fact, for some time after that last lecture, the only consideration that occasionally excited a desire in me to return to my palace—or, at least, a curiosity about what I might find there—was the recollection of Mme Hadot up upon that stage, ravishingly lovely in her evening gown, singing in that positively crystalline *bel canto* voice of hers. I could even, in fleeting moments, allow myself to appreciate the general preference for her over me on the part of the current inhabitants of my memory palace. But, whenever the thought of her rose up in my mind, I quickly reminded myself that she would have been unattainable to me in any world, coming as she did from some exalted heaven far beyond my ken or class. Anyway, she was married, assuming she was not a widow, and I really knew nothing about her—not even her Christian name, or even what Christian names her husband's initials represented. I did, on a few final occasions, make furtive visits to my lost estate, only to find it further changed. Birds now sang in the gardens, for instance—

a feature I had neglected to include in my designs, as I could find no mnemonic value in it—and sometimes I saw visitors walking their dogs along the slopes and terraces. Moreover, the weather had grown unpredictable. During my solitary tenancy, I had effortlessly preserved everything in a perpetual, lushly floriferous springtime. On my last visit, however, snow was falling, the air was briskly cold, the gardens were denuded of their flowers and the trees of their greenery, children were playing on sleds on the slopes above the terraces or building snow castles in the gardens, couples in heavy coats and woolen scarves strolled at their ease across the glittering lawns . . . Really, an almost idyllic winter scene—or it would have been, in different circumstances.

There is not much more to tell, really.

I remarked above that, before undertaking my great interior labors, I had not understood how vastly they would enlarge my inner life. Neither, however, had I understood something I learned only much too late: to wit, that the inner life, when amplified beyond its normal confines, is rather like an empire. The greater its dimensions, the more uncertain the security of its frontiers; there is a point past which the conquest of new territories of the soul becomes indistinguishable from the dissolution of the self. Having retreated as thoroughly into my own inner mansions at it seemed possible to go, I had turned around to find them invaded and, for all intents and purposes, already conquered. Not that I know who these rough multitudes pouring across my over-extended dominion's porous and disintegrating borders truly are. I some time ago abandoned the notion that they were metempsychotic souvenirs from previous lives. There were simply too many of them. Quite a number were obviously one another's contemporaries, and some had even been one another's acquaintances of old. I had seen dozens of grown adults, for instance, whose attire and manners clearly came from the last few decades of the nineteenth century or the first few decades of the twentieth. I could scarcely have transmigrated through so many full lives in a span of, at most, two or three generations.

I did, however, recently recall, for whatever it is worth, that early in my study of mnemotechnics, when I was still casting my nets wide, I had read somewhere that when St. Augustine spoke about "memory" he was referring not merely to the faculty of recollection, but rather to the whole depth of the mind, as it exists in but also transcends each of us—

so much so that, in entering into it deeply enough, one finds not oneself but God, the source and ground of all. At the time, I thought little of it. I find all religion ludicrous and could not be more indifferent to the "brute and blackguard" celebrated in most theologies; but perhaps I should have paid more attention. Maybe the isolated self—the small, finite, self-aware empirical ego in all its absurd grandiosity and pathetic indigence—is only a meager, attenuated, rarefied distillate of something immeasurably richer and vaster, lying for the most part below the threshold of awareness. Maybe the "I" is always only a small island only perilously elevated above the surface of a boundless ocean of consciousness, or (better) of the unconscious. And who knows what dwells in those depths—what ancient remembrances, what dreams and fancies and prophetic visions and magical beasts, what primordial agonies? Maybe to descend into that abyss is to sink back down toward a level of pure possibility, where I am not yet "I" but rather potentially anyone, the one anonymous I common to all, the pure subject, as yet not joined to any predicate by any copula. And maybe this inchoate, endlessly protean self—this self before the self—can only resent being drawn upward into the light of the conscious mind. That might account, at any rate, for the rudeness, the hostility, the—what else can I call it?—*hatred* that I had encountered among those who had taken possession of my estate. Who knows, though?

There is a line from Seneca, as it happens, that is wonderfully apposite to this whole tale. It comes from one of his *Epistulae morales ad Lucilium*. Unfortunately, I cannot recall the precise wording. I once had it inscribed around the rim of a very lovely sundial, in one of the gardens on the western side of my palace, near a border of blue irises. Obviously I cannot go there to consult it. Even if I did not fear for my safety when on those premises, I find the people in the crowds there quite insufferable—especially all those sanctimonious Jacobins or Marxists or *soixante-huitards* or whoever else they are who think they know me so well. I shall never return. The sort of person the place now attracts is not at all to my taste.

8 The Principle of Sufficient Reason

Throughout the thirty-three years of her life, she had never been able to name a cause—emotional, spiritual, material, or otherwise—commensurate to the bitterness that she so often felt. Even as a child, she had been given to frequent and prolonged spells of melancholy, so much so that before she reached the age of twelve she had been thrice treated for depression with medications that, far from improving her mood, seemed only to blur its edges and make it feel all the more oppressive to her. And yet her parents and her older sister loved her dearly, never abused her, never denied her their affection or help, never abandoned her to her despondency. And, in financial terms, she had always been quite comfortable. None of this is to say she was incapable of cheer or laughter, and she certainly had no great difficulty making friends. When she was old enough, she suffered no dearth either of boyfriends or of aspirants to that station, mostly because she was extremely pretty (though she often seemed curiously indifferent to the fact), but also because her habitual sadness had by then acquired a sweetly bleak quality that, from the outside at least, was rather attractive, especially to the sort of young males who believed they alone had the power to rescue her from her dejection. None of those connections lasted very long, of course, and invariably it was she who severed them. Later, first when she was at university and then when she had become an editor at a prestigious publishing house, she contracted and dissolved a long series of diverting but ultimately uninspiring liaisons. She found romance more or less impossible, though not for want of honest effort on her part, and sexual release she found only physically gratifying; she knew that others—women of her acquaintance, in fact—were able to attach emotional significance to the act, and were even in some cases unable *not* to do so, but for her it remained always at most an amiable and relaxing exchange of favors between herself and a man with whom she knew her association would be transient. Sooner or later—sooner, in most cases—her obstinate melancholy would cause him to lose patience or interest, except in those few difficult instances when his attachment to her proved annoyingly tenacious and she was obliged to drive him away. And so she had come, at the last, to resign herself to a life of loneliness sustained by a habit of irrational sadness, convinced that it was simply a fixed and inextirpable feature of her character (and so of her destiny).

He, for his part, had perhaps an even less discernible rationale for his perpetual dissatisfaction, his long and restive spells of anomie, his frequent surrender to a quiet, seemingly unprovoked anger at the world. For most of his thirty-seven years, he had been aware of feeling as if he were tormented by the memory of something unutterably precious that had once been his but that he had always already lost and could not now recover—something he could not name or imagine, because it had been taken from him at the very moment of his birth, or perhaps even in an earlier life (though he did not believe in earlier lives). As a child, consequently, he had often been both gratuitously truculent and incorrigibly listless. He had had a kind father, a doting—though not suffocatingly so—mother, one older sister who was his dearest friend and one beloved younger sister who practically worshipped him. He was born to money, had good looks, was intimidatingly intelligent, had an incisive wit, was utterly charming despite his congenital tendency to sullenness, and was always extremely successful with girls—though also remarkably prodigal in squandering their affection once the initial seduction had arrived at its denouement. The pattern remained unchanged as he grew into adulthood, not because he was indifferent to the succession of lovely women who graced his bed—in fact, he was more than prepared to fall in love should the occasion ever present itself—but mostly because he could not conquer his depression, and neither could any of them. He never sought counseling, and he never attempted to cure (or suppress) his sadness or anger by means of pharmaceuticals. His only chemical palliative was alcohol, which he used with moderation if every day without fail. He had known from an early age that he wanted to be a writer, to the degree that he wanted anything at all, and his natural talent had brought him very early critical notice and soon thereafter a decent measure of financial success (not that he needed the money). But this, when he took the time to reflect upon it, made him only all the more aware of his sense of something absent—something that some nebulous but deep intuition assured him should have been there. So he too had, in the end, accepted his lot as a miserable soul—burdened with an immemorial regret for an object of longing whose nature he would never know.

They met in Milan. He had been living in Paris as an expatriate for the past three years, having decided that America had become uninhabitable, but just then he was renting a villa in the Milanese countryside, and from there had been making regular expeditions through Italy by train and taking notes for his next novel. She had made the journey principally to meet him, although she had also arranged to make something of a vacation of it. Her employers had lured him away from his publisher of nearly a decade, and, though she would not be working with him directly on the book they had contracted with him, they knew that she was the most cultured and most competent (and most glamorous by far) of their editors, and the one most likely to make a lasting good impression. So they deputed her for their first embassy in person to him. Through her secretary, on the day before her departure from New York, he had proposed that they have dinner together on her second night in the city, at a restaurant of his choosing, and she had sent back word that this struck her as a splendid idea. The name and address of the restaurant were waiting in her box at the desk when she checked into her hotel.

They were attracted to one another more or less at once, of course, simply on account of their physical beauty, her elegance, and his subtle, cigarette-scented panache. That they would be spending the night in the same bed was tacitly established between them almost within their first ten minutes at the table together. But soon—somewhere between the second and third course, or at least before the end of the first bottle of wine—each of them realized, with something of a shock of surprise, that the attraction between them was far more powerful and immediate than either had expected. They instantly found conversation not only effortless but also thoroughly enjoyable. They shared the same sense of humor, and both had a gift for wry quips. Their tastes seemed to coincide whenever any reference to any of the arts floated up to the surface of their talk. Each found the other's company at once wholly comfortable, as though they were old lovers, and yet thoroughly exciting, as if each found the other to be an endlessly fascinating enigma. They knew that they shared something essential in common; they might even have suspected, at least at a subliminal level, that it was that damnable propensity for inexplicable sadness; and by the end of the meal each had become almost deliriously captivated by the other.

The following morning she returned with him to the city from his villa to check out of her hotel and collect her possessions; then she canceled her reservations at the various hotels throughout Italy where she had been intending to stay over the next three weeks and moved in with him for the duration of her sojourn in the country. It was an idyllic arrangement. Twice while she was there he resumed his peregrinations by train, but only for a day each time, and each time she joined him. Otherwise, they kept to themselves at the villa, and the rest of the world receded into something vague, unreal, and uninteresting to them. The weather was splendid, the soft breezes were nearly constant, the evenings were clear. They took long walks through the countryside and long baths together afterward. They ate out on the shady verandahs on the villa's western side, or on a blanket spread out on the grass in its olive grove, and exhausted the wines he had had stored in the cellar when he first took up occupancy. They never tired of one another's company or conversation, and their laughter was constant in a way that was quite abnormal for either of them. There was a shallow, well-preserved pool in the eastern garden, tiled with reproductions of Roman mosaics of

Aquarius and Pisces, where they swam naked at night in the bright moonlight. Their lovemaking was ecstatic or languid or (on two or three occasions) delightfully fierce, as the mood or the hour warranted, and in every instance unreserved, emotionally no less than physically. Neither had ever before surrendered to another person so spontaneously or with such guileless abandon; certainly neither had ever experienced carnal pleasures so wholly pervaded—and so obviously and marvelously intensified—by deep affection. As neither had had any experience of authentic romantic love, its sudden arrival in their lives, and at so late a moment, was overwhelming for both of them. Neither had ever so much as suspected that this was what it was like to be wholly absorbed in another's presence, or so fearful of another's absence.

And yet, at the end of those three weeks, she had to return to New York, and he had to return to his writing. They fully intended to continue their affair, as soon as they could contrive to fit their lives together in some plausible way. Perhaps, had they met when they were younger—say, a decade earlier—at a moment when their characters had not yet crystallized into such hard and lucid immutability, or when they had not yet become consciously resigned to who they were, they would have succeeded. For a time, they remained in touch across the vast distance separating them, and made hopeful if vague plans for one of them soon visiting the other. But it was not very long before both of them began to lose faith in the happiness they had known at the villa, and to doubt that it could be renewed—or, at any rate, sustained past a certain predictable limit. They had both become comfortable over the years with who they were, and had come to rely upon the dependable constancy of the loneliness each of them had guarded so cautiously for a lifetime. And perhaps, after they had been apart long enough to reflect on the matter, they both came to feel—if only, again, at a subliminal level—that it had been their sadness that had united them so ecstatically, and so to fear that, if that sadness were now exorcised, their passion would in time subside into something ordinary, imperfect, and miserably disappointing; and then they would be robbed even of the memory of that gloriously enchanted intermission in the Milanese countryside, under the Italian sun. So, gradually but inexorably, they drew apart to a safe emotional distance from one another, and allowed the connection between them to attenuate into a kind of peaceful regret, and finally agreed over the telephone that they should not attempt to pursue a life together. Neither of them was especially surprised to learn that they had both reached the same conclusion, so deep was their understanding of one another.

Thereafter, their lives returned to the patterns that had been established in them before they met. She remained quietly bitter, habitually melancholy, morbidly incapable of forming enduring attachments. He remained either angry or enervated by his sadness and always tormented by that ineffable sense of some terrible, irrecoverable loss. In fact, both were even more miserable than they had been before meeting. But, in one very significant sense at least, everything was now different for both of them, and in an oddly gratifying way. They had both perhaps found something each of them had always craved—something perhaps even more precious to either of them than love. True, neither would ever be happy in this world, but now, at least, both of them knew precisely why.

9 Thresholds

As she did each morning after completing her first ablutions and dressing but before joining her father and mother for breakfast, Lucy sent her maid away and sat by herself in front of her mirror, brushing her hair, applying her powder and rouges with as light a hand as possible without rendering them ineffectual, admiring her own beauty as frankly as she could without succumbing to vanity, and idly imagining some other life far from the confines of the barren, privileged world into which she had been born. Not that she despised those privileges or was so naïve as to imagine that she would have been happier had she come from poor parents; the few glimpses of real poverty that she had been able to catch from the safe distance of her sheltered existence had convinced her that money was by far the best protection against life at its most unadorned and unsentimental. She also knew, however, and just now acutely, that both her station and her sex condemned her to a destiny that society expected for her in a very general way, that her father and mother had recently contrived for her in very specific terms, and that she did not in the least desire; and every day that passed brought her nearer to it without opening any avenues of escape. Now that she was almost eighteen years old—the delectably vendible first flush of her nubility—the marriage that would rescue her family's gradually but inexorably failing fortune had been contracted for her with something less than even her passive assent. Well before the end of next year, 1913, she would be wed to a hale and hearty son of the Empire: broad-shouldered, narrow-hipped, prognathus, eupeptic, the scion of an impeccably inbred noble line (she forgot which title was or would be his), heir to numerous homes and extensive estates (no doubt the patrimony of centuries of enclosures); possessed too of a lavish private income, an officer's commission (she forgot what rank at present), and famously good luck at the gaming tables. (He also rode with an excellent seat—or so he had repeatedly informed her.) Once the hymeneal feast had been celebrated and the vows consummated by her ceremonial perforation—which she was certain would be accomplished by a gallantly unceremonious thrust of his loins, devoid of either kindness or cruelty but not of some measure of delight on his part at taking possession of her and at asserting a right she would be powerless to deny him—she would be borne away by him to India, where he was to be assigned to some general's staff as an aide-de-camp (or something of the sort). She had in fact been born in the Punjab, but had been brought back to England as a babe in arms and so could recall nothing of the place. In a sense, though, she knew much more about India than she did about the man she was going to marry. She had met him on at most a dozen occasions over the past year and a half, during which she had endured several conversations and dances with him (he was adept only at the latter), all at her parents' urging and under their approvingly vigilant gazes, but had gained only the most superficial knowledge of who and what he was. During that time, he had clearly become rather enamored of her without any great encouragement on her part, while she had come to detest him without any particular provocation on his. She found it all somewhat mystifying: that is, both the earnestness of his attraction to her, when she shared nothing like his temperament or inclinations, and the vehemence of her distaste for him, when he was no more intrinsically repellent than many other young men whom she found merely boring. Perhaps the strength of her aversion was really only her dislike of the looming prospect of becoming what her mother was: an indefatigable hostess, her husband's obsequious shadow and echo, heroine of the childbed, priestess of the domestic altar, warden of the household economy.

Lucy noticed an eyelash on her cheek and gently brushed it away, careful not to disturb the color she had just so delicately applied there. She peered at the clock on the mantel above her fireplace, calculating how many more minutes she could wait before her absence from the breakfast table would excite her father's impatience. She would not go down till the last possible second, she decided. Here, before this mirror, she always felt so wonderfully at peace, not because she was generally given to adoring herself—no other mirror had the power to hold her attention as this one did—but rather because of a peculiar quality in its glass that, combined with the morning light, always made what it re-flected seem somehow lovelier, more luminous, more serene. For several years after it had been given to her by Great-Aunt Emma, she had been unable to decide whether the effect was due to some curious imperfec-tion in the glass or some rare virtuosity on the part of the mirrorsmith; she knew only that it provided her a kind of serenity that she would be unable to recapture at any later hour of the day. She took pleasure in, if nothing else, seeing herself removed from the reality she knew and translated into another where it briefly appeared as if neither time nor the expectations of others could find her. Her reflection always seemed to her to be floating in some purer element there—liquid, translucent, silvery, softly glistening. At times, as she stared at herself there, she was sure she caught glimpses of small phantom gleams, faint prismatic flashes, as if the very air surrounding her were a finely faceted diamond; but they never lingered, and they seemed to change their patterns by the day. There was certainly no beveling at the edges of the glass of the sort that might diffract the daylight; and, in any event, it was never at the edges that the gleams appeared. They sparkled in elusive constellations about her head and shoulders just as she was dropping her gaze, like the traces of a melting nimbus. As a girl, she had often attempted to dis-cover whether there were small, almost undetectable flaws in the glass or in the tain behind it that might account for these momentary irides-cences; but the nearer she drew to the mirror, the more immaculate its crystal appeared; and then one day she suddenly realized that her breath did not leave any mist on its surface. It was then—long before any of the other, more mysterious phenomena that manifested themselves later—that she became convinced that her great-aunt had been speaking the truth: the mirror possessed some kind of magic.

She sighed and considered rising from her vanity table, but she simply could not make herself do it yet. She glanced again at her clock and decided that she could wait perhaps ten minutes more, then took up her brush and began slowly and needlessly stroking a single dangling tress. She knew the ritual that awaited her downstairs. The conversation at the breakfast table, conducted entirely by her mother under her father's unchangingly sober and wordless gaze—as though he were the idol in a temple before which morning litanies were being offered up— had of late become exclusively discussions of her nuptials, and of the married life that awaited her, and of her future husband's properties and station. No mention was ever made of his genial but exorbitant stupidity, of course, though it was among his most conspicuous attributes. Not that it was a topic that needed to be avoided. His was precisely the kind of stupidity much admired and enthusiastically cultivated in his circles, particularly among his fellow officers; it only made him all the more resplendent a prize in her mother's eyes. In Lucy's view, moreover, it was far from being his most disagreeable or most inconvenient attribute. After all, she sometimes daringly imagined, if she ever decided to risk scandal and ruin and to take a lover, just for the sake of excitement—as her cousin Mary had done after two years of wedlock and was still doing with great vigor after four—she would have to rely on that stupidity, especially since she might very well have to choose a paramour from among his friends. Not that she thought this likely— she had two or perhaps three other men in mind—but neither did she think it entirely impossible. Certainly she expected plenty of cheerful infidelity from him. He was in his thirties, after all, and accustomed to the perquisites of his class. A new bride, sixteen years his junior, would be scarcely likely to alter his habits. Only four months earlier, at one of his father's country houses, she had caught sight of him down a corridor and through an open drawing-room door giving a pretty young maid a kiss on the lips and a squeeze of one breast before casually dismissing her with a firm apopemptic slap on her backside. Remembering the sight, she felt a small shiver of revulsion at the thought of the license he was soon to acquire of laying those same hands on her, maybe in much the same frankly proprietary way. Mary's explicit descriptions of the wedding night had come with her typically unsentimental counsels—"Don't cry out, even if it hurts very much; if you do, try to make it sound grateful and pathetic at once; flatter him with sighs and murmurs of pleasure; afterward, act as though you appreciated his efforts, however slight they may have been; appear to fall into deep, satisfied sleep . . . "—and it all came back to Lucy now. And yet her distaste, she knew, was a matter neither of principle nor of timidity; the thought of certain other men's hands similarly employed evoked a very different, positively delicious feeling in her. So, once he had opened the gate to her heart (as it were)—chased the cherub with the flaming sword away from it, so to speak—crossed the hitherto inviolable threshold of the mystery—well, why should she not admit a special friend or two into her private garden by secret paths? Mary made it sound so exquisitely wicked, like a game of chance made all the more exciting by the enormously high wagers it involved, rather than a mere indulgence of the appetites, and claimed that the elaborate deceptions did as much as the sensual ecstasies to make it delightful; it was even, she asserted, what rendered married life tolerable, by infusing the dreary domestic sphere with an air of peril and intrigue. Honestly, it had made her marriage a success.

Lucy laid the brush down again on the rose marble of her table and continued to stare into the mirror. The morning's light invariably became gentler, warmer, more limpid in those glassy depths. She had become conscious of this daily, quiet, lovely transformation about two years before, and at first it had been mystifying and marvelous to her. She could swear that, no matter what the weather outside, a perpetual spring reigned on the mirror's other side. On gray, bleak, bitter days, the muted glow that entered her room through the moisture or ice on her windowpanes became, in the specular world into which she was now gazing, a languorous, scintillating yellow, as rich as butter; and sometimes she was sure that from the corner of her eye she had seen the reflection of a cotton curtain's fleecy hem briefly billow out from the sill in a series of ripples, as though the window were open and a warm breeze were issuing in through it; she even fancied that, so long as she kept her eyes fixed on the world in the glass, she could now and then catch a slight fragrance of newly opened flowers and faintly hear the ringing of wind chimes. Of late, moreover—only the last month or so—she had become aware as well of what appeared to be a subtle displacement of proper angles in the mirror's reflection of her room, as if it were capturing the scene at her back in proportions and depths that should have been impossible for it and that it had never encompassed before. Obliquely but relentlessly, parts of the room that had not previously been visible from where she sat seemed to be spilling into view from around the edges of the glass, as though the image in the mirror were not so much a reflection of this world as a slowly expanding prospect opened upon another.

Great-Aunt Emma, to whom alone Lucy would have confided these latest impressions, would have assured her that she was not deceived. Unfortunately, that strange, delightful, perversely unconventional old spinster—an endless vexation to the rest of the family but to Lucy an inexhaustible source of joy—had died the summer before. Why she had insisted on giving Lucy this table and mirror as a ninth birthday present she had not explained at the time; she had merely employed the full moral authority and privilege of her age, as well as the mystique of her legendarily implacable eccentricity, to override the irritated objections of Lucy's parents. She had told Lucy only that the mirror itself came from the Punjab—"Just like you, my love"—and that the family had acquired it many, many decades before from a Parsi mirrorsmith when Emma and Lucy's father's father had been children and they had lived in India in a large bungalow. The luxuriant foliage and flowers of its molded silver frame seemed to confirm its exotic provenance. A year or so later, Great-Aunt Emma had confided to Lucy—and had never afterward deviated from the claim—that there was some kind of magic in its glass. A little while after that, she had elaborated upon this by assuring Lucy that certain Parsis understood the magical use of mirrors, because mirrors had so long played a vital part in their mysteries. When Lucy from time to time begged to be told what kind of magic it was, however, her great-aunt had usually replied that it was rather like the magic of Alice's looking glass.

On one occasion only, on the afternoon when Lucy had told Great-Aunt Emma of how the early daylight was now being altered by the mirror, the old woman had grown more expansive on the topic. By then, she was already in failing health, and her mind had begun to wander at times, and to become sporadically forgetful; and perhaps that day it was her own carefully guarded reserve that she had forgotten, because she spoke to Lucy about the mirror much more freely than she had done in the past. She had observed many of the same strange phenomena when she was a girl, she said, and they had become especially vivid, frequent, and remarkable just as she had passed the threshold of womanhood and had only begun to subside again "after John." Lucy was startled by this name, which had arrived suddenly and from nowhere, attached to no one of whom she was cognizant, but it took only a few moments for her to understand its significance; and at once certain assumptions she had habitually entertained regarding her great-aunt (and perhaps about all well-bred young women of the Victorian age) were dispelled, while certain suspicions she had occasionally entertained were confirmed. Then Great-Aunt Emma had gone on to explain how she had assumed in those days that she had been allowed to enjoy the mirror's secrets because she was a changeling—as of course, she immediately added, Lucy was too. When Lucy reacted to this remark with only widened eyes and a half-formed smile, uncertain whether it was a joke or a sign of dementia, her great-aunt had added that she was saying nothing but what was obvious from Lucy's rather ethereal sort of beauty, just as it had been obvious from her own very similar beauty when she had been young. Then again, she added, everyone is a changeling really, at least in part, but a very small number of us are more aware of it than others are, and all of us are more aware of it at certain times of life than at others but tend to forget it as we age. The truth is, she continued, now speaking as if not to Lucy but to someone only she could see, this world is really just the shadow side of things, and we were all taken from the better, more beautiful world where we belong and were brought here by who knows what sorcery; yet even so, in a very few places or in a very few objects—say, in the waters of an enchanted well or pool under a full moon, or in the glass of a magic mirror crafted by a master mirror-smith from just the right sort of materials, to the accompaniment of just the right prayers or spells, with the aid of djinns or peris or fairies or yakshas, just catching the light of morning—some of us can peer briefly into that other world and see something of its serenity and splendor and loveliness. "Sita explained it all much better," she had suddenly added, and Lucy at once recognized the name of the Indian woman who had looked after her grandfather and great-aunt for several years when they were children. But just then a maid had arrived with tea and sandwiches, and by the time the conversation resumed, Great-Aunt Emma had entirely forgotten what they were talking about.

Lucy knew that a magic mirror should, by all rights, be a surprising sort of thing. It somewhat surprised her that she did not find it nearly as astonishing as she probably ought to have done. Certainly it would have surprised anyone who knew her if she were to speak of it openly as something she really believed in. Had she ever mentioned it to her parents, her father, equable man though he pretended to be, would by now have contrived to have had it removed from her room and destroyed, probably while she was away from the house somewhere; he was intolerant of all "nonsense" and "mysticism"; he even—though he was a respectable Anglican—thoroughly disliked any signs of excessive piety in those around him, or any unhealthy preoccupation with matters for which an hour or so on Sundays more than sufficed. She, however, even in guarding the secret, had come rather quickly to think of it as nothing very extraordinary. Perhaps the pleasure of knowing it was all hers overwhelmed any other feelings regarding it. Anyway, she had never acquired any prejudices against the possibility of real magic in the world, and had always more or less assumed that it was a perfectly reasonable thing to believe in. As a little girl—though not so little that she did not instinctively know to withhold the intelligence from her parents—she had for a year or so been accustomed to hearing disembodied voices out in the garden, among the flowers or in the shade of certain trees, small and high-pitched and always rather musical, and tending always to dissolve into laughter that itself then tended to dissolve into the sound of leaves stirred by the wind or into the songs of birds overhead. If she had ever made out any of the actual words, they had been so few and uncertain that she could extract no sense from them, and certainly could not remember them now. She had told, of course, only her great-aunt, who had been quick to ascribe the phenomenon to fairies and had advised Lucy to enjoy it while it lasted, assuring her that these precious periods of communion with unseen realities tended to come only during certain brief and exceptional seasons of one's life.

If only Lucy could speak to Great-Aunt Emma now. The oddly expanding vista within the glass, as it happened, had not been the only new dimension of this magic to have manifested itself since the old lady's death. In just the last two months, Lucy had begun to observe certain small but unmistakable deviations of detail in the mirror's reflection of her room. In a general sense, of course, every object seemed more attractive, more idealized even—with sharper lines and richer layerings of color—when captured in the strangely pellucid medium of that enchanted glass. But now some of them were altered in more concrete ways. The solid, smoothly white frosted glass shade of a lamp on a small table near her window became a gaudy, jagged carapace of translucent amber. In place of the porcelain kitten at one end of her mantelpiece—a gift from her mother's sister that Lucy despised but felt obliged to keep—stood a vase of milky green jade filled with yellow roses. The colorless arabesques of the room's wallpaper were now tangles of green vines with crimson blossoms set off against a sheen of pale peach. Only there, of course—only in the glass. When she turned her head to look at the room, it was always still merely itself in all its unremarkable daintiness. And then, most fascinating of all, over the past five mornings a recessed portion of the wall at the far end of the room, designed for a wardrobe but now vacant, had acquired (of all things) a door, of an oddly opalescent white, perhaps mother-of-pearl, with bright golden bordering around its panels, a slender door frame of solider white, and a doorknob of chiseled ruby glass. It was by far the most remarkable of the mirror's apparitions, and the first time she had caught sight of it, over the reflection of her right shoulder, she had turned about violently, with a small gasp, only to see—as she had known she would—that it corresponded to nothing in this world. She was caught off guard only that once, however. Thereafter, she had not tried to find it on this side of the mirror again, and after the second day had scarcely paid it any mind at all except during odd minutes when, every now and again, she glanced at it for longer than usual and tried to imagine what was hidden on its far side. All she could ever summon up in her imagination when she did this was a placid country meadow and a shining pond, over which was bent a single drooping willow, the whole scene aglow with a clear vernal sunlight. Surely, she told herself, whatever was there was something far more splendid, far more beautiful. But, not being Alice, she had no way of reaching it to find out, and was resolved not to torment herself with futile curiosity.

Just now, however, on this morning, as she was resigning herself at last to rising from her chair and descending to her breakfast and her father's quiet displeasure—he would, she knew, ostentatiously remove his watch from his waistcoat pocket, inspect it momentarily, cast a cool glance in her direction, replace it, fold his newspaper, and then calmly reach for the bell to summon the maid with the coffee and toast—she found herself dearly wishing she could crawl up onto her table and slip through the glass to the other side and open the door and see what lay beyond. Somehow the imminent prospect of yet another conversation with her mother about the marriage, conducted yet once more under her father's stonily impassive scrutiny, seemed especially depressing today. She simply had no will to be forced to contemplate yet again, under the forms of whatever new auxiliary considerations or subsidiary concerns had occurred to her mother in the night, what would after all be a thoroughly and miserably predictable course of events, which Lucy hated being made to foresee again and again with such perfect clarity while remaining as impotent as Cassandra to avert it: from the formal announcement of the engagement to the commission of her gown to the solemnization of the union by some vicar or bishop to her perfunctory defloration to her being carried away captive to India in invisible chains, not to mention the torrents of tedious exertions and annoyances that would rush to fill in any empty intervals in the schedule. Even so, she rose from her chair, took a deep breath, cast a final forlorn glance at the lovely peaceful world in her mirror, and began to turn away.

Just then, however, something new caught her eye. The white door with golden trim at the far end of the reflected room was apparently slightly ajar. She could tell, even at this distance, because a thin border of pale white light was now visibly showing between the door and the surrounding door frame. She paused and stared for nearly half a minute without moving, one hand raised to her throat and lightly clutching the collar of her dress. Her heartbeat had quickened. She wondered for a moment whether she should feel mocked by this sight—at once so inviting and yet so utterly unattainable. She was even tempted to turn about and look behind her, but she resisted. And then something occurred to her. Was it not the case, she thought to herself, that in fairy tales the key to solving a magical problem was often to employ magical thinking? Childlike thinking, in point of fact, rather than logic? What if, she wondered, rather than trying to approach the door herself, she were to allow her reflected self, there on the other side of the glass, to do so in her stead? She took one last look at the clock on her mantel, though she ignored what she saw there, and returned her gaze to the door in the mirror, then looked directly into the eyes of her own reflection. She was slightly taken aback by the small, curious, somehow knowing smile she saw on the face there, and briefly raised the hand that had been pressed to her throat and touched her own lips with two fingers, trying to tell whether the reflection was simply showing her herself or was instead (rather frighteningly) showing her herself as she was in that other world. But this was too eerie a thought. She set the question aside and took a step backward, slightly awkwardly, followed by another, and then—staring fixedly into the mirror, making sure not to allow her reflection to block her view of that increasingly distant, ever more delicately beckoning glow—she began walking steadily and evenly backward, her house slippers whispering faintly atop the Persian carpet, until her reflected form came within reach of the door in the depths of the glass. Then, slowly, tentatively, waveringly, she reached behind her, feeling for the glass doorknob she saw in the mirror—so far away now that it took her four attempts to align the tiny reflection of her hand with it—until all at once her fingers came to rest upon what were unmistakably two facets of chiseled glass. Her reflection's hand now lay upon the doorknob. Her breath caught in her throat. She trembled slightly, then somewhat more violently. Slowly she closed her hand on the knob and, after a few seconds of indecision, pushed it backward. She saw the door in the mirror swing open into the swelling, pearly light beyond, and felt the door behind her swinging open at the same time, though it made no sound at all. A soft glow now hung in the air about her, pouring in from behind her back. Her heart was beating rapidly, her breath was growing shallow. Yet, even at this distance, it seemed to her that the face of her reflection wore an expression of utter serenity, and an enigmatic—even perhaps slightly wicked—smile. She dared not look for too long, however, as she knew to do so would quickly weaken her resolve. Instead, closing her eyes and taking as deep a breath as she could, she turned around, now holding fast to the doorknob and reaching out with her other hand until she felt the edge of the door frame, which was queerly smooth, like glass, and took a step forward, so that she knew she was halfway through the doorway. Beneath the sole of one of her slippers she was sure she felt grass. Releasing her breath slowly, she opened her eyes. The light now did not seem pale at all, but merely mild; and it took Lucy only a few moments to realize that the world into which she was looking was not only far more than she had ever imagined it might be but also far more than she ever could have imagined—more gorgeous, peaceful, dangerous, pure, amoral, convivial, menacing, ethereal, carnal . . . more beautiful. She gazed and gazed. She let her hand drop from the door frame. Her other hand was now resting only lightly upon the knob, barely touching it with the tips of just two fingers.

Lucy's father replaced his watch in his waistcoat pocket for the third time that morning. It really was remarkably inconsiderate, he told his wife, for Lucy to leave them waiting for so long without at least sending down some word. What on earth could be keeping her? Lucy's mother, from the other end of the table, agreed that their daughter's behavior had been growing increasingly unpredictable of late, and that she constantly seemed to be forgetting things that she ought not to forget, including apparently some of the niceties of common courtesy. But, to be fair, she was still quite young, and no man can really understand how exciting, even dizzying, it can be for a young girl to contemplate her approaching nuptials—so many details to consider, so many happy dreams to dream, so many understandable questions and, of course . . . understandable anxieties. Well, quite, her father conceded, a little uncomfortably and with a bit of an embarrassed cough; but then all the more reason, he suddenly asserted with renewed force, for her to start taking responsibility for her actions. With an impatient shake of his head, he rang for the coffee and toast. Her mother again agreed and promised that she would herself go and find their daughter if they were made to wait much longer. He took no notice but instead only repeated himself: Blast it all, she—"forgive my language, my dear"—but she could not go on behaving like a child indefinitely. In a year she would be the mistress of her own household, with a husband who was accustomed to a properly governed home, and certainly she would not be able to drift about dreamily then, appearing at the table whenever the mood took her. Yes, her mother agreed yet once more and assured him that she would have a talk with Lucy—a very frank talk. Somewhat mollified, her father said that he was pleased to hear it. After all, their daughter was very soon to be a wife, and no doubt a mother in fairly short order. It was time to cease being a girl and to enter fully into woman's estate. She could not go on lingering on the threshold forever.

10 *Pictor Ignotus*

He left us only the one painting, unsigned and unattributed and now vaguely dated as having probably been produced (or, at any rate, completed) at some point in the late 1650s; but this was more than enough to secure his fame—even his legend—if only under the gray, impersonal designation "Master of the Dordrecht Canvas" (or "Dort Canvas"). Of the story of his life there are only fables, devised one imagines by tour guides or popular historians or art dealers hoping to sell other paintings—forged or merely anonymous—as works produced by the same hand to credulous collectors (of the sort who are more investors than connoisseurs), despite the utter inimitability of his techniques. Naturally, the stories contradict one another. According to some, he died young and impoverished, having exhausted himself producing the single work upon which his posterity rests. According to others, he died both rich and very old indeed, with dates spilling over one end or the other of the seventeenth century. The legendary material is all very much of its age, moreover. There are coarse and picaresque tales of his carousals in taverns, the rapier duels he fought in narrow streets, the blasphemies he uttered in public, the husbands he cuckolded in their own beds, the maidens he deflowered in his. There are perfumed and pious tales of his being seized by religious fervor and going down on his knees in the open street to pray, or discoursing with the apostle Paul in an ecstasy, or restoring churches at the behest of angels, or receiving the inspiration for his masterwork in a vision while reading the sixth chapter of Isaiah. According to some accounts, he learned his art in the finest academies of Europe. According to others, he was an untutored genius, warbling his woodnotes wild, whose native gifts far surpassed the most refined skills of his greatest contemporaries. Some stories say that he was extremely tall. One says that he was in fact a dwarf.

Whatever the features of his life, they could scarcely be as enthralling, moving, or mysterious as the one great and enigmatic and astonishing work he bequeathed posterity. And perhaps it is for the best that he himself has utterly vanished from memory, leaving only that one stupendous achievement behind to seduce, humble, frustrate, and inspire generations of admirers. If we knew his name and the no doubt boringly mundane features of his biography, they would seem so trivial and arbitrary next to a work of such unearthly splendor that the effect would be positively absurd—as though one were to discover that the galaxies above had been hung in place in the infinite reaches of space by one Mr Henry Warner, a bank clerk from Omaha. All we really have of the Master, and all we could ever need or want, is the painting itself, which has been on display continuously since 1659 in a tiny private museum in Dordrecht devoted solely to it, like a shrine dedicated to a sacred image that fell one day from the heavens. There it occupies one wall in a large open gallery where spectators can view it from roughly twelve feet away, on the other side of a blue silk rope. Its dimensions are about twenty feet in height and thirty in length. To one side of the frame is a brass plate bearing the painting's original title, *Het Geestesoog*, which of course has long since been eclipsed by the simpler, less enigmatic name by which it is now generally known. To the other side of the frame is a similar brass plate whose inscription records only the artist's posthumous *nom de guerre* and the year of the canvas's unveiling. Perhaps you have visited the place yourself, although in fact relatively few persons ever have done so, and for understandable reasons. The painting's reputation is an uncanny one, and its effect on anyone who sees it is notoriously unsettling. Who among those who have ever stood before it, after all, gazing not *at* but *into* it, has failed to be overwhelmed, to the point of tears or terror or panic or bliss? Who can look at it for long without danger of becoming lost in it, and finding himself or herself still standing there after several hours, scarcely conscious of the time that has passed? To see it is to know a kind of transport that no other earthly object can impart; but it is also to have one's faith in the intelligibility of the world shaken. Such a thing should not be possible. And yet there it is. Consequently, many choose not to subject themselves to the experience. Many others refuse to believe the reports, and argue that visitors to that small museum have obviously been the victims of some sort of hypnotic enchantment or aerosolized hallucinogen. Still others refuse to believe in the existence of the painting at all, and regard even photographs of it as proving nothing, inasmuch as these cannot possibly record everything that those who have supposedly viewed the canvas *in situ* profess having seen in it; they regard the entire archive of scientific data regarding the painting as fraudulent and dismiss all scholarship on it and its creator as an elaborate hoax, a conspiracy of the expert classes, prosecuted solely for their own amusement and for the cruel pleasure of practicing upon the simplicity of the uneducated. And then there are a few religious fanatics who acknowledge that the picture exists but who claim that it must be a work of infernal manufacture and advocate its destruction; some have reputedly pledged themselves to the cause. The museum, in consequence, is vigilantly guarded, and ever more advanced security technologies continue to be installed there at the expense of a few wealthy and devoted patrons.

As for the painting itself, it is a glorious and gorgeous thing when taken in as a whole: an immense, fanciful cityscape with winding cobbled avenues and broad, populous thoroughfares, a crowded skyline of imbricated roofs, two shining domes, and a dozen severe steeples, the whole of it stretching out along a chersonese that slopes down on the left to the sea, under a sparsely clouded vault of brilliant blue. The scene is depicted as if from an elevated position on the other side of a large bay—a facing promontory perhaps, or perhaps simply an idealized vantage angelically hovering in the heaven of the artist's imagination. There are numerous vessels in the bay, as well as in the docks of the harbor along the near shore, and alongside the wharves casting their glassy shadows among the sage-green waves—fishing boats, cargo craft, small swift packets, delicate pinnaces with sails like swallows' wings—while out at sea, beyond the cape, two large rigs underway toward the open ocean are visible against the dazzling, silvery-green water and the nacre horizon. For vividness of color, clarity of line, and ingeniously rendered effects of sun and shade, the image is already a wonder; at first sight, it seems to stand out from its canvas, like a madly elaborate diorama or scale model. Even when one's vision has adjusted to the image and it has retreated into its actual two dimensions, it is all far too rich and varied and complicated in its verisimilitude to make sense of. One longs to violate that sleek cordon and approach as near as possible. But there is no real need to do so; the distance the viewer is obliged to keep from the canvas is a meager one, and it cannot prevent him or her from being quickly drawn into the painting's intricate play of shadows and light, or its exquisite layerings of color. And that first impression is only a hint of what prolonged inspection reveals. The true marvel of the Dordrecht Canvas lies in its superb and delicate particularities, and that marvel has only deepened in its grandeur and mystery—and deepened, and then deepened still further—as successive technological advances have allowed us to penetrate its surface more thoroughly and minutely: the invention of photography above all, as well as ever more powerful and perspicuous lenses for magnifying glasses and microscopes and cameras. As astonishing as the image has always been in the precision of even its most minuscule details, only in the last century have we been able to grasp how miraculous that precision truly is. No modern machine as yet can duplicate it. Indeed, in some respects the image mocks our very latest technological developments. Even the most advanced digital reproductions are too coarse-grained to capture its finer features; inevitably, at some point in the process of enlargement, well before the contours and densities of this or that detail have been plumbed or exhausted, the picture dissolves in a pointillistic mist of pixels. Much of the study of the canvas today, therefore, relies on the best available film photography. And, even then, in our descent into its ever smaller, ever deeper dimensions we are as yet unable to reach the end of our explorations. The best microscopy discloses the smallest strata of interior depiction it can reach, revealing them to be no less precisely and concretely limned in their surface qualities than those of greater magnitude—never thinning out, that is, into gauzy abstractions or dissipating into merely suggestive traces—but it also makes us aware that these same strata appear to be diaphanous to yet deeper strata, still further down within the image. We as yet have no notion how far it may be possible to venture into any of the canvas's discrete details.

Neither can we find any area of the image where this is not so. Even the few hazy clouds that float in the resplendent blue of its sky on closer inspection (through, say, a powerful magnifying glass) disclose depths within depths, successive veils of vapor, sinuous and trailing wisps of atomized moisture, illuminated by the sun from somewhere beyond the upper left quarter of the canvas, and enveloped from the opposite angle in soft blue and dim purple shadow. Then, as one continues to progress into those clouds, they slowly resolve into individual droplets of precipitation, limpidly hovering in their own ghostly sheen of watery iridescence. The exactitudes and precisions never relent, no matter how deep one goes. Even here, in the seemingly empty sky, among the most apparently vapid and undifferentiated of the painting's effects, one can easily become lost. How much more absorbing, though, are the concrete and fully articulated shapes and figures sprawled under the canopy of that sky. There is one house, for instance, among the many hundreds the painting depicts, that occupies less than a square inch of canvas; yet it is impossible to say how long and how intently one could examine its sleek clay roof tiles, counting the rough places where their surfaces have flaked or have been chipped, and where the light glistens in their cracks—or gaze at each of its mottled bricks in turn, with its asperous texture and the variegated red and dull blue of its colorations—or look at the dove nestling against one of the chimneys, each of its feathers' barbs perfectly delineated and shimmering like dull pewter, its eyes like glistering opals in the clear sunlight. There is a walled garden attached to the house, and the vantage at which the scene is rendered allows one to peer down into it and see glossy laurel leaves bathed in pallid sunlight, white roses with satiny petals, a cankered lily drooping on its stem, countless blades of grass depicted in all their individual variances of shape and hue. There is a pool there too, with ripples expanding in crystalline circles from the dorsal fin—protruding just above the water's surface—of a red and gold ornamental carp, each scale of which is edged by a tiny prismatic gleam. Below the surface, sinuous weeds coil and uncoil in the golden-green water. The carp's gills are fully dilated; its lips are parted as if it has just taken in a morsel of food. Beyond the pool, a gardener is entering through the far gate; his worn, loosely woven woolen coat has six plain wooden buttons running down its open front; there is none, however, on the stained and patched shirt beneath but only three limply tied strings between his throat and sternum; the buckles on his shoes are so scored and tarnished that the now unrecognizable metal might be either brass or lead. There are many windows in the house as well, catching the slanting rays of the sun in the old, uneven, faintly greenish glass of their panes. Through the one farthest to the right on the highest floor, one can see (if one employs a microscope) a daintily furnished room where there are several chairs upholstered in white satin with blue floral embroideries, all turned to face an elegantly fashioned spinet, atop which two pages of sheet music stand open. Closer inspection reveals the score to be from one of Frescobaldi's *Fiori musicali*. A faint fingerprint is visible in the margin of one page where the scribe evidently touched the paper with an ink-stained thumb, and a little lower down the page the same print, identical in pattern, is repeated more faintly still. The paper is of a creamy color with very fine fibers.

A darker, denser glass occupies the frames of the windows in the stern of the nearer of those two ships out at sea. Still, it is clear enough to afford a good view of the sunward side of the interior of the captain's cabin, and shows him—an old man with a severe face and dark gray eyes stippled with flecks of hazel—bent over a large bound volume open on a small table of polished oak. For years it was assumed that he was reading a chart or an inventory of the goods in the ship's hold, but now the text has been captured by a camera with an especially powerful lens, and it has been revealed to be a passage from Joost van den Vondel's play *Lucifer*, performances of which at the putative time of the canvas's completion were still banned in the Netherlands (scholars of the canvas disagree, sometimes quite volubly, over the significance of this discovery: whether, that is, it indicates surreptitious impiety on the painter's part, or wry mockery of the hypocrisy of the Calvinist authorities, or is intended as a commentary on the characters of the officers of the Dutch merchant fleet). Needless to say, all the furnishings of the cabin are rendered in infinitesimal detail, as is every plank of wood in the slightly lemon-hued hull, every frayed thread of every hawser, the weave of the sails, the obviously young and inadequately seasoned timber of the deck (still beaded and, one can almost sense, redolent with sap), the brilliance of the scoured and polished brightwork, the fabric of the seamen's shirts and hats, the badly scuffed polish on the shoe of what appears to be a ship's surgeon (to judge from the old bloodstains on his one visible cuff). The marine life observable in the smoothly vitreous, unfurling wake of the ship turns out to be a school of sea bass whose scales shimmer in wavering lines of blue, pink, and green. Two gulls are perched on the railing of the bow. One of them has a damaged lower beak.

There is another house with an open prospect on the sea, from which those ships could be watched till they vanish over the horizon, and one can gaze obliquely into its seaward sitting room through the side panel of its large bay window, and find among the many items there a convex mirror on the far wall in an oval frame of silver, and see among the objects it distortedly reflects another mirror, this one with a flat surface facing the sea, and then glimpse in that second mirror the reflection of the large central panel of the bay window, and discover there the ghostly, almost indiscernible reflection of a lovely girl who is otherwise obscured from view and hidden from the convex mirror by a black and gold lacquered folding screen, wearing a dress of what appears to be rose-pink and milk-white blended silk and cotton and a lovely dangling teardrop earring whose single lustrous pearl captures the attenuated glow of the daylight reflected off the water with excruciating delicacy . . . And still, we know, we could go further in. One day we shall. Some have come to believe that the depths of detail may be, for all intents and purposes, infinite. Perhaps we shall find, they suggest, that we can descend to the molecular level without the image dissipating— perhaps down to the atomic if we ever possess a technology capable of capturing images at such unimaginably small levels of magnitude. And they mean not the strata of the real molecules and atoms composing the pigment and canvas, but those of the *depicted* molecules and atoms that compose the objects portrayed in the painting, miniaturized in exact proportion to those objects. Perhaps we could theoretically descend as far as the Planck scale of the quantum level, where only the gods can see the craftsman's diligence (and where perhaps we will find that it is their gaze that collapses the potentiality wave into the fixed image on the canvas). This is all no doubt absurd, but such is the painting's power that it can induce exorbitant credulity in even the sanest of minds.

It is easy, then, to understand how some who have never seen the painting and who refuse to see it on principle might reject all reports of it—from the most scientifically sober to the most mystically rhapsodic—as lies or delusions or the ecstasies of madmen. And it is just as easy to understand how some of those who have peered into its mysteries have come to believe it a product of sorcery. By what arcane means, after all, and by what esoteric craft, could the Master have achieved such unimaginable exactitudes? Pigments did not then exist—nor do they now—capable of such ethereal, even disembodied tenuousness. Cohesive compounds with oleaginous and particulate bases simply cannot, especially when applied to the fibrous surface of an artist's canvas, be rarefied to the point that they can assume the visible quality of sunlight penetrating one corner of a single cell of a leaf on a tree in a garden, and that an already miniature garden in one tiny quarter of a picture. The paint would have to have the consistency of light itself. And how can any glaze be as pellucidly transparent as that used by the Master, betraying as it does no striations from the hairs of a brush and no irregularities of thickness and none of the discolorations one would expect as a result of time's passage? Neither can human eyesight, even when augmented by the most powerful of lenses, penetrate into realms so minute; nor can human hands wield instruments capable of working at such inaccessibly tiny scales. In perfecting details so far below the threshold of his senses and physical faculties, the Master must have employed methods not so much technically accomplished as divinatory, more feats of thaumaturgy than of practical craft. And yet is it not a barbarism or an infantile surrender to the irrational to invoke magic as an explanation of a phenomenon that resists our comprehension, no matter how prodigiously it does so?

Some think that if only the image's meaning—what the artist intended, that is—could be discovered, then much of its mystery would be dispelled. This seems a curious supposition to me, since merely demonstrating what purpose a thing might serve surely gives us no better understanding of how in itself it is possible. But there are those—functionalists, they call themselves—who argue vigorously that this is not so; if only we can establish the *cui bono* of the thing, what process it subserves, then the mechanism of its creation, evolutionary or artificial, will become self-evident. In fact, the object itself, they say, at least as we conceive of it and imagine we perceive it, may prove to be only an apparent phenomenon, generated by the syntax of its function. But interpretation is elusive. Some see the image as an allegory, others as a fantastic exploration of certain subtle moods or affective atmospheres or mere color schemes, others as a satire on an excessive and slavish devotion to realistic representation, others as an ironic demonstration of the interminability and therefore wasteful prodigality of such representation. For some, the sublimity of the canvas lies in its very pointlessness, the grandeur of the thing in the sheer triviality of its compulsive precisions; for these critics, the picture says everything in meaning nothing. In recent years, a particularly radical style of interpretation has arisen that sees the image not as the representation of a secret meaning but as the effacement of a deeper text, one that can exist only *as* effaced; thus the image exists only *as* our necessarily unremitting examination of it, our endlessly dilatory search for an absent signifier that nothing can bring to utterance or representation, or for the sublimely ineffable object of a desire that can never be appeased; and it is this insatiability of longing that is in fact the generative "inscription" of the image's ever finer and ever emptier details.

There are more conventional theorists, of course, for whom the picture is an aesthetic philosophy *in nuce*, and yet others for whom it is nothing less than a total metaphysics; among these latter, the preponderant majority regard the image as a practical demonstration of one or another version of idealism. There are some, however, who eschew interpretation altogether as a category error and a species of mythic thought, but who also go further than the functionalists in subordinating the contents of the image to its physical occasion. These are the "eliminativists" or "disapparitionists," and they claim that a properly scientific account of the image—one that reduces it to its chemical and then molecular and ultimately atomic constituents—will render otiose all our normal talk of a "picture" and of an "artist," or for that matter of "spectators," or indeed of representation or depiction or recognition as such, and will expose all such language as just so many relics of a primitive folk aesthetics and folk psychology, which must be eliminated altogether if the image—if "image" is even a useful term here—is to become an intelligible object of scientific scrutiny. Then we will see that any putative "experience" of pictorial details is an illusion, and that all talk of a continuous field of representation—like talk of a continuous "I" who is the subject of the experience of that representation—is a figment of grammar, the obstinately ineradicable residue of a folklore haunted by such mythical entities as intentionality, perception, recognition, and subjective mental states.

Inevitably, of course, there are those factions for whom the chief significance of the Dordrecht Canvas is either theistic or atheistic. For some believers, the image is miraculous; it defies all naturalist or physicalist explanation and therefore disproves materialism; it is evidence of the supernatural and of the reality of God. For certain militant infidels, the canvas is manifestly a natural object, one composed of physical parts and possessing a documented material provenance, and that very fact, they say, demonstrates the fatuity of arguments for divine design, even in cases of the most intricate complexity imaginable, and renders the idea of God—"that hypothesis"—altogether needless. Then too there are a few daring theorists who have gone so far as to argue that the image may have had no painter at all, exhibiting as it does a degree of minute coordinated complexity found nowhere among human artifacts but everywhere in nature; rather, it is quite possibly an emergent phenomenon generated by an incalculable succession of antecedent, purely physical causes, progressively refined over vast epochs of time by Darwinian processes of mutation, attrition, and selection. A few others, rejecting this view but still refusing to take the leap of faith into arrant supernaturalism, have advanced the thesis that, precisely because the picture is undoubtedly a natural phenomenon, it obliges us to call into question the residually mechanistic views of nature that bedevil so many of our philosophies and scientific presuppositions, and should probably prompt us to reconsider sympathetically the logical solvency of certain ancient notions of nature's intrinsic intentionality and teleology (chastened, of course, by a firm resistance to any sort of either panpsychist or design theory).

None of these questions interests me anymore, I have to admit. At one time they did. As I have grown old in the vicinity and shadow of the

Dordrecht Canvas, however, I have ceased attempting to understand it or the artist who painted it. And this has allowed me to appreciate the very mystery of the thing as perhaps its chief beauty. Of the Master, I need know nothing more than I do. In recent years, I have begun to have dreams about him—or rather one dream about him that has passed through several variations while remaining, *mutatis mutandis*, the same. In it, he appears as a dark figure, more silhouette than substance, and his back is always turned to me, while I feel as if I am gazing at him from some narrow crevice, as if attempting to hide myself. Usually he is standing in a shadowy doorway, framed against the twilight, clearly in the act of leaving me behind, wherever it is I am. Sometimes instead he is at the end of a long open colonnade, also at twilight. At other times, he is standing in a trellised arbor by the gate of a twilit garden. He is always quite tall, but, beyond that, I can discern nothing about him; he is wearing a cape or cloak with a high collar over his shoulders, as well as a hat with a wide crown and jutting cockade, all of which largely deprives his form of any distinctive features. I know it is he, however, even if I cannot say how I know. I reach out to him and begin to speak, but no words come to my lips. He starts to turn his head as if he is going to look back at me but then halts, adjusts his hat, and walks away into the evening—through the doorway or out the end of the colonnade or by way of the gate. The scene then melts away, and I either dream something else or awaken. I do not know what it means, of course, any more than I know what the painting means. I am always relieved, however. I realize each time that I do not truly desire to see his face, at least not in my present state; I dread that it will be too real, too living, and nothing like what I might imagine, or even like what I dare not imagine. I fear that he will prove monstrously beautiful or exquisitely terrible, and I am prepared for neither possibility. The thought of looking into his eyes carries with it a special terror for me, if also a strange elation. I am glad that he departs as he does, in silence and mystery and in the dying light. For now, I am content just to dwell in the wonder of the Dordrecht Canvas, and to accept that the secret it keeps will never be revealed to me in this life. I am at peace with that knowledge. I simply visit that small museum whenever the mood comes over me, never fewer than three times a week, and take in the spectacle each time with a sense of deep gratitude, always finding something new to admire. I expect I shall go there tomorrow, as it happens.

11 *Ensō*

Perhaps, he thought to himself as he rose from the bench, placed the strap of his canvas valise over his shoulder, and began his walk home, this was indeed the day he had been waiting for. Certainly the weather was ideal: a mild, balmy, early autumn afternoon in the Pacific Northwest, a sky of particularly limpid—even diaphanous—blue, altocumulus clouds of dazzling white; yet also a slight, cool dampness in the air, the keen, faintly metallic fragrance of approaching rain, and a brisk and constant breeze raising soft deciduous sighs and coniferous whispers in the woods to the right of the gray gravel path and stirring the grass in the meadow to its left, so that its wide, low expanse looked like a sea of crawling tidal combers with aquamarine crests. The evening, moreover, promised to be pleasant, with a few light showers and an early moon only three days removed from full (the perfect degree of imperfection). He would be able to leave the French doors leading to his garden open, so that the night breezes could issue in, now and then perhaps bringing in a few raindrops.

His last seminar of the semester, moreover, was two hours in the past and the campus half a mile behind him. He had already recorded grades for all eight of his graduate students—an "A" in every case, of course—even without having received their final papers, since there was no question but that they would all acquit themselves brilliantly; he had admitted only his best disciples into the seminar. So, then, no professional obligations remained that need detain him now, if indeed the right moment had arrived. And he was quite satisfied that he had, by the semester's conclusion, duly impressed upon his students the three lessons he had been most anxious to impart: First, that Japanese aesthetic theory simply presumes the beautiful, but exhausts itself in ever subtler reflections on the mysteries of the sublime, in the original classical sense of that latter word—that which lies *sub limine*, below the threshold—the plain, the unadorned, the nobly restrained. Second, that this yields an implicit metaphysics of aesthetic experience quite unlike the Platonic notion that the eros for corporeal beauty leads the soul upward to the contemplation of eternal beauty; it is rather a metaphysics devoted to a studiously refined if often quiescent appreciation of everything most delicately subdued and withdrawn in nature and artifice, most marked by time and use, most expressive of the sheer thereness of the world in its unimposing simplicity, and so devoted also to the pure temporality of being's disclosure of itself. And third (and this had been his sole critical contribution to his discipline over twenty-five years of teaching and writing on Asian arts), that the best and most "systematic" approach for Westerners like himself and his students to the host of largely untranslatable terms that constitutes the indigenous glossary of Japanese aesthetics is to try to situate them along a continuum between the experiences of *mono no aware*—the "*Ah!*" of aching enchantment at the utter dewlike evanescence of everything lovely, the gasp of wistful awe, the pang of a melancholy mastered by thankful detachment—and *yūgen*—that gracefully grave transport induced by a sense of mist-veiled distances, shadowed depths, darkness, things hidden or at most suggested by the faintest of traces, things concealed, mysterious, always further away, always barely recalled, always ineffable.

A few dozen yards ahead, at the edge of the path, a young maple whose leaves were already bright crimson and mellow purple except on the lowest branches where they were a golden pink, stood out against a larger, overshadowing eastern red cedar—not a cedar at all, actually, but rather a variety of juniper—whose thin, darkly green scaled leaves and sprawling clusters of small, midnight-blue "berries" produced a hue of extraordinary richness, one that reminded him of a color—both emerald and azure at once, in alternating but somehow distinct layers—he had once seen the ocean briefly assume just after dusk, as the last blush of the sunset was departing from the horizon and stars were beginning to appear in the sky. Still further along, enveloping the cedar's outline in a kind of nimbus, there was a yet larger tree, perhaps a poplar, all its foliage now a dark, parched gold. And directly ahead of him on the path, twenty yards away perhaps and walking in the same direction as he, was a girl—one of the college's undergraduates undoubtedly—with an admirable figure and long straight brown hair, carrying a small black pocketbook over one shoulder and clad (in obvious defiance of the changing season) in a light, tightly fitting white knitted blouse and a pleated red tartan miniskirt. Just as she was passing the maple the wind rose and lifted the hem of her skirt, wholly revealing one hip and exposing quite a good deal more than that, not at all concealed by the purely ceremonial wisp of lavender undergarment she was wearing; and she, promptly but casually, reached down to stroke the hem into place again, glanced over her shoulder, graced him with a radiant and whimsically hapless smile, and simply continued walking onward at the same leisurely pace. And then a number of leaves from the maple came spinning down in her wake from the high branches, momentarily hiding her from view in a cloud of flickering red. He paused for several seconds, watching the leaves settling on the path and then looking up to follow her with his eyes as she continued, with her very fluid stride, to draw away from him. How enchanting, it seemed to him, and touchingly so, the sheer insouciance—the want of haste—with which she had adjusted her skirt, and how impressive the calm confidence of someone so assured of her own loveliness that she felt no embarrassment whatsoever at the small indisposition her minimalist choice in attire had caused her. It had imbued the moment, however fleeting, with a kind of perfection that no one could have planned. An excellent illustration, he thought, of the unrepeatable, irretrievable, and for that reason all the more precious beauty of the ephemeral. Never again in the whole expanse of eternity would this precise orchestration of elements—that girl and this moment, blossoming youth and the dying year, innocence and sensuality, elegance and absurdity—recur; never again would this vanishingly transient instant of charming equilibrium be achieved with this same fortuitous grace and always already melting immediacy, or precisely this arrangement of delightful juxtapositions; all of it was irrecoverable and for just that reason pervaded by the softly sparkling beauty of death.

Here was what he had tried to impress so often on his students: the elusiveness of the present moment experienced not as the moving and fragmentary image of eternity's unchanging fullness, but rather as the most poignant image of the luminous void—though, perhaps, he had also tried to tell them, Platonism's invocation of eternal beauty and Japanese aesthetics' praise of exquisite transience ultimately express one and the same apprehension, albeit in inverse aesthetic grammars. One need not choose sides here. Or, perhaps, the ecstasy of that Platonic aspiration, the enthusiasm of its divine afflatus—that complete surrender to rapture from glory to glory and from delight to delight, that nisus into eternity—concealed a deeper melancholy within the very superabundance of beauty that it sought: a fullness beyond pleasure, the sadness of an always too precipitate leave-taking of the things of earth, the loss precisely of the particular and ephemeral; and perhaps it was precisely this traumatic violence of the beautiful that the Japanese tradition had wisely learned to resist, or at least to contain. Surely this is what Sen no Rikyū must have understood at some level when, in the ambit of Hideyoshi's gaudy teahouse of gold, he had striven to refine the *cha-no-yu*—the tea ceremony—into *wabi-cha*, an ever more limpid exhibition of serene simplicity, of both the fine and the coarse grain of nature . . . of pleasure in the pensive surrender to *mujō*—impermanence—of dedication to *miyabi*—the elegance of restraint—of the cultivation of *fūryū*—gracious propriety without ostentation . . .

Yes. More and more, he was becoming convinced that this was indeed the day.

He continued for a minute or so to contemplate the red and pink and cerise of the maple's leaves, those still on their branches and those spread out on the path before him, and the sere, dark gold of the poplar's. There would come a period of perhaps twenty minutes, he knew, just before twilight, when their colors would seem to become more intense, as if they were glowing from within with a mysterious light of their own. He was almost tempted to wait to see it before going on. But, after less than a minute more, he resumed his journey, through and over the scattered leaves, continuing on to where the footpath terminated at the top of a gentle rise and issued out into the small residential avenue at whose end he lived. There, as he was turning toward his own house, he decided that he would order a sushi dinner for himself from the small, excellent Japanese restaurant that had opened on the main street two months earlier. He had an excellent bottle of *sake* at home that he did not wish to leave unopened if indeed this was to be the day. It would be a pleasant prelude to the act, as well as an ideally delicate last taste of the world he would be leaving behind.

All along the avenue, trees were turning red and yellow and purple; some had already fully assumed their final autumnal colors; others were pale gold and pink along their lower boughs and crimson at their peaks; others were still mostly green. The fragrance of the approaching rain was becoming more acute. The breeze was growing more constant. The leaves falling from the branches, not as yet in torrents as they would do later in the month, turned in graceful spirals or—more enchantingly still—swung back and forth on the air as they sank downward. He strolled onward for the remaining mile or so to his house in its particularly quiet corner of the neighborhood, among trees a century old and more, trying to think of nothing but this moment, this vanishingly momentary eternity—or, rather, trying not to *think* at all, but only to be aware of the aromatic, rain-laden breeze, the gently swaying treetops, the bright leaves floating to the earth like flakes of fire.

There were certain things he could not convey to even the best of his students, he thought to himself nearly two hours later as he dried the delicate, concave ceramic oblong of his sushi dish, with its images of white cranes in flight through a sky of soft blue glazing, set it atop its stack on the kitchen shelf, and then hung the damp dishtowel on its ring beneath the cabinets. He lingered for a moment, staring at his own reflection in the darkening glass of the window above the sink, luxuriating in the slight but pleasant floating feeling in his limbs that a little too much *sake*—chilled, not warmed—had induced in him.

It was when he tried to impress upon his students the other side of an aesthetics of impermanence—the transience of transience's charms, as it were—that he invariably discovered that they were simply too young to understand. Their sensibilities were still as yet too un-formed, too innocent. None of them could as yet even imagine the peculiar tone and texture of times long past, of vanished decades, of memories transformed over many years from burning emblems of a life still full of countless unfathomed mysteries into the cold embers of ex-hausted possibilities. Hence, he tried to explain to them, the wisest con-noisseurs of evanescence were also those who at the last sought a retreat from the ceaseless flow of things to the higher stillness of *ensō*, and sought to cultivate within themselves a yet deeper detachment: a quiet, constant, imperturbable concentration of the will upon a transcen-dental object as perfect as the Sun of the Good, yet as cold and silent as the moon.

It was time, he decided, to bathe and change for the evening. He wavered ever so gently from side to side as he left the kitchen. Once he had gone into the cedar bathhouse that he had had added as an annex to his home seven years earlier and had set the hot water running from its copper tap into the deep, resonant wooden *furo* installed there, he went to his wardrobe and chose a kimono—a white cotton *yukata* with a simple indigo camellia pattern—and a pair of single-strap sandals with straw soles. Then he returned to the annex, hung the kimono on one of the brass hooks by the door, placed the sandals on the mat below them, undressed, left his clothes from the day in the wicker hamper, went into the small tiled alcove with the large drain in its floor and the two shower heads—one overhead, one at the level of his midriff—and washed him-self thoroughly with the bamboo-charcoal soap and the bar of rice shampoo he kept there, both of which he had become accustomed to as a student in Tokyo and had had regularly sent from Japan ever since. When he felt thoroughly washed, he turned off the shower and left the alcove. He shut off the tap at the *furo*, which he had made as full as pos-sible while leaving room for himself, stepped up onto the low cedar platform surrounding it, tested the water tentatively with one foot, and then slowly eased himself down into the hot bath. Immediately, he felt the *sake* in his limbs again, as a delicious tingling. He rested back in the *furo*, against wood sanded to an almost silky smoothness. The fragrance of cedar, the languidly rising steam, the heat soaking into his flesh, the diffuse but constant glow of the alcohol in his veins and muscles—all of it was unspeakably pleasant.

Shibusa, he thought to himself after a few moments, casting a casual glance at his kimono on its hook. *Shibui*. An unobtrusive and subdued palette, simple patterns. Subtlety, a hint of bitterness like the taste of an unripened persimmon, as well as an astringency, the aridity of fine, fragrant wood, slightly weathered in the open air. This his students had always found it very easy to grasp. He had often wondered whether the shrill glare of the late modern world of luminous screens and electric lights, and the incessant blaring of mechanical sounds, even mechanical music, had not endowed them with an appetite that only something like the traditional Japanese fascination with the quietly austere could ever possibly sate. So often they had seemed to embrace the aesthetics of the restrained and elegantly unadorned with a kind of paradoxical passion, as though it were a saving refuge from the modern age's storm of plastic and electric glare and incessant noise. Each successive wave of graduate students seemed ever more desperately and gratefully infatuated with the idea of *wabi-sabi*, for instance, and ever more sensitive to all its nuances. One certainly never had to labor to persuade them of the reality of that curiously serene loveliness that *sabi* connotes: desolation wrought not by disaster but simply by time; senectitude, loneliness, the waning of the year, of the moon, of the harvest; rust softly smoldering along the edges of old iron, time's patina laid like a translucent gossamer upon wood and metal and porcelain; stillness in empty places; the chilly beauty of *hie*, the dim beauty of *yūgen*, the remote beauty of a fading prospect in the gathering twilight. Neither were they mystified by *wabi*: beauty in its austerest and most understated simplicity; the impassive acceptance of the vicissitudes of life; cold light; the appeal of things that are *wabishi*—deserted, isolated, abandoned— or of things gradually vanishing away, dwindling; the sound of light rainfall on thatching or tiles or among leaves; a garden strewn with faded flowers, a green branch not yet in blossom, a simple wooden gate standing open on its quietly creaking hinges.

Again, though, they were not yet able to see the other side of the matter. They were not ready yet to raise their eyes in weariness from the broken cup of *wabi-sabi* to the unbroken circle of *ensō*.

Sinking further down into the water, until it reached his lower lip, he allowed his gaze to linger for a time simply on the grain of the cedar paneling of the nearest wall.

Of course, the most amusing of his students were the young men who thought they could grasp the essence of *iki*, that most urban and late modern of Japanese aesthetic values, which he suspected no Westerner could ever really comprehend as an integral concept. Was it really a concept at all? He could see, however, why it might seem so tantalizing to the current generation, with their small, fiercely trimmed beards and their thin curled mustaches, and why they might convince themselves that they too could hold its farraginous elements together in a single clear idea—uniqueness, spontaneity, novelty, but also resignation, composure, gallantry, nonchalance, and then too a certain stylish loucheness, detachment, an alertness to possibility, somehow all expressed in a partiality to gray or brown or dull blue attire, perhaps decorated with simple stripes, as well as a preference for indirect light and secluded corners . . . and so on. And perhaps they could. It seemed implausible to him; but then again, perhaps it is a value for which *only* the young can feel an immediate, intuitive penchant. Maybe they did understand it better than he did, and probably better than they really understood those older values that emanated from the natural world. For all that they could grasp of *shibui* or *wabi-sabi* or *mujō* and so forth, they could not possibly, he once again found himself thinking, know the true desolation that came when the enchantment of transitoriness gave way before the brute reality of the relentless advance of the years. They surely could not fully appreciate how memory can slowly transform a delicate sense of transience into the mere dreariness and vacancy of the irrecoverably lost, or into quiet mourning for what never was and now never can be. At that point, every unbidden association that springs up between the present and the past carries with it the peril of a devastating weight of regrets, and a painful awareness of how far the joys of the past have already receded along the corridor of memory. These webs of recollections, these echoes of transience within transience . . .

That girl he had seen on the way home—her momentary indisposition in the breeze, her guileless indifference—it reminded him now of a time years before when he had been an undergraduate in England, at Oxford, on a particularly lovely day in spring, and he had looked down from a window (in what building he could no longer remember) to the broad stairs leading up to the front of . . . (again, he could not remember which venerable edifice), where several other students were seated on the steps, among them an extremely attractive girl with flowing red hair, wearing one of those long floral print skirts (Laura Ashley, perhaps?) that were all the fashion then, and the wind had lifted it in a sudden billow and raised its hem back almost to her hip, momentarily revealing her long, lovely legs and elegantly slight white shoes with flat soles; her hands were momentarily occupied with keeping her hair from her eyes, but she soon put the skirt in order again. In an excess of boldness, he had descended to the street and gone to talk to her. Nothing came of it except a short and pleasant conversation, in the course of which he discovered that she had a charmingly quick sense of humor, a radiant complexion, enchanting green eyes, and a boyfriend who was even then on his way to meet her for lunch. But it was all superb at the time, and the memory of it had remained a source of happiness for him, whenever it rose up again in his thoughts, for a good while thereafter. But today, when the memory had been revived by chance, the sheer remoteness of that afternoon seemed to imbue the recollection with a cruel emptiness, a bitterness, even a kind of banality. Now it felt as if the memory were nothing but a souvenir of exhausted possibilities, exhausted youth. She must be a middle-aged woman by this point, with two or three grown children. And that thought, he found, was really rather horrible. There's the rub, he thought. Too much duration is the death of beauty, *precisely* because in memory the transient refuses to pass away in that lovely way it is supposed to do; instead, it insists on enduring, as perennial as bronze. Even the most serene experience of impermanence, when prolonged and periodically reiterated by memory, can become a painful fixation. The transient vanishes like the dew, he told himself, but the transience itself often lingers on and on. If only one could oneself somehow fade with the moment every time—could draw the evanescence into oneself—and then begin always again, without the gravity of memory persisting and persisting . . .

And then what awaited him, he thought, once all the empty years ahead were done? He had watched both of his parents wither away at the end, each becoming ever more immured in pain and idiocy until at last death came; and by then it came as nothing more than the cessation of an undignified and imbecile organic momentum, the body's degrading habit of enduring amidst its own ruin. It came far past the point when it could be welcomed gracefully . . . much less freely summoned.

Perhaps the prospect would be more bearable if he were not obliged to face it alone. But he had never married. None of his romances had ever taken root or proved to be more than fleeting attachments. The most promising among them—lasting twenty months or so during his years in Tokyo—was ultimately defeated by distance (and perhaps by other things) once he had returned to the States. And thereafter . . . well, nothing but occasional and occasionally intense liaisons. And now nothing at all.

For a moment his jaw tautened as he fought back a wave of distasteful self-pity.

And all the cats he had kept over the years, he then thought to himself, and how they had delighted him, and how terrible it was when they had died, and . . .

He had drunk too much *sake*, he decided. It had rendered him fatuous. And the water in the *furo* had grown tepid. It was time to leave the bath.

   Forty minutes or so later, now dry (apart from the lingering, fragrant dampness of his hair) and clad only in his kimono, he sat upon the large *tatami* mat that served as the carpet of the airy, enclosed, window-thronged sunroom at the back of the house. The effects of the *sake* had passed, apart perhaps for a slight and pleasant laxity in his limbs and back. The French doors were open to the garden itself, now quite denuded of its flowers; the moon above was nearly full but mostly hidden behind clouds, shedding only a very weak radiance on the bare flowerbeds and barren branches; but the small, sharp glow of the two lawn lights at the garden's far end and the drifting haze of rain still gave the scene a ghostly quality that he found curiously soothing—even inviting. And the effect was greatly enhanced by the darkness in the room where he sat; those lawn lights provided what little illumination he needed to see the items laid out on the low, polished teak table beside him: the small green porcelain *yokode kyūsu* in which his tea was steeping, the matching cup without any handle, the black ceramic bowl filled with ice cubes, two neatly folded strips of white linen, and the coldly gleaming *tantō* removed from and resting at an upward slant upon its black lacquered bamboo sheathe. To his left, a few feet away, a single plush golden cushion lay upon the *tatami*. As he had foreseen, the rain had come not long after he had reached home earlier in the afternoon, and had paused and resumed many times since then without ever becoming anything but a gentle shower, and at times little more than a faint silvery sheen of mist. It was falling now, as it happened, and at irregular intervals—also as he had foreseen—the breeze rose in a gust, filling the room with the fragrance of wet grass and leaves and sprinkling him with a few pleasantly chilly droplets. Not far beyond the garden's end, at the boundary of his property, the woods resumed and the ground sloped downward toward a shallow ravine; here not only the avenue, but indeed the whole neighborhood and town reached their end; but it was all invisible in the darkness just now. At the moment, those two wan lights marked, for all intents and purposes, the furthermost limit of the world. He poured his tea, lifted the cup to the level of his lips, blew gently upon the liquid for several seconds, and finally took a hesitant sip. It was still hot enough slightly to burn the tip of his tongue, but the soft richness of the *gyokuro*—at once floral and faintly smoky—instantly filled his mouth and throat.

Yūgen again, he thought. *Yū*—the shadowy, obscure, dim. *Gen*—darkness, night. A very particular kind of mysteriousness, more enthralling than frightening, more captivating than terrible. The pale green of early evening in the western sky. A lake in the twilight, surrounded by a forest into whose dim beryl-hued shadows one can see only a little way. Subtle evocations of things hidden, unspoken, merely suggested. A feeling too deep or too opaque for words. A depth that cannot be plumbed, a question that cannot be answered, something concealed and yet ever achingly near. Nature as seen through an atmosphere of lush and enigmatic beauty. Always subdued, however. The beauty that Chōmei says is like that of an evening in autumn, as one stands beneath a colorless expanse of silent sky and feels tears springing to one's eyes for reasons one should be able to recall, but cannot. Or a beauty like that of autumn mountains mostly hidden from view by a heavy mist, with only a few muted leaves indistinctly visible in the middle distance, beyond which the imagination conjures up boundless vistas. In all of it, an inexpressible sense of surfeit—of all things being disclosed while remaining hidden, coming to light by remaining obscure, being given by being withheld. Something is always withheld in Japanese aesthetics, of course—almost always more than is given, in fact, and thus whatever *is* given becomes ineffably precious.

He drank more of the tea, now in long swallows rather than sips, and then set the cup down on the small table.

Surely, he thought, the inner horizon of *yūgen*—the secret within the secret—must be death—must be a sense of life's fluidity, its fragility—a sense of graceful release into what is unknown but always just there, on the other side of every surface of the palpable world. Therein lay the lilting lyricism in the thought of suicide: the dream of simply slipping away peacefully into the shadows, mingling with them, merging, passing into and through that veil of mist, actively *choosing* to do so before the mystery of life has wholly waned away and only disenchantment and humiliation and pain remain. An intuition more than a hope, perhaps, that one will find welcome there past that boundary, and a place of rest; still, a hope nonetheless.

He breathed in deeply, slowly, closing his eyes and rising onto his knees as he attempted to compose himself, and then exhaled and opened his eyes again. The rain was so soft that it was nearly inaudible, but there was an exceedingly faint susurrous pattering on the leaves near the open doors, and the fresh, damp coolness of the air was soothing. The day really had been perfect in its way—or as perfect as one might have any occasion to hope. Moments of beauty, moments of charm . . . one touchingly whimsical moment . . . the glowing leaves, the silvery rain, the coldly fiery moon behind the smoldering clouds . . . the *sake* and the tea . . . the languor in his limbs, the shadows at the far end of the garden. It really was time. This really was—this must be—the day. Nothing had marred it, and nothing now would. Again the breeze briefly rose, and the rain brushed his cheek. Delicately he took up one of the folded lengths of raw white linen, laid it open in his left hand, took three dripping cubes of ice from their bowl with his right hand, placed them upon his still open palm, and folded the linen over and then around them. Then he raised the wrapped ice and placed it against the left side of his neck, on the carotid artery. He was not, he told himself, excessively afraid of pain; but he should not like it to be so great that it was the last thing he was thinking about when death stole in upon him. He was no samurai, after all, and he had neither any shame for which to atone nor any enemy to fear; and he would not have known how to commit *seppuku* even if he had inexplicably conceived the desire to do so. Not to mention, of course, that without a second to sweep his head from his shoulders with a *katana* before the agony could become intolerable it could only be a miserable and grotesque conclusion to an otherwise flawless day. No, he thought, glancing at the dreamily glimmering steel on the table. This would suffice—a quick, smooth, even slash of the *tantō*, a gout of blood that would soak his *kimono* and the *tatami* mat with stains like crimson blossoms as he lowered his head onto the cushion, and then at most a few seconds to continue gazing into the rain-glazed garden, followed by a peaceful lapsing away into . . .

The ice on his neck, even through the linen, was more uncomfortable than he had expected, and as he shifted it ever so slightly a drop of chilly water trickled down from it and ran unpleasantly under the collar of his kimono. The hand in which he held it, moreover, was beginning to throb a little painfully. He set it down on the mat and gently probed the side of his neck with the fingers of his other hand. Cold but not nearly as numb as he had hoped. He adjusted the linen wrapping around the ice, trying to make it tighter and folding it more thickly underneath, where it would rest in his palm, and then applied it to his neck again. This time he forced himself to endure the discomfort for as long as he could, until the now-constant drops running down his neck and wrist and soaking into his collar and cuff became insufferable. Perhaps he should have used a freezer bag, he thought to himself, but the sheer hideousness of anything plastic would have irreparably disfigured the whole ceremony. He certainly could not have departed this life if it meant that something that tawdry would be found near his corpse. Everything must remain perfect to the end. He laid the wrapped cubes of ice back in the bowl and quickly took up the *tantō* by its sleek black-lacquered handle. There was of course no reason to wrap the lower half of the blade with the other length of linen, since he was not going to eviscerate himself and had no need to grip the steel directly; but he did it anyway, for purely aesthetic reasons, and the milky white linen did in fact look very fetching against the lambent steel. But then, knowing that the numbness in his neck was already ebbing, he raised the *tantō* to his carotid artery, the handle in his right hand, the back of the blade steadied by the fingertips of his left. He felt the steel's edge—honed almost to the sharpness of a razor—ever so lightly scrape his skin, and then felt it poised delicately against his only partially insensate nape. He took another deep breath and tightened his grip on the handle. He gazed vacantly ahead, out into the garden. The rain had once more become little more than a slowly precipitating mist. From the woods beyond the garden and the boundary of his lawn, the call of an owl sounded out, three times, then a delayed fourth time, and then there was silence. Surely that was the perfect final note, he thought to himself, that lovely, soft, plangently plain voice in the darkness. The last and utterly poignantly fitting element of a day without flaw. He ceased breathing, closed his eyes tightly, summoned up all the strength of will he possessed, felt the muscles in his arms growing rigid, and then . . . then . . . yes, and then . . .

A faint spasm of exasperation caused him to release his breath. This was vexing, to say the least. He did not know what it was that still delayed him. It was only a little thing that was required now, after all, a slight instant of pain, as Marcus Aurelius would have told him, and then that final, easeful, luxurious repose. If one would desert one's station on the battlements of the world, as all the Stoics insisted, one need only pass through a door that stands ever open. Again the muscles of his right arm grew tense, his wrist stiffened, again he closed his eyes, and now he knew that, yes, this time he would do what he intended. His breathing was growing rapid, a strange thrill was passing through the fingers of his right hand, his left hand was beginning to quake. Slowly but resolutely he began to apply greater pressure to the blade, ever more insistently . . . Or so he meant to do. But the blade, in fact, was for some reason making no deeper impression upon his flesh. If anything, its touch was becoming lighter, more delicate. It felt almost as if it were trying to float away from him. He realized that his left arm had become weak, almost fluid in its yielding pliancy, as if the effort of holding the blade steady and pressing it against his neck was simply far too onerous. This was absurd. Now he was growing angry. For a moment he gritted his teeth, suppressed the urge to curse himself, slowed his breath, tightened his right hand on the hilt of the *tantō* until it was positively painful for his fingers and the heel of his hand, and with one final enormous exertion of will—one final great surge of resolve—one final . . .

Suddenly, jarringly, in a way that sent a sudden painful shock up his spine and into his neck, the sound of a car's horn blared loudly from the street outside; then came the sound of a man's voice hoarsely shouting something ferocious and probably obscene at someone else, perhaps a pedestrian, perhaps another driver. With the French doors open, it was all quite surprisingly loud even here at the back of the house. Instantly, he released the *tantō*, and it fell onto the bamboo of the mat beside him with a dull clatter. His breath issued from between his teeth in a sharp hiss. There was the screech of a tire, the groan of an engine, the sound of a car lurching forward and speeding away, squealing curtly against the asphalt, splashing through the water running in torrents beside the curbs and pooled in depressions in the road. Now he did curse. This was wholly unprecedented in his experience, here at the end of his shady avenue, right where the lane terminated in a small cul-de-sac. None of his neighbors had ever behaved in that manner, certainly. Perhaps the driver had become lost on his way somewhere else and was angry at finding himself in a dead end. But, really . . .

He was trembling now, he realized—perhaps had been doing so for some time, in fact, even before he had been so rudely interrupted. And then too his breath, he found, was labored, and his chest hurt. He held out his hands before him and saw that they were quivering. He remained like this for half a minute or so, before laying his hands in his lap, shaking his head, breathing deeply, and turning his eyes once again toward his garden. The rain was heavier now, though still no more than a light shower—and it was really quite beautiful. But it was too late. The moment had been spoiled beyond rescue. It was quite impossible now to finish what he had begun. As on previous occasions, he would have to resign himself to waiting for another day like this one, when he might try again to bring everything to its proper conclusion without any unseemly disruptions.

He did not move for several moments. Then, suddenly, he laughed. Then he laughed again, and continued doing so for several seconds until the laughter was curtailed by a sound like a sob that rose in the back of his throat. He closed his eyes tightly and strove to contain his tears. It was all nonsense, he knew. Why he kept striving to convince himself that he really meant to do what he had planned, and had now attempted four times without success, he could not say. Yes, he wanted to be rid of life; but no, he could not bear to depart from life. He knew it so clearly now. He might forget again at intervals in the future; he might even reenact this silly little drama. Who could say how many times? But just now his mind was luminously clear. He would never bring it to its end, never sever the cord that bound him to this world.

He shook his head again, opened his eyes, and stared out toward his garden. The sound of the rain was really quite delightful. The cool air, the soughing of the trees in the darkness beyond, the pale light of the thinly veiled moon—all of it was beautiful, and mysterious, and somehow timeless.

After ten minutes or so, the trembling in his body ceased. With some effort, and feeling far weaker than he expected, he rose from the mat, stretched his limbs, and walked nearer to the open doors, coming to a halt only three feet or so from the threshold. Here cold drops of rain began to strike him with greater frequency, though still only very lightly. Now he could see the red and yellow leaves of trees strewn across his garden by the winds, wet and wanly shining in the agate grass. He gave vent to a soft sigh, almost inaudible even to himself. Really, he thought to himself, to be perfectly honest, he had no particular right to pass through that "door ever open." His suffering was no greater than that of most persons, and was far less than that of very many. How could he take himself so seriously? No. A night like this was enough for the complaints he had against the universe, small and petulant and ultimately absurd as they were. *Yūgen* was enough. He did not need to cross over the threshold at all if he could only learn properly to dwell at the boundary, to cultivate that precious, elusive appreciation of the mystery—of the hidden prospect that lay on the other side of the darkness.

Just then, there was a parting in the clouds, and he glanced up to see the moon—almost but not quite full—shine out like flaming silver in a crucible; for a few seconds, its brilliance turned the raindrops into sparks of cold fire; and then the clouds closed over it again and its light once more became merely a diffuse, gauzy glow in the shrouded sky.

But then no, he thought, lowering his gaze again, not merely *yūgen*, but rather also, more profoundly, *ensō*: the empty circle, the perfect form, the universe, the void—*mu, śūnyatā*. Purity of form and will, graceful humility—and then, too, the absolute, that which is absolved of all things and so hospitable to all things, yet remaining beyond everything. The vacant lunar light that presides over this world of shadows. The gentle light that summons forth the tremulous, wavering, transient forms otherwise forever concealed in the darkness of *yūgen*, and then soon sends them on their way again, back into the darkness. The nothing that makes room and so lets all things be.

Perhaps, he thought, it was time he once again attempted to paint that circle. His brushes and ink and ink stones and rice paper all lay neatly arranged on their shelf in his studio upstairs, untouched for at least three months now. That would have been the better way to bring this day to its end. He smiled, somewhat forlornly, and lowered his eyes to the floor. A stray leaf blown in from the garden, its mottled purple just barely distinguishable in the dim light, clung to the rough linen selvedge of the mat, fluttering slightly along one edge. *Ensō.*

Ensō.

No matter how many times he might temporarily forget in future, he knew perfectly well that he would never advance beyond this point—and maybe that was as it should be. To dwell just here in certain intervals removed from time's flow, where the difference between the momentary and the eternal, as between memory and oblivion, disappears and is replaced by what is at once neither and both—this would have to suffice. This must be the form he would labor to perfect. *Ensō.* For how long, though? How long could he sustain it? He looked up again to the bright moon, now once more beginning to emerge from behind the drifting clouds above. As long as he must, he told himself. Obviously.

The wind rose again, shaking the leaves that still hung upon the branches of the bushes along the garden's verges and upon the flowerless stems in the garden beds, stirring the fallen leaves that lay in the grass, rousing a few from their resting places and sending them rolling across the lawn, and driving the continuously descending mist of rain toward the invisible east.

12   *Dramatis Personae* II

"Now, then," she said, "if I've satisfactorily discharged the task you gave me, and supplied the beginning of your story for you, you can do me the reverse service of supplying an ending to a little vignette I've dreamed up about a stage actress in the 1880s, somewhere in the Austro-Hungarian Empire—one of the more civilized parts of it, that is—performing the part of an aristocratic English beauty of marriageable age, pursued by a host of suitors, in a light melodrama written especially for her."

"I see," he said. "That's already quite an exact premise. I'm not sure I can enter as effortlessly as you can into someone else's imagined world."

"Certainly you can," she replied. "You do it every time you write a new story. You become someone else on each occasion, after all, with every new story you tell. This one shouldn't tax your imagination to a crippling degree. Although—and this is maybe a bit unkind on my part—there is one aspect of the tale that I want you to provide at the very beginning. I want you to decide on her physical features for me, and maybe some of her mannerisms."

"Why?" he asked. "Haven't you a picture of her already in mind?"

"Of only the most fluid kind," she said. "But, whether I do or not, I have a wicked ulterior motive for making the request. I want you to paint her portrait for me precisely so you'll have even more of an emotional stake in what becomes of her in the course of the narrative. I want to make you that much more an accomplice in her fate. I'd like you to, so to speak, *confect* her out of your own memories, especially from some you cherish—or even some that haunt you. I also want you to conjure her up out of your imagination, of course, but you should endow her with characteristics of girls and women you've known . . . or wished to know. Maybe the charms of a woman you dared admire only from afar. You know . . . eyes, lips, figure . . . the special timbre of her voice . . . a certain laugh or gasp of delight . . . "

"Yes, all right," he interrupted. "I understand. I already know which woman from my past she resembles. Shall I describe her to you?"

"Later, perhaps," she said. "But have her in your mind's eye as the story unfolds."

"At least," he said with a sigh, "let me mention the beauty mark just above her left upper lip, and her deeply green eyes . . . and her auburn hair."

"Very well," she replied. "But remember that her hair, however you remember it being worn, must in this case be arranged appropriately for the era. Anyway, that's all as may be. When the story begins, she's only just arrived in the city. Don't ask which city. It's somewhere in Austria proper, I imagine, though my own historical and geographic ignorance makes it basically a fairy tale setting rather than a realistic portrait of any actual place."

"A large city?" he asked.

"Not really," she answered. "It's populous but not immense, a commercial city with a thriving prosperous upper middle class whose members are wealthier in many cases than the old landed aristocracy but still deferential toward and deeply envious of their social superiors. It's a very respectable bourgeois city now, one that's grown up on the edges of the ancestral estates of a few noble houses. You can imagine it easily enough. In the propertied Brucheium, so to speak, virtues vie with virtues, while in the lower city vices clash with vices. Yet between all those virtues on one side and all those vices on the other there's only harmony—a peace bred of mutual dependency. The decent and socially impeccable inhabitants of the city's richer, northern districts are edified and sustained in their polite and abstemious ways by the knowledge of the debauched and deplorable rabble to the south, while the denizens of the poorer districts are encouraged in their coarse and dissolute habits by the knowledge of those humorlessly proper, desiccated householders to the north. Moreover, the vices of the city's southern side and the virtues of the northern curiously coincide: both tend to be variants of concupiscence, avarice, pride, and sloth, differing only in style. Everyone has a station and is aware of it. Everyone is baptized, save for a small Jewish community, but no one is devout.

"The most enterprising among the rising middle class are always vainly hopeful of elevating their status in society through the exercise of patronage; they compete at purchasing paintings and sculptures for their private collections or for donation to the city's small *musée des beaux arts*. They all also share a naively vulgar appetite for sumptuously decorated homes. The wealthiest of them all are the northernmost of all, living in the exurban neighborhoods where paved avenues yield to cobbled roads and dusty lanes and quaintly prosaic façades are supplanted by daintily palatial homes with moist, brightly green lawns bordered by hedges. It's a sheltered little arcadia of a neighborhood, far from both the squalor of the working poor and the *déclassé* tawdriness of the still-aspiring middle class, and yet no less removed from the mist-crowned Olympus of the landed aristocracy, from whose unscalable slopes only an occasional fragrant and clement breeze descends. In this little terrestrial demi-paradise, contradictory though it seems, acting is still a very suspect profession, and yet the most famous figures of the theatre are objects of almost servile fascination; and happily our actress is just such a figure. As a result, for the duration of her play's run in the city, she's staying there as the guest of a rich widow who has only a hazy notion of what divides the high arts from the low in the estimation of polite society, and who's very proud of having so glamorous a visitor. The soiree her hostess threw in celebration of her arrival two weeks ago brought out what passed in these circles for a glittering company—bankers, prosperous merchants, manufacturers, speculators, and so forth—including a large number of young men who spent the evening practically falling over one another in their eagerness to capture her attention for a few moments, and who were to a one dazzled by her radiant smile, the practiced fluttering of her eyelashes, the trilling gaiety of her laugh, the elegance with which she lightly turned her head aside in restrained elation or clasped her hands together in polite amusement."

"All right," he said, "but who's in danger of sounding like a poor man's Henry James now?"

"Merely setting the scene," she rejoined. "Don't be impatient. Anyway, you have a better picture of her than I do, having plundered your memory for her. Just realize that she knows how to enchant without for a moment having the least interest in those on whom she works her charms. She's still young and in the first flush of her beauty—just—but she's also experienced and knows how to shine like the sole bird of exotic plumage among a flock of crows."

"This is more appropriate than you know," he remarked. "I mean, to the woman I'm . . . recalling."

"Good," she said. "So, as our tale begins, she's more than midway through her stay. It's early spring, still so cool that in the shade of the hedges around the house the dew lingers till late morning as a pale gauze of frost, but also balmy enough that everything is coming into blossom, and all about those shaded boundaries blue lobelias are in flower and look like dark sapphires in the light of either dawn or dusk; irises and marigolds fill the garden beds at the front of the house, and glow with a positively painful richness in the mild afternoon sunlight; and so on and so on—you can arrange the grounds as you like. You're fonder of flower descriptions than I am. We meet her for the first time strolling with an open parasol resting on her shoulder, late in the morning, in the park across from the house where she's staying; she's accompanied, four steps behind, by her maid—who also happens to be her *costumière*—but is otherwise alone, having managed to slip away from her hostess for a blessed half hour or so of liberty, and hasn't as yet been descried—or, at least, intruded upon—by any of the neighbors. She's thinking of an attractive young man who caught her eye a week ago when she was on stage and whom she has seen again at each subsequent performance. He keeps a box at the theatre, you see, one near to the stage and overlooking it practically from above the left wing. Not one of those oafish sons of industrialists and bankers and merchant moguls she can captivate so effortlessly, and can conquer with a coquettish smile and dominate with a sigh, but someone altogether more refined, mysterious, remote, and fascinating to her—someone who conducts himself with the practiced reserve of the very well bred, and someone she's frequently observed gazing at her with a contained intensity quite unlike the guileless brashness and canine eagerness of any of those privileged yokels. He's obviously a man who has command over his own thoughts and feelings, and some depth of experience they could never even aspire to. Obviously also a son of the aristocracy. The first time she noticed him was midway through the play's second act, when she had been obliged to cast her gaze upward dramatically just before pronouncing an admission of the love felt by the character she was playing—whose name, if I omitted to mention it, is Lady Jessica Wolford, which our Austrian dramatist thought sounded very British—anyway, just before pronouncing the love Lady Jessica feels for the chief male character— who's, at that point, absent from the scene—and suddenly there he was—not the male protagonist, that is, but the handsome young aristocrat in his box, gazing down directly at her. Not at the stage in general, that is, and not merely at the action of the play, but at her; he was leaning out far enough over the edge of his box that the diffuse glow of stage lights illuminated his features, and he was staring intently into her eyes, quite frankly and obviously even across the shadowy distance separating them. She nearly forgot her line, he was so very strikingly handsome, and seemed so preposterously young. Several times thereafter, as the play traipsed along toward its vapidly happy conclusion, she had looked up to that box only to find his eyes still fixed on her, an expression of rapt attention on his face. And all of this even though he was not alone that night; there was a splendidly, glitteringly glamorous woman in the box with him, with dark hair and copious jewelry, always quite near at his side, leaning toward him. At least three times, on looking up from the stage, our actress had noticed this woman whispering something in his ear with a wide smile, obviously trying to divert his attention from the stage by some sly observation or seductive witticism, or perhaps some slightly sensational remark about some other woman in some other box. But the whole time he barely acknowledged his lovely companion, except perhaps with a fleeting and forced smile, and instead continued to gaze down at our actress. Clearly he was spellbound. As I say, he has returned to the theatre each night since then—twice with other women, once with a friend, once with what it seems reasonable to assume from appearances are his father, mother, and younger sister, and otherwise by himself. And each time he has spent nearly the entirety of the time gazing at her with that same intense but also somehow pensive, withdrawn, and enigmatic expression of fascination and quiet delight."

"Is this to be a story about a love affair thwarted by class disparity?" he asked. "I dislike those."

"I hope not," she replied. "Surely you can do better than that. Anyway, that's not *my* intention certainly. At the point where I leave the story hanging I've left room for more interesting possibilities than that."

"Where's that, then?" he asked.

"Realize before all else," she said, "that our actress is no dewy-eyed ingenue. Her heart's her own, and her bank accounts more so. She's young and gay and charming and so forth, especially on her very effervescent surface, but she's also practical and prudent and has a fine sense of irony. And she's not at all adverse to the sort of arrangement men of that class regularly make with actresses, as she has a keen appreciation for the advantages one can extract from them—especially if one keeps a firm grip on one's emotions—both sensual and pecuniary."

"I see," he said.

She smiled. "Naturally, she assumes that sooner or later a note attached to, say, a bouquet of white calla lilies will arrive at her dressing room door, requesting a backstage audience, and thereafter an accommodation will be reached. But, while she's certain this is the direction in which things are tending—and this is what's occupying her mind as she strolls through the park in the morning freshness amid the chorusing birds—things are certainly taking longer to sort themselves out than seems necessary to her, or even healthy. As far as she's concerned, the terms of the compact have already been firmly established between them, perhaps silently but several times, in all those frank gazes they've been exchanging for weeks now. All that remains is the customary overture, the verbal agreement, the ceremonious night of dinner and dancing and demurely salacious banter, and then the inevitable and—one would imagine—quite enjoyable 'surrender to passion.' A few faint and invitingly insincere protestations first, a seemly but brief reluctance, of course; but then the agreed upon services, presumably as much a delight to tender as their tangible rewards will be to receive. He is, after all, far more handsome than her other temporary paramours have been, and she has an eye for male beauty. Then the attentions, the gifts, the increasingly expensive displays of devotion, the caresses and tender exchanges and clandestine assignations, and finally the inevitable, wistfully heartbreaking—but, she would hope, amiable and less than absolute—parting. After that, she will take stock of her spoils from the episode, both material and sentimental, and move on. She smiles to herself here, incidentally, at the memory of one of these young . . . benefactors who, in a sudden eruption of earnest mawkishness, had asked her to abandon the stage and marry him. He didn't care, he ardently professed, what his family or society would think. She, of course, had known that it was sheer fantasy and had gently dissuaded him from his abrupt resolve. It had been very sweet, however. But that's all in the past. In the present she's growing restless at her current suitor's—or presumptive suitor's—continued failure to bring the situation to its obvious resolution, and she's coming to believe she'll have to take matters into her own hands if anything's to happen at all. The trick here, of course, is to avoid giving any impression of being meretricious or unladylike or wanton, but nevertheless to prompt him to action, ideally making him think he's initiated it all."

"Yes, all right," he said, "but are we nearing the part where I take over?"

"Yes," she replied. "Don't be impatient. I'll have the baton in your palm in just a moment. But the scene must change first. Now it's the night of the same day, after the evening performance of the melodrama, and she's out for a late dinner at the very fashionable restaurant across the street from the theatre, escorted by one of those oafish young men who're so anxious to be seen in public with her on their arms—in this case, an industrialist's son . . . or perhaps a banker's. And, unexpectedly, she sees him there—her handsome young aristocratic admirer, I mean—dining with a friend who had been with him in his box during the evening's performance of her play. He has not seen her now, however. And this, she decides, is when she must take the game into her own hands and make whatever move she can. Somehow, without degrading herself in her admirer's eyes—without surrendering any of her air of feminine propriety or the advantage it gives her—she must detach herself from her gauche companion (and from the miasma of unctuous pomade, mustache wax, coal-tar soap, and *eau de cologne* that hangs about him) long enough to make some contact with her real opponent but must also do so with sufficient subtlety to make the latter believe it's he who controls the board. And . . . that's it. *There's* where I leave things lying for you to pick up."

"You want me to decide which move she'll make?" he asked.

"That," she said, "and all the consequences that follow."

After a moment's reflection, he said, "Yes, I think I can oblige you. The first part is easy enough to imagine, though it'll have to be somewhat contrived. Decently speaking, there's no way for her to circle in any more closely on her prey without being noticed, and perhaps restrained, by her escort—not physically, that is, but according to social usages. So it comes down to timing and positioning. Let's say that the mysterious young aristocrat with the box has either finished his meal or has not yet been seated, but is standing with a friend near the bar to the, ah, right of the entrance. She tells her escort that she wants to leave—they've eaten already, after all—and absolutely craves the fresh air outside, and perhaps—here an enchanting smile and tilt of the head and small batting of the lashes—a stroll at his sheltering side along the pavement while the city is still awake. She has a fan with her—that's absolutely crucial—folded in her hand. She pauses in the open between bar and door, adroitly positioning herself just behind the young aristocrat, and sends her young oaf to find why no one has brought their coats and hats, and as she does so she says something amusing, affects a gay laugh, and 'carelessly' swings her folded fan to the side, 'accidentally' striking the young man on the shoulder. As he turns to her, she turns to him, laughing charmingly and immediately beginning to apologize even before her eyes have quite met his. When their gazes do meet, she pauses, still smiling brilliantly—oh, by the way, she pinched her cheeks as she rose from the table—anyway, she's still smiling, as I say, and pauses and asks whether they've met. When the young man stares back at her, oddly impassively, she remarks that, oh, of course, he's the young gentleman she's seen from the stage, gazing down from his box on so many occasions—my goodness, she can't help but remember him, since he seems to be there every night—in fact, is it perhaps, actually, *every* night?—what a faithful devotee of . . . of the *theatre* he must be. Here she gives him a slightly conspiratorial—in an amused and gently affectionate way—smirk. And then another small, enchanting laugh. She orchestrates it all to perfection. And yet, to her consternation, she's not having the effect she'd hoped. The young man seems neither delighted nor intimidated by this unanticipated encounter; either reaction would please her, but neither comes. Instead, he seems merely discomfited and a mite embarrassed; once she's addressed him, he drops his eyes and refuses to meet her gaze with his again. Instead, he continues to look down for several moments and then, when he does lift his eyes, he looks about the restaurant with a somewhat abashed—but also somewhat displeased—expression, saying nothing. After several seconds of unrequited attempts at repartee, she becomes self-conscious, falls silent, and merely looks at him quizzically. Her incandescent charm is beginning to dim. The effusive smile has become merely pleasant. She's already issued as much of an invitation as she dare, marshalling as best she can the musical laugh she can still summon up from her throat and her best demure but frank gaze and her most ebulliently lilting tone of voice. Yet nothing is coming back her way. Still not quite looking at her other than with a quick, oblique glance, he murmurs almost inaudibly that yes, he's seen her very often on stage . . . he's enjoyed the performances. Then, turning his eyes to something seemingly somewhere off to her left and arching his brows as if responding to some signal, he says that he's just seen a friend he absolutely must go to greet, and will she please excuse him, and . . . He doesn't even finish the sentence; he simply stops speaking, unceremoniously steps around her, and strides away. She doesn't turn to watch him go—she knows how humiliating it would be to do so if anyone had observed the scene to that point—but instead, after a tense pause during which she resolutely assumes an expression of amusement, she slowly turns toward her escort, who fortunately is just now returning, and smiles at him with renewed vigor. Secretly, she's dumbfounded. Perhaps the young man is still too tender in years or temperament to know how to present himself to a woman he desires. Perhaps he's far shyer than she could have guessed. Perhaps there's some more complicated and arcane explanation for his behavior—the presence at the restaurant of a friend who's already been mocking him for his constant attendance at the theatre and his obvious infatuation with an actress—a friend he doesn't want to see him responding warmly to the very woman in question. Who can say? Whatever the case, if anything is to come of all those ardent gazes he's poured down on her from his box, it may require more ingenuity from her than she had anticipated, and more persistence. The young oaf is with her now, however, and she's obliged to go for that damned walk with him. At least he has money. The meal was excellent.

"The next night, there's another performance of the play. At her first entrance, treading the boards as Lady Jessica and softly aglow in her hazy nimbus of limelight, she immediately glances up to see whether her admirer is in attendance. There he is, as always, alone this time and leaning forward with one arm on the ledge of his box, his expression as intent and unwaveringly fixed upon her as ever. She greets his eyes with hers and smiles at him, albeit somewhat more uncertainly than she intends. He does not react. He merely gazes and gazes. She lowers her eyes. And so it is throughout the performance: when she looks up, she sees him looking at her with quiet, intransigent fascination, but none of the enticingly tender little smiles she sends back his way rouse any discernible response. And when she comes out after the final curtain to take her bows with the cast she sees that he's already gone. Briefly she entertains the hope that he'll be waiting backstage in her dressing room—her maid has instructions to admit him if he should come—having at last found the courage to accept her unspoken invitation. But, when she arrives there, he is nowhere to be seen. Now she must decide whether to leave matters there or to make one last attempt to run her quarry to ground. It may be a matter of pride or, worse, of a sudden anxious fear that perhaps she's not still quite as young and utterly entrancing as she fancies herself to be in men's eyes—who knows how men see things, since they're so childishly attracted to bright and flawlessly pretty things?—but she resolves upon at least one last effort to draw him out of his reserve, just to reassure herself that she's still able to work her magic. She spends some time examining her face in the mirror, and then—letting the silk dressing gown she's wearing slip to the floor—examining her figure, from every angle she can. She finds nothing amiss."

"I should have expected you'd find a way to get her out of her clothes," she remarked.

"Simply striving for psychological authenticity," he said with a feebly ironic smile. "After dressing, she delays her return to her lodging long enough to write out a note on the rather fine linen stationery she always has with her. She destroys a first draft out of dissatisfaction with some of its wording and a second out of dissatisfaction with her hand-writing (which does not look either unhurried or feminine enough to her), but the third strikes her as perfect. When it's blotted and dried, she folds it and places it in an envelope, leaves it in her dressing table drawer, and returns with her maid to her hostess's house. The next night, after having applied a touch of the perfume she wears to the en-velope's edges, she tells her maid that if the young gentleman should ap-pear as usual, she must take the note to an usher on that floor and have it delivered to him in his box near the end of the first act. He does ap-pear, and the maid does as instructed. Near the end of the first act, our heroine happens to glance up to see the young gentleman stirring from his trance at the sound of something at his back, rising, opening the door of his box so that his figure is momentarily framed in a narrow ob-long of yellow light, and then returning to his seat, envelope in hand. She delivers a few lines and then glances upward again to see that he has extracted the note but is evidently having some difficulty reading it in the poor light. He rises and retreats to the low-burning gas lamp en-sconced on the wall at the back of the box. She is obliged by the play, however, to exit the stage just at that point. When she enters again some several moments later and then finds an apt moment in the action for raising her eyes in the desired direction, she sees that he has resumed his seat again, and that now the expression on his face is even more in-scrutably impassive than ever. His eyes still meet hers, but somehow they seem to do so from a greater distance than before.

"The note she had sent to him had been impeccably delicate and elliptical, even in its candor. She had written that she now found it im-possible not to notice that he had faithfully attended every performance of the play for three weeks or so without break, and she felt she could not err in assuming that this indicated some degree of admiration on his part—for her acting or, perhaps—dare she imagine?—for herself. This being so, after so many nights of being gazed at by him, and of meeting his eyes so often across the space separating the stage from his box, she would be very glad of a visit from him after the play, so that she could at least learn his name and thank him for his devotion. She quite felt that by now he was not a stranger but a friend, and it seemed odd to her to have a friend whose name she did not know; it would be only polite of him to supply it. Then she had signed off with a simple 'Your Friend' followed by her full name, not just her Christian name, which would have of course seemed a little too presumptuous and forward. And that had been it. She could be no more frank than this without losing all advantage and without forfeiting the illusion of her social respectability. But, for heaven's sake, she tells herself now, wedging the thought into a small interstice between two of her lines, if he's still unable to understand what's being offered to him, practically reclining naked on a Turkish divan, or is too unmanly to avail himself of the invitation, he's probably too stupid or pusillanimous a specimen to bother with. At least, she briefly comforts herself with that thought. The play goes on to its end. Not once, on glancing up, does she observe any change in his expression. At the curtain call, she again finds he's left his box. This time, however, when she comes to her dressing room, he's there. Her maid modestly, if a little too hastily, excuses herself. At first assuming she has at last breached the wall of his diffidence . . . or taciturnity . . . or whatever it is, she positively scintillates at him for several moments, with her gayest smile and most carefree manner and a stream of enchanting babble about how lovely it is to meet him properly at last. But then once again she begins to realize that something is wrong. He's not responding in an *enchanted* way at all, whether awkwardly or boldly. She has extracted a name from him but only in a vague murmur. She's heard of the family and is impressed. But that's of no importance. He remains oddly, adamantly unemotive, apart from that expression yet again of discomfort and general displeasure. When she realizes at last that he intends neither to beg nor to seize her favors—that he has come neither as suppliant nor as conqueror, though she has implicitly given him permission to assume either role—she becomes quiet, even grave. As he obviously has no intention either of wooing or of ravishing her, she now must strive at least to rescue her dignity. Plainly, even a little icily, she asks whether he is quite well. Why is he so . . . bashful . . . so aloof? Why has he come, precisely, since he seems so little at his ease?

"He hesitates for a moment to answer, not meeting her eyes. After a moment, he responds—in a dry and soft voice—that he has come for the purpose of preventing any further misunderstandings, and if possible in order to remedy a situation for which he alone bears the blame. He cannot allow matters to continue in the direction they seem now to be heading. Well, then, she asks coldly, what is it he wants to tell her? That her note, he replies—gracious as it was—was prompted by a misapprehension. Yes, it's true, he comes each night, and does so out of a deep . . . admiration . . . more than that . . . He pauses here. Well, she prompts after a moment, and so . . . ? Yes, he continues, but not a fascination. 'Not a fascination with *you* . . . as such,' he says, his voice dwindling pathetically away on those last two words. Her brow furrows. 'Well, with whom, then?' she asks. 'You certainly seem to be staring at me constantly—and me alone.' Well, yes and no, he tells her. Yes, he's gazing at . . . but it's not . . . He pauses, closes his eyes, and then draws a deep breath. 'It's not you I'm interested in . . . fascinated by. It's . . . Lady Jessica.' She stares at him in astonished silence for several seconds. 'Lady Jessica?' she finally says, pronouncing each syllable slowly. But don't be preposterous, she expostulates. 'I *am* Lady Jessica. She's nothing but . . . ' Oh, but that's not so, he interrupts at this point. She waits. After a few seconds, he dilates upon his protest: Lady Jessica is . . . well, a lady, not an actress. She's a woman of impeccable morals. But, more than that, she's as perfectly refined as any woman could be—exquisitely so—but also witty, and yet passionate. She's not like the empty-headed women he knows among his own class. But this is absurd, our heroine says. He's enamored of a character she plays on stage . . . a fiction she merely performs for the entertainment of the crowd? At this, he looks abashed and falls silent. Then, after several tense moments, he quietly remarks that he should go. He has come only to ensure that there will be no further misunderstanding. He could never—would never—take an interest in a woman of the stage, who travels about unescorted in the company of men and other women of her . . . of her profession. It's unthinkable. And he could never trade the pure affection he cherishes for that lovely, divine, angelic creature for some dalliance with a . . . with a . . . Silence falls again."

She said, "I see. This is amusing, I have to admit. So, what . . . is she shattered?"

"Oh, no," he replied. "That's not like her at all. No, after a moment or two she begins to laugh. After a few moments more, the burden of her anxieties has quite fallen away. She's not stung by his obvious horror at the thought of mingling with a woman beneath his class—which apparently he idealizes with an innocence she would have thought impossible. After all, she entertains no illusions about herself. She was perfectly willing to exchange carnal and sentimental favors for the material benefits this young man might have provided her, and would have enjoyed herself as much as she could in doing so, feeling free to delight in his body no less than he in hers. She's not offended. She's relieved, in fact, to find that her charms have not begun to desert her, after all. They've simply on this occasion happened to beguile an imbecile. When all is said and done, it's still her beauty and her charisma and her effervescence—to say nothing of her ability to command the stage—that shines out of the character she plays and that holds this poor young idiot Adonis in thrall. And he truly *is* in her power. With only a slight alteration of style in her portrayal of Lady Jessica, she could dash his love to pieces. Not that she would dream of doing anything so cruel, or so injurious to her own performance.

"In any event, her laughter surprises him. He looks about uneasily and then asks whether he must refrain from coming to future performances. He will submit to her wishes in this matter, whatever they may be. She'll not hear of it, she tells him. Why deprive himself of something that so evidently makes him happy? She's delighted to know that her rendition of Lady Jessica brings him such pleasure. She promises—and she means it—to continue to infuse her performance with all the life and gaiety and elegance he has found in it to this point. She has no desire to part him from his love before it's absolutely necessary. At last he looks up fully, and stares at her wordlessly; but the gratitude in his eyes is poignantly obvious. With another laugh, she dismisses him, as a lady might her maid or a queen her subject. Or maybe like a governess sending her charge to bed. 'Go along now, young man,' she tells him with a touch of condescending imperiousness in her voice, actually turning him about by his shoulders like a small boy and only just suppressing an impulse to pat him on either his head or his bottom as she sends him away."

"I see," she said. "She has a generous nature."

"I prefer," he said, "to say she's a realist. And she has a sense of fairness. She'd always intended to play a part for his private delectation, so she feels no great sense of injured dignity on discovering that she's already been doing so. It simply isn't the part she'd expected. What is it that she does each time she appears on stage, after all, other than attempt to make men adore her? After he's gone, and before her maid returns, she seats herself at her dressing table and stares into the mirror. She had quite forgotten till now that she's still in her stage makeup—is still wearing Lady Jessica's face, as it were, though in this light and seen so close up the effect is more garish than pleasing. But she continues to regard herself in the glass, with an irrepressible smirk of amusement. Whatever arrogance that young gentleman might be accused of, it's not so much his as that of his class; and perhaps it's to his credit that he believes in the standards he obeys. What's more, amusingly enough, his passion for Lady Jessica is obviously a pure one, to which he will remain faithful in years ahead, even when he's taken a wife; his heart having been pierced by the arrow of so unadulterated and lofty a love, he'll never succumb to the nagging counsels of conscience or reason (those two withered harridans) when he thinks about her, and he'll tell his wife—when she asks why he's so distracted—that he's trying to recall whether he's written that letter to his lawyer, or something to that effect. Really, he's to be admired—though, of course, pitied as well.

"As she continues to contemplate the painted face looking back at her pensively from the glass, it occurs to her as well that, after all, the role she plays every day before the adoring eyes of the world is no less a fiction—no less a fabrication and feat of deception—than those she plays on stage. Not because she's an actress, moreover, or in any special sense disingenuous. We're all of us fictions, she tells herself firmly, hiding who knows what from view? Perhaps nothing at all, other than some sort of formless will to exist as . . . something . . . somebody . . . and to deceive others into loving us, or admiring us, or fearing us. The simple truth of the matter, it strikes her just now, is that to be anyone at all is already to be a creature of fantasy. There's the real folly of that young idiot. Were his discernment nearly as great as his passion, he would be drawn to her no less than to the woman she plays on stage, *not* because she's in some fuller sense a real woman; he would prefer her because she herself is a richer, more ingenious, more exquisitely artificial fiction than that ghostly figment whose name and personality she assumes for a few hours every night—that sketch of a person into which she briefly breathes a miraculous and luminous life and then allows to dissipate again in gales of applause. If only he had the taste to do so, he would appreciate the artistry with which she has crafted the particular self she is out of all the countless possibilities that lie in the depths of her nature, as well as the virtuosity with which she sustains the illusion of being who she is. *If*, that is, he were less of a philistine, and less of a child with a child's fondness for simpler fictions, rather than the more complicated fictions preferred by more seasoned sensibilities."

After he had been silent for several seconds, she remarked, "And you say my eye is cold. Yours is colder."

"You may be right," he replied. "In any event, she's at peace, and even somewhat more pleased with herself than usual. She begins removing her stage face. Soon her maid returns, having seen the young gentleman depart, and is disappointed to learn that he will not be returning. Our heroine laughs kindly at this, pronounces herself delighted, and instructs the girl to help her change. All is well—though, realist that she is, she does pause before leaving her dressing room for the night to look into her mirror once more and take stock of her features, now restored to their normal tones, and thinks to herself that in five years or so she'll have to begin considering securing a prosperous husband for herself and retiring from the stage. Seven at the most. That will mean assuming yet another role, of course—another fiction to inhabit and sustain—but she's equal to any part, she tells herself; and, needless to say, the one she's playing now can't go on indefinitely."

13 Transformations

Nicolò Gonzaga of Mantua had arrived just before dawn, when the path beneath the apple boughs in the orchard of Rabbi Johannen ben Isaac's home had still been filled with coins of moonlight, and the dew had gleamed like polished silver along its borders. Now, as he was leaving, the deep golden sunlight of the early evening was spilling across the grass and glowing among its green shadows and glittering amid the flavescent leaves and glossy autumnal fruit overhead, while in the house candles and lanterns had been lit by the rabbi's servants. The kindly old man had repeatedly tried to prevail upon his visitor to stay the night, for thieves were known to lurk along the way. "My lord Gonzaga," he said, even as the two of them were walking by one another's side toward the high orchard gate, "I know that you're not one to disdain the shelter of a Hebrew roof."

"Heaven forfend, *mio maestro*," Nicolò replied. "But neither am I willing to seek shelter within reach of my own lands, two hours from my own door. I shall be well. My horse and men are refreshed, you've fed me twice, my blood is still warm with your wine—and, too, the moon will be nearly full and should be up before we have traveled far, and the sky is clear. Anyway, I'm well armed, and I've three strong attendants. That very tall one with the iron-tipped staff—the ostler's son Luciano—well, I think I should pity any brigands so foolish as to fall upon him."

"At least let me send some of my men along with you as well," the old man implored, even as a servant boy drew back the bolts of the gate and opened its doors.

Nicolò laid his hand lightly upon the hilt of his rapier and affected a confident smile. "I have traveled this road often by night."

With a slight shrug, Rabbi Johannen relented. Waiting until Nicolò was in the saddle of the small, sturdy, but handsome palfrey, the old man merely raised a valedictory hand, almost as if bestowing a blessing. "Peace be with you, my lord," he said.

Nicolò smiled again, now more wryly. "*Et cum spiritu tuo*," he replied and then turned his horse away and began his leisurely journey home, his servants accompanying him on foot, one at either stirrup and the third—Luciano—a few paces ahead of the horse, leading the way with a lit lantern, not because there was any need for it as yet, but only to have a flame ready to hand when darkness fully fell. Within ten minutes, the party came out of the border of trees that hid Rabbi Johannen's home from the roadway and from whatever scandal it might have caused those who disliked the idea of a Jew owning so desirable a freehold and enjoying its entailed usufructs. When the old man had decided to retire to his native Lombardy to devote his final years to his great commentary on the Song of Songs, *Solomon's Desire* (*Heshek Shelomoh*), it had been Nicolò who had negotiated the villa's purchase from one of his cousins. This he had done at the behest of a more distant relative, now deceased—Giovanni, youngest son of House Pico della Mirandola e della Concordia—who had studied with the old man in Florence in the company of Fr. Marsilio Ficino. Nicolò had chosen the property specifically because of its relative inconspicuousness: it was nearly surrounded by two large private estates and sat well back from any common roads, along an obscure and wooded byway. As Rabbi Johannen was also known by the vague title "Alemanno" (even though he was not actually of German descent), that was the name in which the purchase had been made. It was a fairly humble villa but one that Nicolò had known all his life, and one in which he would have been more than pleased to spend the night under normal circumstances; now, however, he found himself in such a state of exhilaration and mental ferment that he needed to retreat for a time into his own thoughts without any interruption, and the journey back to his own villa was the best way he could contrive to do this without discourtesy to his teacher. He had learned so many marvelous secrets in the course of the day that he felt as if his heart could bear no more for now; instead, he must ponder all he had received until he could contain his excitement.

For the first half hour or so of the journey, as the descending sun's beams became more lateral, the light deepened in hue, turning a darker, richer gold—almost like honey by the time the sun reached the horizon and began to melt away into ribbons of yellow and red. For much of this part of the journey, the fragrance of bay trees and the whispers of the breeze among the pale leaves, overhead or already fallen along the way, were constant; and, when the party had emerged from the cover of the woods, where the road issued from between twin copses of arbutus and ilex onto a low long hill above an open plain, the western horizon had become crimson and the sky high above had become like an ocean of liquid sapphire in which the mild gleam of the Evening Star was floating all alone. There below them, somewhere along that stretch of ground, the southern boundary of Nicolò's own estate insensibly divided common from private land. But he was scarcely conscious of where they were, or of the scene laid out before them. His mind was still too full of the old man's words, so much so that his hand trembled upon the reins.

"It is a pity that true magic," Rabbi Johannen had said early in the day, when the morning light was still pouring in through his eastern windows and making the dust on his study's table shine like gilding, "the *magia naturalis* of which Father Marsilio has so well written, is so often confused with its counterfeit simply by virtue of the careless abuse of an innocent word. Men foolishly speak of 'magic' so indiscriminately that the true *artes magicae*—which are, when all is said and done, merely arts of efficacious prayer—seem to many indistinguishable from their absolute opposites, the goetic arts of influence over lower potencies . . . or even the diabolical arts. The men of ancient days suffered from no such errors. They knew to differentiate between *mageia* and *goēteia*—that is, if they were conscious of the latter at all. The Magi of Zoroaster and the Chaldean mysteries certainly would never have imagined that their holy rites or the hidden wisdom imparted to them by God—whom they called Ahura Mazda—could be mistaken for the petty sorceries devised for fallen souls by the devil—by the one they called Ahriman, that is. So too all the true practitioners of the magic arts—the Hebrews from at least the time of Moses, greatest of magicians, or the Egyptians since the days of Thrice-Great Hermes, or the Arabian, Indian, Persian, Hellene, and Romani sages—ah, my lord Gonzaga, none could have imagined such a thing. Between the magical and the goetical there is an absolute difference in principle, no less than in purpose."

Nicolò had asked the old man please to say more. "Forgive my ignorance; I am as yet only a neophyte in these mysteries."

Rabbi Johannen had smiled at him gently then. "Sometimes I think I confuse you with your kinsman Giovanni," he said. "Lord Pico. He was your age when he . . . Oh, well. What I mean is that the two practices do not draw upon the same power, or even on related powers, and in the event resemble one another not at all. The goetic is all craft, the exertion of power over chaos . . . the coercion of the lowest principle, the material substrate of the *Assiah Gashmi*, the realm that lies far below all the kingdoms of the spirit that emanate from the *Ohr*—the light—of *Ein Sof*—the limitless, that is. The malign force reaches down into the void of material potency . . . its chaos. *Goētia* is the hand that in the darkness forcibly molds obdurate clay into misshapen vessels. But true *mageia* is not coercion. It is invocation of that divine light—that highest of all principles. It is prayer. Not mastery of chaos, but devotion before the throne of the Plenitude. And the highest kind of prayer at that. Thus magic is the final, the most difficult, and the purest stage of the soul's spiritual formation. One who has ascended the ladder of the angelic *elohim* or embarked into the *Merkavah*, the divine chariot, has become all prayer; his every utterance, his every desire calls upon the unutterable name that exceeds all desiring. He calls down the divine— he divinizes the world—by himself becoming one of the channels of God's manifestation . . . one of the channels of the creative power of the radiance of the divine *Ohr*. Thus, too, the sages of the Hellenes, Copts, Abyssinians, and Syrians call it theurgy."

The hill's ridge sloped down gently to a shallow brook running among scattered hornbeams, their delicate teardrop leaves mostly light yellow or a yellowing green and a good many of them already scattered in the grass. Nicolò took appreciative note of the babble of the water among the smooth stones and of the gentle plashing and clopping of his horse's hooves as he crossed over it; and, coming out from the trees again, he saw the glitter of the stars emerging from the deep blue darkness above. On the next hill's ridge before him, lower than the one he had just descended, he saw the small, sleek form of a running fox briefly set off against a night sky already luminous from the moon just breaching the horizon. Still, though, the world about him seemed barely more than a dream by comparison to the thoughts coursing through his mind.

"Recall," Rabbi Johannen had gone on to say, "that it is only here, in the region of unlikeness, where the heavenly forms of the Great Age on high are meted out in fleeting reflections caught in the shadowy flow of time, and where all things are finite and posed over against one another, that contraries ceaselessly contend with one another without accord or union. This is the realm of finitude. But it is posed, as it were, between two infinities: that above, the infinity of light and life, and that below, the infinity of formless primordial matter, utter darkness and privation, the pure patiency of the substrate before any impress of form has been made upon it. In both, contraries merge, but for totally opposed reasons. There above, there is what the Christian philosopher Nicolaus of Kues has called the 'coincidence of opposites': that is, the supereminent actuality of all things together in the absolute simplicity of the divine light—in the infinite plenitude of the *Ein Sof*, that is, which the Christian philosophy knows as God the Father, the One that is more original even than the Godhead's self-determination in the unutterable name . . . *ha Shem* . . . which the Christian philosophy calls the *Verbum Dei* or the *Logos tou Theou*. In the realm of matter, however, in the infinity lying below all forms like an ocean of shadow, the darkness that the light of spirit has never yet wakened to form, contraries are again all one but only in pure indeterminate potency—in the privations of chaos, untamed by the breath of the One who is seated above. So this material realm is poised between the abyss of light and the abyss of darkness—between utter plenitude and utter dearth . . . infinite wealth and infinite poverty . . . and in between them rise the worlds of beings. The transformations worked upon this world by goetic sorcery differ from those worked by magic just as vastly as the one infinite differs from the other. And this is why I say that the difference in principle between them is absolute. Sorcery effects changes in the world by violently severing and banishing form from the abysmal darkness of matter, and then wresting new forms—or diabolical parodies of forms—out of the chaos that remains, wholly by force of will and with words of dark power whose every utterance is blasphemy. By contrast, magic frees the form from the constraints of matter, elevates it again into the primal simplicity above, then prayerfully summons down a new form in its place, out of the inexhaustible wellspring of the eternal light, and thereby resurrects the same matter into this new manifestation of the divine, through true supplication and through the speaking of holy names. For all things truly formed are, you surely know, reflections of the divine. This is true especially of the soul of man, but so too of all that is alive; and all things are alive, for the world itself has a soul. This was even one of the acroamatic teachings of the Stagyrite, it is said. Magic is merely life here below calling out to life there above, and most powerfully when it is done through those righteous ones, *tzadikim*, who have become conduits of light—especially the *tzadikim nistarim*, the hidden righteous men who in each age wait to receive and welcome the *Shekhinah* on earth. As for them, and the magic they work, and their mission here below . . . well, I shall have to tell you also of the Breaking of the Vessels and of the Restoration of All Things—the *tikkun olam*—but that must wait for now."

Later in the day, when the sun had stood at its zenith and the rabbi's study was submerged in cool shadow, Nicolò had again asked about creaturely "channels" of divine light.

"All creative power," the old man had replied, "all that works the beautiful changes in things and brings light to darkness, flows down from *Ein Sof*, and in all the worlds there are channels of that power that spiritual creatures may command, as intermediaries between the inaccessible light of Godhead and the lower orders of being. There are chains of such agencies reaching down to us from above—call them gods or daemons or angels, all are servants before the throne—and we join them in the work of creation and restoration—of transfiguration and sublimation—when we too become vessels of that light. Even the unutterable name is an angelic intermediary. He who is enthroned on high—whom some say is the Great Angel Metatron, who in elder days was the great magician Enoch whose power and knowledge became so prodigious that he was at last ravished bodily through the heavens into the very Presence—presides over the highest of the four worlds as God's viceroy to all below. God is himself the greatest of magicians, of course. All power of change flows from him. All true practitioners of magic merely, as it were, inflect the flow of that divine effluence, and draw it into this the lowest world in miraculous ways. Human deeds of power are nothing but the influence the spiritually pure work upon the descent of the divine light from the higher worlds. Moses, for instance, drew upon these channels of power to part the Red Sea, or to turn the waters of Egypt to blood. And so . . . ”

Here, however, Nicolò had begun to tremble in excitement, and perhaps in fear also, and had asked whether a brief respite might be allowed him so that he could absorb what he had learned, and Rabbi Johannen had called for food and drink—wine, bread, cheese, apples— and they had eaten together, at first practically in silence, until Nicolò had felt able to begin asking questions again. Only after the rabbi had assured himself that his young visitor was at peace, however, would he resume his discourses. “It is a great deal to learn all at once, perhaps,” he had remarked. “If it troubles you—perhaps you fear it is heterodox— we can speak of other things.”

“I have no such fears,” Nicolò had answered in a quiet voice. “The inner doctrines ever differ from the outer, as does spirit from flesh. So my kinsman Giovanni always said. I am merely moved with awe.”

Rabbi Johannen had nodded knowingly and, after another few seconds, continued: “True magic is at one with natural transformation, you understand. It isn't to be sought or practiced in order simply to wield power over nature, but should be used rather to bring nature's potencies to fruition in new and holier ways, in keeping with divine ordinance and natural good. It certainly isn't to be practiced for the purpose of compelling nature to violate itself, or for gaining power over other souls, or for acquiring wealth or eminence . . . ”

"This I know."

He had spoken honestly. It was neither power nor wealth that he desired—and anyway, he reflected as his horse descended another gentle slope down to a place where the path grew more level, he already possessed both in abundance—but only knowledge of the higher secrets . . . the higher truths.

"So, too," Rabbi Johannen had continued, "the alchemist who succeeds in transmuting base into noble metals does so not to create a treasure hoard; the labor is greater than the profit, and the yield is smaller than a persistent beggar could wring from the hand of a miser. Rather, he is merely cleansing one small corner of the darkened mirror of this material world, so that the higher forms may shine more brightly there . . . that the heavenly be made a little more visible in the earthly. It is but a visible and palpable allegory, as it were, of the much nobler transmutation, the theurgic metamorphosis of flesh and soul into intellect and spirit . . . and of how intellect and spirit are called to be sublimed into the divine source in which their fuller reality is eternally present—into God, that is."

The two servants who were keeping pace with Nicolò on either side of the horse had now lit their lanterns also, though he had been too preoccupied to notice when they had done so. Only when he noticed the soft sallow glow that fell across a stirrup and one of his boots did he briefly and vaguely register the fact. He noticed also a certain pleasant chill in the air and, on raising his eyes to the eastern horizon, a pale luminosity along the edge of the world. But then he was lost in his thoughts again as he swayed gently from side to side in the saddle.

"*Ein Sof,*" Rabbi Johannen had said to him when the aurous afternoon sunlight was pouring in at the western window, casting their two elongated shadows across the floor and onto the opposite wall, "reveals itself in withholding itself, by emanating the ten attributes of deity—the ten *Sefirot*—through which creation is continuously generated and sustained, while yet appearing nowhere among them. As I say, each *Sefirah* is a channel of the divine creative energy. Still, even though the One yields the All, the All cannot aspire to the One in its primordial limitlessness and unity—as the philosopher Plotinus too has said, in imitation of Moses. Rather, the *Sefirot* constitute the chain of the worlds—the *seder hishtalshelut*—the chain of celestial aeons—of *olamim*—

between the transcendent God and the created world. And so true magic—the natural magic of Father Marsilio, for instance—is nothing other than knowledge of and communion in the Sefirotic hierarchy, under the countless names that have been revealed among the nations. Which is to say that true magic is therefore nothing but true religion in its most exalted expression: the depth of knowledge and purity of soul necessary to summon down the spiritual agencies of the supernal realm in ethereal bodies to aid in bringing about the Great Work, which is the subliming of the lower into the higher at every level of being, and ultimately the transformation of matter into spirit."

"How many such levels are there?" Nicolò had asked. "How long an ascent must the soul make to achieve full mastery?"

"Ah," the old man had answered, nodding knowingly, as if he had expected the question, "there are the four worlds of the *seder hishtalshelut*—four aeons, four *olamim*—and within each of them the powers proceed according to their natural hierarchy. First, on high, there is *Atzilut*, the world of emanation, the radiance of incomprehensible wisdom; and then from that great perpetual lightning bolt descends *Beri'ah*, the first creative world, the aeon where the souls and the angels of the Most High as yet have no form but are conscious of themselves purely as wisdom born of wisdom; from there descends *Yetzirah*, the *olam* of form into which the spiritual realm above flows ever downward, and which in turn emanates and impresses itself upon the physical world below itself, *Assiah*, the region of action. But, of course, in and through all these worlds the divine *Sefirot* emanate according to the fixed hierarchy of their powers and manifestations, until they reach the lowest level of all, the *Malkuth*—the 'Realm'—of this material order. At the very apex of the Sefirotic tree is the *Keter*, the 'Crown,' the first emanation of *Ein Sof*, in which as yet there is no division of knower from known . . . no estrangement of the One from itself but only pure knowing . . . the walled paradise of divine innocence, into which no eye with plural vision may peer. From there, however, the divine power manifests itself by division into the male and female principles—the agent and patient manifestations—that form the nuptial syzygies from which the lower emanations are born. And each higher level is then in turn the agent power in regard to the patient power below. This is the mystery of the great love of the higher for the lower, and the burning desire of the lower for the higher, which in scripture is expressed as a mystery, under the veil of the story of the sons of the Most High smitten by the loveliness of the daughters of men, and descending to take them as wives."

"Yes . . . I see," Nicolò had interjected, in very nearly a whisper. He had felt for a moment like a fool for not having ever considered the allegory, which now all at once seemed so obvious.

But the old rabbi had simply continued: "From *Keter* proceed *Chokmah* and *Binah*, Wisdom and Understanding, and the one sires upon the other the *Sefirah* called *Da'at*, Knowledge; here *Keter* knows itself not simply under the aspect of the fused oneness of *Ein Sof*, but as a distinct duality of knower and known. These are the three levels—the 'Crown' and the syzygy it emanates—of the divine intellect that presides above all the worlds. From there, what descends are the divine affects or drives: *Chesed* and *Gevurah*, Lovingkindness and Might, the fruit of which is *Tif'eret*, Adornment; then *Netzach* and *Hod*, Eternity and Glorious Majesty, giving birth to *Yesod*, the Foundation; while below the *Sefirot* there is only *Malkhut*, the 'Realm,' the purely feminine patiency underlying things . . . the barren womb waiting to be made fertile by the descent of divine life . . . the dark waters upon whose surface the eternal splendors shine."

Here the old man had paused, staring away with an enigmatically serene look on his face toward the light entering at the western window.

After several moments of this silence, Nicolò had diffidently asked, "Can such knowledge be gained—I mean, the knowledge of true magic—by the unscrupulous . . . and avaricious? Surely the art of the alchemist, if nothing else, could be mastered for gain."

Now the rabbi's impassive expression had yielded to a smile of gentle amusement, and he had turned his eyes again to Nicolò. "To what end?" He had then removed a ring from his left hand and laid it on the table before his guest. It was a simple slender band, but clearly of gold. "It was lead once. I turned it to gold after many long nights of study and trial. But, as I've said, the effort it cost me, if turned to some humbler employment—perhaps tailoring—would have earned me more wealth than that poor pittance, at least as such things are normally reckoned. But, no, since you ask, I do not believe a venal man could master any of the *artes magicae*. Perhaps, yes, some might use force and craft and diabolic aid to wrest wealth out of corruptible matter . . . though I suspect it would resolve again into corruption quickly. But high magic is prayer, as I said. One cannot obtain that knowledge without holiness, for that knowledge simply *is* holy desire made transparent to the divine *Ohr*, divine Light. And that knowledge is hard won, and these small achievements—that ring, for instance—are laborious."

"Will you teach me, though?" Nicolò had asked.

"If you wish, my good lord Gonzaga," Rabbi Johannen had replied with equanimity. "You are a generous benefactor, and though I am a Jew I even dare to call you a friend."

"You honor me in so doing. Though I'm a Christian, I dare call you friend as well."

"That's gracious of you to say, my lord. Do understand, however, that when you learn the arts of transformation you will find that, at the last, I've taught you nothing more than a way of return . . . a new way of becoming a child. Therein is the Great Work achieved. I can only ever show you the way back to the beginning, and to the state of wonder at all things you knew before your infantine innocence was taken from you; but now it will be filled up with the wisdom of experience . . . and art. At that point, you will find that all you can ever do has always already been done in the fullness above. That's the deepest alchemic mystery I can impart."

This Nicolò had *not* understood, however, and the old man could read the perplexity on his face.

"I myself rarely practice the magical arts these days," Rabbi Johannen had continued. "I more often pray without words . . . without gestures. There is, of course, a greater magician by far whose works of transformation in every hour"—here he had momentarily and vaguely lifted his hand in the direction of the light entering the window from the descending sun—"dazzle me . . . enrapture me . . . beyond all longings for the things my lips and hands might conjure. I'm old, of course, and have found that the great surprise that awaited me as I aged was that, when the highest wisdom of magic is attained, the magic itself becomes needless and simply returns into its source in nature . . . and then nothing more is required. All is already accomplished. Names—even the names I've disclosed to you today—fall away. One knows God in his namelessness . . . *as* namelessness, perhaps . . . in everything. Then one can even glimpse his eternity in any passing moment, however ordinary."

It was at this point—perhaps because he did not want to hear these words, excited as he was at the prospect of learning the very arts for which the gentle old rabbi seemed now to have little use—that Nicolò had become conscious of his need to depart, to vanish into his own thoughts, until he was calm enough to come again and begin his tutelage. Yet it was also this final, somewhat baffling exchange that increasingly engrossed him as his homeward journey neared its end; he was so deeply submerged in the recollection of it that he felt as if he were being wakened from a dream when Luciano—who had apparently brought the horse to a stop, holding the slack of the reins below its bridle—quietly called out in his low rumble of a voice, "My lord, see."

They were halted on the brow of another hill, the last one in fact before the long level road that led to his own gates; and when he raised his eyes he saw that Luciano and his other two servants were staring away to their left, toward the broad, fertile plain belonging to the Villa Gonzaga. Nicolò turned his eyes in the same direction. It was immediately obvious what had arrested their advance; it would have been impossible to catch sight of the scene laid out below them and not pause to take it in. The old, gigantic oak that stood there at its center, majestically isolated from the sparsely distributed trees and low hills that formed the plain's far margin, was always an impressive sight: so much so that it had long since become popularly associated with the glory of House Gonzaga, and local legend had gestated a spurious "ancient" prophecy to the effect that, should the tree ever fall, that noble line would soon follow it in ruin. But now the sight was far more than merely impressive. Nicolò had not seen the tree for some time, as he had been staying in the city for more than a week before having traveled from there to Rabbi Johannen's door; and in that time it had changed wonderfully. The massive trunk and lower branches and enormous gnarled roots shone like dark copper. The great, extravagantly spreading pavilion of its crown, almost perfectly in the shape of a wide, high dome, was no longer green, but entirely gold and golden-red, and was radiantly visible in the night because the moon now stood well above the eastern horizon, in a clear sky of almost miraculously lazuline blue, blazing like white fire, casting its glow over everything—hills, fields, trees, stones—making the huge expanse of grass look like a glaucous sea with turquoise crests and transforming the leaves of the giant tree, stirred by the faintest of breezes, into a riot of sparkling flames. The lunar brilliance rendered the patterns of the constellations illegible in the glassy heavens, but also made such stars as were still visible shimmer meltingly in their depths. Everything shone. The view scarcely appeared to be real. Or, rather, it seemed more than real, like the eternal idea of itself; it made everything else Nicolò had seen in recent memory seem unreal and shadowy by comparison.

"Isn't it magnificent, my lord?" asked Luciano.

Nicolò, however, did not reply. He could think of nothing to say. And now the various reflections and recollections that had preoccupied him all along the way from the old rabbi's house had vanished from his thoughts in an instant. It did not matter, though. For this moment, and all at once, he had no use for words. He had no words at all. And he was perfectly at peace.

14   Recognition

Philippe, third son of the Duc de Montmorency, stood in the last of the twilight on a terrace of his house—located seven miles outside Paris—resting one hand on a marble balustrade and gazing westward. At his side stood his mistress of three years now, Marie-Anne de Bourbon, niece of the Prince de Condé and by marriage second cousin of the Duc d'Orléans. Neither had spoken any words for some several minutes; they had been absorbed in their enjoyment of the cool evening air, and of the fragrance from the first woodbine blossoms of the year, and of the waning evening's progress through the spectrum of twilight—pale green, citrine gold, violet, scarlet—and neither had wished to break the spell. Now, however, that the last of the daylight was just a thin silvery glow at the edge of the world, he remarked how exquisite the spectacle of the dying day had been. "So rich a purple in particular," he observed, "and so gorgeously deep a red."

She offered a small, inarticulate murmur of assent.

"It quite makes one believe in a heaven of the angels," he said.

"Or of the gods," she replied.

"Better still." A few moments later, when the night had fully fallen, he looked up and observed, "Not a cloud in the sky. See how Juno's breast milk streams across . . . "

"I thought it was Minerva's," she immediately interrupted, tapping the balustrade twice with her folded fan.

"The myths are inconsistent," he answered. "Anyway, angels or gods or what have you, they've graced us with a lovely night. Clearly it's out of admiration for your beauty, my love." He straightened one of his cuffs. "Did I mention," he asked in as insouciant a tone as he could affect, "that I killed a man this morning?"

"Did you now?" she said with practiced listlessness, not turning her eyes to him. "Not out of carelessness, I hope."

"No, though I might as well have done, for all the effort it cost me."

"Another duel?"

"Only barely. It lasted for all of one pass." Here he pretended to yawn, albeit very daintily, raising one bejeweled hand to his mouth, palm outward and only two fingers extended.

"Yes," she said, briefly glancing at him in the faint glow of three dozen or so candles emanating from the room behind them, through its open doors of beveled leaded glass, "I can tell you're tired."

"Bless me, madam," he replied, "I was up well before dawn and haven't had a chance to sleep since then."

"I find your enthusiasm for duels all very trite and tedious, you know," she said. "One day you'll lose."

"Perhaps, but there was certainly no danger of that this morning. A more maladroit swordsman I've never seen. His blade shook in his hand like a leaf on a storm-tossed twig when he stood *en garde* . . . and then half a moment later it had dropped from his hand into the grass. He didn't utter a sound as he fell. I'm not entirely sure he didn't die from fear before my blade ever pierced his heart."

"A man of good family?"

"So I was led to believe."

"Well, if you must go about slaughtering the nobility of France, why not kill my husband for me?"

He waved a limp, dismissive hand vaguely in the direction of Orléans. "Why go to the trouble? He's half a cadaver already. Besides, I've nothing but affection for the dear old cuckold. He's never treated me with anything but generosity. Goodness, my love, he surrendered you to me without a whisper of protest, even as the horns sprouted from his brow—almost as if he were glad to make a gift of you."

"Which, good my lord, is precisely why I often wish him dead. I have my pride, after all. He's not so prodigal with any of his other possessions." She breathed in deeply and again tapped the railing with her fan. "Though I suppose I shouldn't be spiteful. The old . . . darling has never even spoken crossly to me. And I imagine the real reason he doesn't resent our liaison is that age has robbed him of the necessary vigor . . . or rigor, shall we say, to please me."

He smiled but said nothing.

"Morbidity at the vital root," she continued. "The sap all dried up. I imagine it's a relief for him to hand the responsibility on to you."

"Well, then, be kind. He clearly has a decent regard for your needs. Admirable in any husband, I say."

"Which is all quite off the point. I do wonder if some miserable day news will reach me that one of your countless affairs of honor has left you dead or maimed. Then I'll have to find another lover."

"Not if I'm only maimed, surely."

"Most definitely if you're maimed. You know how I detest damaged things. I won't even allow a seamstress to repair a small tear in one of my dresses. The entire gown must be thrown away. Oh, honestly, why must you duel? It's such a bore."

"In this case, because I was challenged. I'm many things, my love, a good number of them quite deplorable, but I'm no coward, and I would sooner die than be thought a recreant to the field of honor."

"Men are such pompous children," she said, now laying her fan down on the balustrade and turning at last to look at him directly. "Clearly it's something you enjoy."

He smiled, though in the darkness and with his back to the light she heard it in his voice rather than saw it on his face. "If you could have seen it," he said. "Dawn's first light in the Bois de Boulogne. The dew glittering like tens of thousands of tiny cut diamonds, a white mist rising from the earth and hovering above the grass, the trees like looming gray giants . . . Oh, and if you could have heard the choruses of birdsong. And there's always something so soothing in the solemn ceremony—the grave, precise instructions issued by a second in a sober voice . . . the ceremonious appeal for reconciliation . . . 'I exhort you both, as you are gentlemen and Christians, to seek terms of amity' . . . then a whispered refusal, then the clash of steel ringing back from the woods, or the echo of pistol shot . . . It's almost like a dream. If one's to die, I can't imagine a sweeter setting or a more dignified final hour. Better, surely, than withering away in bed as a decrepit vestige of a man."

"Even if I'm in that bed alongside you?"

"Oh, you'll have long since abandoned me if it comes to that. I shouldn't respect you if you didn't."

"More likely I'd be too old and withered myself, and you'd have expelled me from your bed long since. I shouldn't respect *you* if you hadn't."

He permitted himself a deep sigh of satisfaction. "It's such a comfort to know neither of us would expect the other to be bound by love. There's nothing so vulgar as demanding loyalty once pleasure departs. As for the dueling . . . as I say, if you could only see it. The purity of the thing . . . the poetry."

"Except that I'm a woman, so I'll never have the chance of doing so."

"Perhaps some morning we could arrange for you to accompany me, if the opportunity should arise again. You can discreetly watch from the carriage window. Keep your fan open before your lovely face. Torment my antagonist with the mystery of your identity, and the need to acquit himself well before a woman. It would be very . . . quaint."

"I may hold you to that. I've never seen a man killed. I expect it would turn out to be boring after all, though. Most things do."

"It's never that," he said after a momentary pause, briefly abandoning his part in the game of wit, his voice becoming uncharacteristically serious. "It's never that. The idea isn't necessarily to kill, you know, but only to see that honor is satisfied." He sighed. "Mind you," he added, at once resuming his tone of airy cleverness, "this morning's engagement with the young fool who challenged me came as close as possible to being utterly tedious. Happily, it didn't last long enough for that. To be frank, had he possessed even a shred of skill he might have escaped with no more than a wound. I was much too confused by his challenge to feel any special desire to do him harm. I had no idea my very first thrust would strike home unimpeded. I was as surprised to have killed him as he was no doubt surprised to have died." He laughed curtly.

"Surely, if he was the challenger, you must have given him cause. What had you done?"

"You know, oddly enough, I'm not entirely clear on that. I can't remember meeting him more than once or twice, and then only in passing. I'd seen his face before, I know that, but I doubt we ever even spoke to one another before he accosted me. Whether we had even previously conversed I can't say. I certainly have no memory of giving him offense. But then, two days ago, he came up to me in the street in the city, outside my own house, spoke abusively—clearly indignant at something he imagined I'd done or said—and even struck my hat from my head."

"How absurd. Perhaps he'd mistaken you for someone else."

"He addressed me by name."

"Some other mistake had been made, then. He'd been given some false report about you—some insult directed at him."

"No doubt. But I was now the offended party. And a challenge had been issued and . . . as I say, I refuse to be cowed."

She turned again to face the western sky. For several seconds neither spoke. At last, however, taking up her fan again, she casually asked, "This young fool—what was his name?"

For several seconds, he pondered the question, placing a finger to his lips, as he tended to do when trying to remember something. Then at last he shook his head helplessly. "For the life of me, my love, I can't recall. I've no doubt he told it to me, and it was surely uttered aloud at some point by his seconds or by mine . . . but I honestly haven't the slightest recollection. Rather ridiculous of me, I suppose. My memory is growing so wretchedly feeble. Anyway, it hardly matters. Come, my dear, let's go in. I'll have dinner laid now if you have no objection. I really must retire early."

As they returned inside, the phantom floating unseen at some distance behind them realized that he also could not remember his name, though he had borne it all his life, right up to the moment when the sword of the third son of the Duc de Montmorency had severed his aorta early this very morning. Everything else that had led to his death was still fixed in memory, as were the name and social station of the man who had killed him—which, he reflected with some gratification, could scarcely have been more elevated. He could even recall the details of his life in the years before he came to Paris. But his own name—that now eluded him entirely.

He drifted behind Philippe de Montmorency as the latter briefly took leave of Marie-Anne de Bourbon—who arranged herself very ornately on a divan—went to ring for a servant, and issued instructions for their dinner. Then, as the two lovers reclined together on that same divan, the phantom hovered idly in their vicinity, listening to the flow of their persiflage—which was apparently their only way of speaking to one another—and envying its fluency and wit. Though he himself was now only a fleshless revenant, he could sense the lambent carnality flickering through the seemingly casual airiness of their conversation; as it was about nothing as such, it was clearly about something other than words; he was even aware of a strange throb of longing in himself at the sight of the woman's beauty and the sound of her delicate laughter, though he felt no trace of an actual physical excitement. But what did it matter? he thought to himself. The third son of the Duc de Montmorency had everything a man could want, and everything any other man might justly envy, whereas he—a poor phantom, a revenant, a wisp of a departed soul—now had less than nothing.

He had arrived in Paris a little more than a year earlier, accompanied by one servant and bearing a letter of introduction from his father to the man who would eventually kill him in the Bois de Boulogne. There was some remote tie between his family and the Montmorencies (or, to be more accurate, the Beauforts), though his house had in recent decades fallen on lean times, following upon two or three generations of decline as a result of poorly managed estates and a gradual loss of favor with the court; but in kindlier days its name—whatever it was, if only he could recall—had been a resplendent one in its own right, nearly as good as that of any titled ramification of the Bourbons . . . especially so in the days of the Valois . . . and his father still maintained the standards of the house and the honor of its escutcheon, even if the manor was in something of a condition of disrepair. Yet he had still felt like something of an oaf from the provinces when he had reached the city. His father had more or less sent him there to make a reputation for himself and enter into the kind of society that his lineage warranted, in the hope perhaps of finding some means of partially restoring the family's fortunes. So it had been with more than a little trepidation that, three weeks after establishing himself in rooms he could afford, he had donned the best coat he owned and presented himself at the door of Philippe de Montmorency's city residence, the letter of introduction in hand. There he had been told by a coldly phlegmatic footman, barely restraining a look of suspicion or disdain or both at the sight of a slightly shabby stranger arriving unannounced at the door, that Seigneur Philippe was not at home, and was not in fact expected back for more than a week. Though he had told the footman that he was in fact a relation of the master of the house, he had elected not to try to leave the letter at the residence. He had then returned three weeks later, having acquired somewhat better and considerably more fashionable habiliments, and had again requested to be received. On this occasion, though met by the same footman, he had been somewhat better treated, and had been ushered into a drawing room where another man was already seated, resting a somewhat worn leather portfolio in his lap and clutching it fast with both hands.

This person, it emerged from a few subdued exchanges of words, was a lawyer who had come bearing a variety of deeds and other papers that required the review and signature of their host. About twenty minutes passed before the footman reappeared to lead the lawyer in. Then better than an hour and a half passed, during which . . . whatever his name was rehearsed again and again in his mind the things he would say, the ease of manner he would affect, as well also as the deference he would surely display, and the small—exceedingly small—favor he would ask, or at any rate hint at. When at last he heard the lawyer being led again from the inner parts of the house and across the foyer and then being seen out, he prepared himself for the meeting and was just rising eagerly to his feet when the footman entered to tell him that Seigneur Philippe could receive no more visitors today, having business elsewhere in the city to conduct. The temptation to protest was strong in him; his sense of injury at this casual dismissal without even a tepid gesture of insincere courtesy had then momentarily deprived him of breath. But, curiously, a deeper impulse almost immediately overrode his anger: not prudence, though he had that in abundance, but rather a perverse and inexplicable feeling of admiration. All at once, he understood what it truly meant to belong to the most exalted social echelon—to exist, that is, so far above common notions of right conduct that one could act in a way that in a lesser man would have the character of vulgar incivility, or even of malice, and yet do so with perfect impeccability of intent. The higher innocence of the gods, he thought to himself, far from us in their heavenly abodes. Now, more than ever, he craved recognition from the Duc de Montmorency's third son; more than ever, he wanted to be such a man. So, after a few moments of indecision, making no complaint, he asked for pen, ink, and paper and wrote out a calling card bearing just his name—whatever it was—with no address; this he left in the care of the taciturn footman along with the letter of introduction.

Night was now completely fallen. He followed the two lovers through the shadowy rooms and corridors into their dinner, laid at a small table in a private chamber well away from the center of the house, and floated idly in the soft golden light of the candles as they took their seats, and then with something like hunger and thirst—though yet, again, without any actual physical sensations—he watched them eat and drink, through several leisurely courses, for nearly two hours. All the while their badinage continued to flow, leaping and glittering, seeming to grow droller and cleverer as the wine enlivened their wits, and he could only listen in rapt fascination.

He never received any acknowledgment of his father's letter of introduction. For some weeks after that abortive interview, he waited hopefully, even expectantly, for a reply, and even after three weeks only very reluctantly admitted to himself that it would never come. Now, he had begun to reflect, his circumstances were becoming considerably more uncomfortable. The allowance he received from his father was anything but ample, and he had intended to request Montmorency's assistance in procuring some sort of situation in the city not below—or not far below—his social station, and had even hoped for some small period of favor and patronage while he strove to find his way. In truth, he had no prospects to speak of. His only friend in Paris—a young scholar named Stéphane who had grown up near his family's estate and who was now a tutor of Latin and Greek to a wealthy household—was without influence of any kind. He was aware of another relation also in the city, a remote cousin named Hélène who four years before had married a very dull but prosperous merchant prince by the absurdly evocative name of Bourgault and who had then been rewarded for her sacrifice with an early widowhood; but his father had warned him to expect no help from that quarter and had hinted at some intrafamilial estrangement whose details were too painful to bear open discussion. And so, humiliating as it was, he presented himself one more time at Montmorency's residence; and on this occasion he was told at the door that the latter was not at home to visitors today. He was persistent in his demand that his presence must be made known to the master of the house before he would consent to depart, only to be informed again ten minutes or so later that no visitors would be received today.

The memory of that final humiliation tormented him continuously for several weeks, and then tormented him at irregular intervals thereafter, until more than four months had passed. And yet still— *still*—his resentment was repeatedly surpassed by an even more spontaneous and sincere admiration for his tormenter. Not envy, really, but something closer to reverent longing: a deep, wounding craving for *that* man's recognition. And then, quite unexpectedly, he received an invitation to a daylight gathering at the home of Madame Bourgault—something on the order of a garden party, it seemed, though exactly how to characterize it was not clearly specified. She wrote to him in her own hand rather than sending him a more formal invitation, graciously informing him that she had only just learned of his presence in Paris, and playfully scolding him for not having sent word to her as soon as he had arrived from the provinces. Though they had never actually met before, she addressed him in terms not only of familiarity, but even of affection; he was genuinely moved. He accepted the invitation without delay. Still not entirely certain of the currently fashionable manners of the city, he took the wise precaution of turning himself out as well as he could, purchasing a new suit of clothes for the occasion at (for him) considerable expense. He attended the party chiefly in the hope of forging a connection that might at least win him greater security than he now enjoyed—even decently honorable employment—and expecting to meet only an assortment of *grands bourgeois* there. He even thought that he, by virtue of nobility, might prove the most distinguished of his cousin's guests. He no sooner arrived at Madame Bourgault's home, however, than he discovered that her wealth was far greater than he had ever imagined, and was more than sufficient to erase any gap that might have been thought to exist between her social position and that of her putative superiors. In fact, his cousin turned out to be a woman of extraordinary elegance, charm, and taste: a true daughter of the aristocracy whom, he later came to understand, the flower of Parisian society regarded as one of their own, and in fact respected for having remade her family's failing fortune through a clever and mercifully transient alliance with a man of inferior but still presentable rank; and everyone also knew that in time she would contract a second marriage that would procure her a better surname. The guests he found at *chez* Bourgault proved an illustrious company indeed; and among them—pointed out to him by his cousin—was none other than Philippe de Montmorency.

This revelation left him briefly stupefied. As Madame Bourgault turned away to greet a newly arrived guest, he stood staring across a large room at the god who had already thrice spurned his entreaties, just then holding forth to a small circle of resplendently attired men and women and eliciting from them a constant torrent of laughter. He was transfixed; he felt weak, especially in his legs and loins, trembling with an excitement composed from equal parts dread, indignation, and adoration. Montmorency's every mannerism now—an ironical tilt of the head, a flamboyantly casual wave of a hand, a recurrent mischievous smile—fascinated him, to the point that his mouth grew dry and he felt a kind of fluttering in his stomach. His delight in looking on, his longing to be looked at in turn, his hunger to be what he saw, his need to be seen in the same way—all of it caused him to become lightheaded, and he had to turn his eyes down toward the floor until he recovered his balance. Then he gazed again at that glorious man and—summoning up what strength he still possessed—crossed the room, quaking so intensely that he felt as if he were at sea, unable to find his balance. He hovered just outside the circle of admirers and silently listened to the ceaseless stream of witticisms and ironies. After several moments, Montmorency noticed him and responded to his presence with a slight nod of the head, though also with an expression of uncertainty. Several minutes then elapsed before "an angel passed" and he was able, in a voice a little too loud and in phrases a little too rapid, to beg to be allowed to introduce himself. His name elicited no sign of recognition, so he explained who he was, recounted his earlier visits to his interlocutor's house in the city, and mentioned the letter of introduction he had left with the footman. At this, Montmorency expressed seemingly sincere regret and told him that all such correspondence would of course have gone first to a secretary, who was not especially efficient at distinguishing between what required immediate attention and what did not, and that no doubt the letter had been misplaced—but, oh dear, this was at any rate a happy if belated meeting, and certainly the acquaintance would be renewed in the very near future. And then the glittering flow of Montmorency's wit resumed and the circle of listeners began laughing once more. He lingered for a while, joining in the general mirth, until Madame Bourgault called him over to her side to introduce him to her late husband's sister. All at once, the anger, despair, and sense of humiliation had vanished; only the adoration now remained, amplified by the elation he felt at having at last received the recognition he so craved. He then had to do his best to master his palpitating heart and shallow breathing. Half an hour later, Philippe de Montmorency departed the gathering, but blessed him with a gracious smile and bow of the head from across the room as he was doing so.

When the two lovers at last rose from the table and, conducted by a servant bearing a candelabrum in which three candles burned, retired for the night, the phantom did not follow. Instead, he soon found himself moving slowly through the corridors of the house, around its great rooms, up its grand staircase, still trying to remember what his name was or had been. And then, somehow, without noticing how he had got there, he found himself again on that terrace. A bright gibbous moon had risen and stood high in the sky, like a frozen tongue of flame. The darkness seemed ineffably desolate: not so much the natural darkness of night, but rather, somehow, sorrow made visible.

Needless to say, he received no word from Philippe de Montmorency in the many weeks that followed the gathering *chez* Bourgault. And, while he was twice more a guest at his cousin's house, on neither occasion did he find Montmorency in attendance. Soon the giddy hope that had briefly relieved his misery faded away, and a deeper resentment and a more unrelenting despair than he had ever before felt took root in him. As weeks grew into months, his anger increased; and in his mind he again and again revisited the offense he had suffered, until the bitterness of it was with him in some measure during his every waking hour. He even began to fancy he had taken umbrage at the insult visited upon his father (for whom he had never felt a particularly deep affection before), whose name—whatever it was—was just as good as that of Montmorency. Better, in fact, since the current legatees of the Montmorency *duché* were not really true heirs to that ancient name and its appanages; it had been a gift of the damnable Bourbons, those parvenus from Navarre, as his father liked to call them—those rude bucolic Huguenots. And, through all his torments of indignation, the still deeper motivation that made all of it even more intolerable were those inextirpable, contradictory cravings he felt: the desire at once to be recognized as a man of worth by his tormenter and also to be himself the kind of man who could withhold such recognition from someone like himself. How he hated Philippe de Montmorency. How he yearned to be Philippe de Montmorency. But what could he do? And in this way more months passed, more disappointments accumulated. At last, a year to the day since his first visit, he returned one final time to Montmorency's city home. He never reached the door, however, because as he arrived (on foot), the man himself was outside the residence, attended by a valet, about to embark in a private coach. At the sight of this—and especially at the sight of that luxurious coach and its team of four—he felt a surge of pure rage rise up in his breast. Calling something out and dashing across the distance between them, he came within five yards of his tormenter and, unable to contain his emotions, more or less demanded that the latter turn to him and answer for his cruel discourtesies. Then he saw that his words were being met with an expression not merely of alarm, but of total mystification; and he realized that he was speaking to someone who had no idea who he was. Now he lost all control over his actions. He called Montmorency a rogue, a liar, a man without honor, moving forward as he did so in a manner so menacing that the valet and the coachman both interposed themselves between him and their master; but Montmorency—in a way that he would later realize he had found stirringly grand—immediately parted the two servants like a pair of curtains, strode directly up to him, coming within two or three feet of his face, and angrily demanded to know what all this lunacy meant, and who he was or imagined himself to be. He was unable to answer, however; he merely stared into his tormenter's eyes, trembling as if he had a fever. After a moment, Montmorency knitted his brows, laughed tersely, and began to turn away from him, obviously convinced that this was just some madman. He frantically reached out to lay hold of Montmorency's shoulder but did so with such an awkward lurch that he instead struck the latter's hat at the edge of its broad brim and knocked it to the ground. At this, Montmorency turned suddenly back around, eyes wide with astonishment, and, while the valet hastily stooped to retrieve the hat, again demanded an explanation of this insane effrontery, concluding with a furious, "Who the devil are you?" And then it happened. Unable to reply, deeply mortified that such a question had even been asked, he issued a challenge. The words seemed to spill from his mouth before he was even aware of having formed them in his mind. All at once, Montmorency's expression became cold and reserved and then gave way—like ice on a pond cracking in the sunlight—to a small, grimly amused smile. "I cannot oblige you tomorrow, as I've business to conduct in the morning, but thereafter I'm at your disposal. My man here will make a note of your name and tell you where your seconds may call upon mine." Then, without so much as another glance at him, the Duc de Montmorency's third son turned about majestically, replacing and adjusting the hat, and ascended into the waiting coach.

The situation was, of course, a hopeless one. Only after another hour or two did he pause long enough in his thoughts to consider the impossible position he had placed himself in. He was well aware of the deadly reputation, with both rapier and pistol, of the man he had challenged, while he himself had never been better than an indifferent fencer, even when he had tried as a youth to attend to his lessons in a way that would please his perpetually displeased father. As for pistols, he had fired one only once before, had missed his target by several feet, and had burned his hand. He also knew nothing about the etiquette of duels, since he had never before met anyone who had ever engaged in any. As for seconds, the best he could contrive to do was to call upon his friend Stéphane—who was utterly appalled on learning that he had challenged a man whom local lore credited with as many as a dozen dead adversaries—and to dress his own manservant in the same coat he had worn the day of his first visit to Montmorency's residence, charging the poor anxious fellow to remain silent at all times. There was no question of his winning the duel, or even of making a good showing; he decided, for reasons obscure even to himself, that he was more likely to survive a sword fight than an exchange of shot, but he knew he could prevail in neither. He would certainly not agree to a reconciliation before battle was joined; but, if he could successfully parry any assault within the narrow area of his torso, loins, and upper thighs, and accept a wound only to one of his extremities before conceding defeat, he would have achieved enough. Then again, if he should die, so be it. Continued life in his current state would have been intolerable. And so, quite contrary to his every experience of his own character and every estimate of his own bravery up until that moment, he felt oddly unafraid of death. At least, the thought of death seemed strangely abstract by comparison to his burning longing to be acknowledged, to be recognized for who he was, to be known by name by the third son of . . . (Here he trembled with anger at the thought of the man.) No one, he was certain, could possibly fail to recall the identity of a man met honorably at sword point or fail entirely to be insensible of his worth. It was only as he set his feet and raised his sword *en garde* that he all at once became conscious of the true peril of the moment, as well as of the sheer absurdity of his own behavior. He began instantly to shake. It took a mighty effort of the will on his part simply to keep his hold on his sword's hilt. And then the most humiliating imaginable denouement to the whole affair: it required not so much as a preliminary feint by his opponent to entice him into making that single awkward attempt at a parry with which he permanently disgraced his own memory; Montmorency's initial, almost teasingly tentative sword thrust at his breast struck home without obstruction. He died nearly immediately, though in his last instant of consciousness he glimpsed an expression of genuine bemusement on the face of his killer.

The moonlight shone down on the mottled marble of the balustrade and the smooth flagstones of the terrace with a wan, bleak glow. The fields beyond the barren autumnal garden looked like iron and ice. The stars seemed to stare down disdainfully from a desolate sky. And then the phantom understood. Of course he could not recall his name, for it was no longer his, and could never be his again until it was given back to him by the Duc de Montmorency's third son. And that great gentleman could make such a gift only by happening to remember what that name was, and by speaking it aloud, and this now seemed vanishingly unlikely. Until and unless that should happen, the phantom would be condemned to continue to dance this spectral attendance upon the man who had killed him, at least until the latter died. Thereafter, who could say what might come? For now, whatever the years ahead might bring, it was his own insatiable desire that imprisoned him in his present state. For, truth be told, he did not wish to be released on any other terms. As he pondered his present condition, he became aware that he no longer suffered from the rage that had driven him so idiotically to his death. All that now remained of those tempestuous passions that had tortured him throughout the final months of his life were his yearning to be known and his deep admiration for this great and intrepid and elegant man who could not be bothered to know him. He certainly felt no resentment at having been so unceremoniously killed. How could anyone have foreseen how poorly he would acquit himself at arms? He was not even particularly appalled or alarmed to find himself now transformed into a nameless ghost, hovering unseen at the edges of another man's life, as it seemed to make very little difference in the larger scheme of things; at most, it had merely disencumbered him of a great many superfluities of personality. After all, really, what else had he ever been?

15 Empire

I pray you, tell the Emperor of my service. I do not deceive myself that he should ever read this dispatch, or recall the face of one so lowly and insignificant among his countless servants under Heaven. It is as it should be that he sends us wheresoever he will, to every quarter of the Middle Kingdom, and thither we fly, expecting no further attention from him. We are content to be his words upon the wind, his instruments and symbols, his ensigns and devices, and nothing more. Mine is a humble petition: I ask only that my name be spoken aloud, if not in his august presence, at least in the hearing of the court, and that it be recorded in the annals of the empire as the name of one who has remained faithfully at his station, here at the far edge of the habitable world. And this I ask only so that the Emperor's wisdom in his delegations and deputations might be made manifest. I ask it only for the glory of him who requires no glory.

It is now eight years since I was sent as a magistrate to these cold borderlands, far from the splendor and high walls of the Forbidden City, and farther still from my own native district. Even Linhuang is many, many days' journey to my south. I repine at nothing, even though I have not seen my wife or my two children since the day of my departure for this place, and have received since then only sporadic and strange communications from home—fewer and fewer as the years have passed. I also, however, have received no new instructions from the court for nearly three years now, and my dispatches have elicited no reply. Not that an unworthy servant such as myself need receive acknowledgment of his labors. It is honor enough to be charged with fulfilling the Emperor's will among his subjects. More honor than I could possibly merit.

It is a simple people among whom I live—or, I might better say, beside whom I live, if at a necessary distance. I cannot dwell in their midst, of course, or walk freely among them. The dignity of my office forbids familiarity, and the dignity of my class makes easy commerce with the peonage unthinkable. When I must pass by them on a street, their voices fall silent, they back away from the thoroughfare with bowed heads. I do not turn my eyes to them, lest the spell be broken. Moreover, the dialect spoken here is unknown to me, and even after eight years my tongue cannot mold itself to such harsh and ungainly syllables. Even brush and ink are of no avail with this folk, as they are all quite illiterate, apart from one servant of my house who can understand a certain number of ideograms and take them as instructions. Otherwise, all my interaction with the locals is conducted through my private secretary, who speaks both our dialects. He is even my only means of issuing directives to the small local garrison of soldiers, as all of them come from this same region and are no better educated than the peasantry; this is so of even the two remaining officers. I rely entirely on my secretary, in fact. If he should ever die, I shall be bereft of any means of communicating my needs or wants to those around me. He is young, it is true, but his narrow chest and pallid complexion—to say nothing of a certain febrility to which he is prone—suggest to me that he may be of a hopelessly frail and tabid constitution, destined for an early grave; I fear some harsh winter wind will one day steal his breath away for good, and then how shall I fare in this wild and desolate and uncultured place? What authority can I wield if I have been rendered mute?

I watch them, of course. They are a placid and oddly cheerful folk, the villagers. The men, I perceive, speak gently to their wives and children, and rarely ever beat them. In all my time here, there have been only three instances of an altercation that has required my adjudication, all occasioned by wine and none especially violent. In every case, thirty strokes of the rod for each of the parties involved was more than sufficient remedy. Not once have I so much as had cause to suspect any of them of avoidance of taxes, or felt the need to issue a warrant for perquisition of anyone's property, such as it is. They are by nature of a docile disposition. They endure punishment equably, without resentment or complaint. A refractory child is a thing all but unknown among them.

Much of this I attribute to the simplicity of their way of life and to a diet that never excites or unbalances their corporeal humors. Rice or millet is their daily staple, as well as the aromatic cabbages and lettuces that thrive in this soil, wild and cultivated alike. They are judicious in the use of herbs and eat with moderation. Peppers do not grow at these latitudes, it seems. Moderate too is their indulgence in the raw rice wine they ferment, except on certain nights when they gather to sing. The only music they know, of course, is the beating of rough hide drums and clapping of hands and clashing of small, shrill cymbals. Their voices are raucous and uncouth, and their songs are pitched in severe intervals, strange to my ears; and naturally the words are unknown to me. But the sound is one of robust merriment, vulgar but with a certain guileless charm. The tea that reaches them in hard cakes from the south is of variable quality, but is wholesome and calming. Fruit too comes up the river upon the boats of merchants, and even sometimes jugs of plum wine, but these transports arrive irregularly, often only lightly laden by the time they reach this place. There are succulent wildfowl to be had here, and the local rustics are skillful in laying nets for them. They are fishermen too, of course. The river winds down to us through shallow vales among the hills beyond the border markers, beyond the grassy plains, and flows so slowly through the lowland—smooth and gleaming, sliding past banks of slender rushes, pale green fen grasses, sinuous weeds—that the water often seems almost still, even as it spreads out serenely into marshes all along its way. At times, it is all so pure a mirror of the sky—apart from a few glassy ripples and the spare dark reflections of bending reeds—that the flat fishing boats seem to float upon light. Only when the rains come does the water rise up and dash along in surging and splashing and babbling currents.

I was still a young scholar, only a few years from having completed the imperial schedule of exams, when I was commissioned to come to this place. It was to be a temporary posting, or so I was told, and as the way was long and travel along the roads in the north was notoriously arduous I could not bring my wife and my two sons with me. (I have a daughter also, who would have been an additional burden on such a journey.) My second son was still an infant and would likely have perished on the way. Even if they had all arrived safely with me, wife and sons alike, how could they have survived the austerity of this region, its barrenness, its savagery? I thought I should return to them in no more than a year, and now nearly a decade has gone by.

These country-folk, with their rude agrestic ways, are brutes. Placid, contented, submissive, but little more than livestock to be herded and grazed. Had my family come with me, it would have been an exile for them, as bitter as any penal banishment. And from whom would my sons have learned the arts of gentility?

Tell the Emperor of my service. I have received no instructions from the capital these past several years. No word has come to me at all, either along the post roads or upon the river. Still I conduct the business of my office. I send my reports faithfully. See how assiduously and meticulously I compile the records for the district: of produce, of taxation, of deaths, of the births of males. Faithfully too I send detachments of soldiers southward with the imperial revenues I have so laboriously wrung from this wretchedly indolent people. And faithfully I execute the Emperor's justice, which reaches out like a great canopy to shelter all things under Heaven in its cooling shade. I do not repine. To serve him, be it in ever so lowly a station, is my highest honor, contemptible wretch that I am.

The plains beyond the river, stretching out to the low hills of the horizon, are vast and ominous in their emptiness. This is especially so on days of clouded skies, when the long grasses there look like dark green jade, or in certain twilights, when they become gold and purple, and then briefly seem haunted by elusive traces of crimson, just before darkness falls and they become a gulf of susurrous shadow. Sometimes, in that soft crepuscular light, the standing pools amid the marsh grasses are like emerald, but when soft breezes ruffle them the scudding cockles are like amethyst.

Beyond those hills live the barbarians. I have never seen them. But at times their voices drift down to us from those slopes, over that undulous ridgeline. Savage cries. Laughter, bellows of rage. And then too the distant thundering of their horses' hooves. The glow of their fires along the skyline, dull and rufous against the night's blackness. The scent of smoke upon the wind. Sometimes the ringing of swords. Sometimes the remote and terrible sound of wailing brass, and the pounding of great, deep drums, and of music far more uncanny and atrocious than the harsh songs of the villagers here.

Beyond the border markers.

They hunt with falcons, it seems—the barbarians, that is. Sometimes one sees the great birds soaring over the hills, or across the plains, near to the river, and can occasionally even faintly descry the leather straps fluttering out from their legs. A shrill, keening cry, forlorn and terse. Dark and menacing shapes against the opal sky.

The woman who cleans my house and sees to my laundry and prepares my meals—the one who can make out a dozen or so ideograms—has a husband who tends the vegetables in my garden. He lacks even his wife's meager literacy, and when I direct him to do this or that with a gesture of my hand he usually only stares stupidly and nods;

occasionally, though, he emits a small curt murmur as well, to signify that he understands, but whether he is pronouncing a word or making a mere animal sound I cannot tell. The dialect here is so bestial that it barely approximates the syllables that naturally fall from human lips.

I have had no true conversation with anyone for time untold. My secretary, efficient and capable though he is, is a man of disappointingly deficient culture. He barely now remembers even a few of the odes he learned in preparing for his exams, and neither his family histories nor his private thoughts provide anything diverting enough to bear more than a moment's discussion. He bores me. Yet if he should die—if he should die, Heaven forbid—I shall be like a man stranded on an island far out at sea.

The woman and her husband, like all the villagers here, live in a simple house, roofed with rushes. I believe they have children.

In my study, I have a small bowl of glazed white bone-ash ceramic in which I keep a number of smooth white pebbles flecked with quartz, gathered from the sand in the river shallows. They are strangely poignant in their simplicity. On more than one occasion, I have found tears coming to my eyes as I have gazed at them.

I am removed from the common folk here, as I have said, and as is appropriate. Though I have had no conversation for so very long, I hold to my silence as to a precious treasure, or as to an unshakable tree amid a driving tempest. To this people I must ever remain a presence awful and mysterious, like a ghost.

As I say, merchants arrive irregularly, and for years no messages from the capital have come to me by way of the imperial posts, or in the boats that come up the silver river, gliding past the marsh grasses and catkins and reeds.

I should mention that, when seen through the grasses, the sparkling of the water seems to merge with the flickering silver of those long pale green blades. One can become entranced by the sight.

Do, I implore you, tell the Emperor of my service.

There are ghosts here. Many, in fact. Sometimes, if one listens intently, disembodied voices are carried on the winds that sweep across the plains and stir the grasses like a turbid sea with thrashing crests.

What they say, I cannot tell; the words elude me; they are most certainly in some other tongue. But that this is a haunted place, I am told, all who dwell here know.

The distant cries of the barbarians. The fading moans of hungry ghosts. Prophecies.

My dreams since coming to this place have all been surpassingly strange, full of omens and incomprehensible portents. And strange figures, without faces, veiled in deep shadow, who seem to know me but who will not speak.

There is a palpable darkness that lies over these regions, a dread. The barbarians will not stay forever beyond the borders, beyond the hills; and the darkness emanates from them. Something savage and inexplicable, contrary in every manner to the Way of Heaven. They consort with demons—this none should doubt. I am told by my secretary that my predecessor in this office, less than a year before he contracted the pleurisy that killed him, after two of his horses had bolted across the plains, sent an embassy of three men beyond the border markers and over the distant hills, to the barbarians, bearing gifts of jade, ivory, silver, and porcelain. Two were officers of the garrison, one was my secretary's predecessor. None returned.

I confess, I have begun to forget the life I knew before coming here, so much time has passed; and what remains in memory is now very like a dream.

In my mind, I see my wife. Her back is to me. I can no longer summon up the image of her face in thought; and no doubt she is now very much changed. The flower of a woman's beauty fades so swiftly; in its transience it is like the shadow of a cloud. But what I see is clear and moves me deeply. She is combing her hair with an elegant comb of mother-of-pearl, kneeling upon a bamboo mat in a garden, beside a still pool whose surface is a flawless argent sheen; lying at her side is a mirror set in a frame of white jade.

Is this a memory? Did I ever see her thus, or have I only dreamed it?

Cranes with wings outspread or languidly flapping, soaring over the marshes, under clouds the color of pearl. Hoopoes burbling among the grasses in dulcet voices. In the evening, the ghostly moaning of wolves.

They are a gentle folk, I repeat. They have mournful eyes, but they laugh with sincere gaiety. And yet I have a horror of them. How would it be to be like them? A people without poetry? A people who sing by howling, like wolves, and who know no other music than dull hide drums and brashly tinkling bells and tiny jarring cymbals and the slapping of callused palms? A people without civility?

None among them has ever felt the caress of a silk sleeve, or the dampness of a cuff made wet by tears that have been shed at a tender recollection. None has ever known a moment of delicate wistfulness or exquisite grief. None has ever been moved to sighs by dew upon a white jade parapet at dawn, shining beneath the morning moon.

White jade. Tears. Dewdrops. None of it evokes anything for them.

How often I yearn to see the city again. It is like a great thirst. I do not repine, however. The mind is a city, is it not, into which one may admit all the wonders that abide under Heaven?

Please, be so kind as to tell the Emperor of my service.

Blue lightning sometimes falls from the stars here.

Wild, lean deer, red and brown, bound through the grasses. Sometimes one sees them on the plains, untroubled, grazing, like the deer in the imperial parklands, traipsing across glistening lawns, through the azure shade below the deep green boughs, along the margins of ponds in whose plumb-blue depths golden carp lazily swim.

I have seen them running also, in terror, under a sky like bronze from smoke, through which the sun shone dimly, a glowering gold. Bright embers on the air, gently falling, above the coursing of the wind-stirred grasses, now all turned a sullen red. Locusts swarming under the violet haze hanging above the ridgeline, against the gray-green screen of the early evening sky. Brittle shadows clinging to jagged rocks. Dry reeds hissing in the wind.

Or was that a dream? It was, I imagine. But surely it was an omen as well. There is a darkness gathering beyond the hills, out past the border.

In truth, there is great beauty here, I cannot deny it. If you were to see the plains transformed by the rushing wind into wave upon wave of a vast incoming tide, you would be at a loss for words to describe it. The late autumn brings the rains, and the waters descend from the higher elevations in scintillating freshets to fill the narrow, shallow winterbournes hidden among the grasses. They glimmer and flash everywhere amid the green, like liquid glass, like bright veins of flowing light. The pools of the marshes rise and spread. The fragrance of wood smoke wafts from the villages. There are days of white sunlight, smoldering among the dark sedges, making the silken heads that crown the russet marsh reeds gleam the color of moonlight. The wind falling from the slopes of the distant hills sometimes sweetly stings one's cheeks and lips with minute ice crystals.

Rains come in the spring as well, though they are gentler. They too become shimmering runnels and branching streams amid the green, but they—unlike the rains of winter—are soon followed by an indescribable profusion of nodding wildflowers, of every hue, especially in the meadows to my south, but also in those vast plains to my north. During those brief days, one knows such beauty as the gods enjoy in every hour.

Early in each autumn and then again when the winter yields to spring, I cannot help but wonder whether this will be the year in which the barbarians break the peace. The common people here would be swept away in an afternoon. The garrison would not survive more than a day or so; its poor fortifications, with their low ramparts and aging wooden gates, would prove as fragile as a clay cup before the onslaught of those abominable hordes.

Such thoughts assail me also on those chilly days when mists roll down from the hills, so dense that the plains disappear, lost to view behind veils of gray. At such times, the unnatural powers that ride in the barbarians' vanguard do not scruple to disport themselves, moving as great soundless shadows across the immense spaces, misshapen and terrible among the billowing, dim, and shifting vapors.

It is known that these are haunted lands. There are ghosts here, upon the plains. And there are signs.

In every season, I am faithful in my observance of the rites. My ancestors never want for tribute and veneration. I need never fear that they will ever doubt my piety or turn deaf ears upon my supplications.

All correspondence reaches this place only irregularly, official and personal alike. I have received no letter from my wife these last two years. When I parted from her, my younger son had not yet taken his first steps. Soon he will see his tenth summer.

I do not repine. What higher honor than to serve my Emperor, lord of all things under Heaven?

I find myself ever more often wondering: What are the barbarians? What kind of creatures? Whenever I try to envisage them, I entertain such dreadful—such impossible—thoughts. This is what terrifies me most: not the threat of their indomitable savagery, their great numbers, their martial prowess, their cruelty toward the conquered, but the thought that there where they dwell, out past the border markers, there is no Emperor. I can scarcely write those words: no Emperor. I certainly cannot speak them aloud. The shadow of his provident hand does not reach out so far as to cover them, to shield them from the pitiless sun and the bitter winds; and I—who dream so often and so longingly of being drawn back further in under that hand's Heaven-spanning might—I know of no thought more horrible, more unimaginable. How can it be? How can I dare to imagine it? How do they live, so exposed to the abyss?

Where they dwell, out past the border markers, there is no Emperor.

And then, too, I sometimes wake in terror from dreams I cannot recall and find myself alone in the darkness thinking that perhaps the reason that I have received no instructions from the imperial court is that it has passed away, all in an instant perhaps, like a momentary mirage on a distant mountaintop, or like mists driven away before the wind. Perhaps the capital has simply vanished. In my mind, I sometimes see an empty horizon where once the soaring prospect of the city stood. And then, far more intolerably, I wonder whether it was ever there to begin with—and even wonder whether the Emperor is himself only a dream. Is the imperial court real at all? Is the Forbidden City? Or have I only imagined it all from the very first? I have received no word for so very long. Perhaps I have never received any word, ever. These are impious thoughts, I know. Blasphemies. In those hours, I can only wait for the light of dawn to chase the horror of them away.

See how with this letter I send all the records and registers I have so faithfully compiled, here at the end of my eighth year in this posting. I affix my seal of office, and know in consequence that my dispatch will come inviolate to your hands; for now the Emperor's own ward and sovereignty lie upon and protect it, and surely nothing bearing the mark of his beneficent power can ever perish or be lost.

Tell the Emperor of my service. I pray you.

16 *Theophania* (a fragment)

Those who have seen the gods can never again be unaware of their presence in all things. To have seen them is ever thereafter to be blessed and cursed with the terrifying and ravishing knowledge of that beauty—that merciless power. I know whereof I speak.

I was only a student at Marburg when I was granted my vision. As a philologist, I should perhaps have been better prepared than I was, seeing as I had all the testimony of antiquity, Western and Eastern alike, to instruct me in the meaning of what I saw. But the gods show themselves to us only rarely now, in fleeting and mysterious glimpses, often no more than a shadow caught out of the corner of an eye. Certainly they never now reveal themselves in the fullness of their glory, like Zeus before Semele or the LORD before Moses. Oh, but at one time they showed themselves to us freely, prodigally. The world shone with

183

their presence; in every natural form their figures could be discerned; the wind and water and echoing valleys and sounding woods were full of their voices. One could not turn one's eyes from them, or seal one's ears against them, or be insensible to their caresses in every idle breeze, every living touch. They flowed within all things flowing, lived within all things living, stood immovable within all things great and changeless. They were ever near to us—closer, often, than we were to one another.

Then too there were places of meeting, mysterious and enchanted places where gods and mortals stood in peace before one another, sometimes even face-to-face—clearings, grottoes, mountaintops, tabernacles, shrines. For a very long time, the gods even consented to dwell among us, in houses we had built for them, inhabiting the great images standing in the shrines of our temples, showing us their visages—stern and benevolent—but veiling their glory lest we be destroyed by their unbearable beauty.

As gods and mortals continued to draw near to one another in those places, moreover, we became more divine and they more human.

Perhaps I am not being clear. I should simply tell my tale. I—

But let me note, first, that what I saw that night was only a fading image of what at one time no one could fail to see.

Each year, in the winter months, Apollo was absent from his house in Delphi. During that time, Dionysus dwelt in his place within the temple's shrine. Instead of the Apolline paeans, the Dionysian dithyrambs were sung. Then, in the spring, when Apollo returned from his Hyperborean retreat, the feast of *ta Theophania* was celebrated. The inmost sanctuary of the temple was unveiled before the gaze of the faithful. The divine images were revealed. The gods themselves were revealed to mortal eyes.

That, though, was only a mystery within a greater mystery—a revelation within a greater revelation—for it was ever thus with the gods. They were always at once hidden and manifest, unapproachable and intimately present. And it was their beauty—for which we longed so achingly, and in which we delighted so constantly—that continuously fashioned us into something ever more like them.

It is our fault that they have grown so distant now. They granted us, over many epochs and with ever greater liberality, the very power by which in time we would dispossess them of their empire. Now we attend to them rarely and without reverence, and they condescend to know us scarcely at all. That estrangement was the shattering of the world.

Enough of the philologist remains in me that I can tell some part of how it all happened. Our race learned to tell stories about the gods long before it ever occurred to us to tell stories about ourselves. And even when we first learned how to tell our own tales, we still at first could do so only by speaking of ourselves as mortals living out the brief spans of our lives in the presence of the immortals, under their kind or baleful gazes. It was a very long time indeed before we began to grasp that we could tell tales from which the gods might be absent, or at least within which they could remain safely hidden, without rendering the tales incomprehensible to ourselves. Until that moment, which no doubt lasted a great many centuries, the only histories of which we were conscious were of events that had happened in a time beyond time, before and outside and above the passing hours by which our days are measured. Or really, one might better say, not in time at all—not in *tempus* or *chronos*—but rather in that age—that *aevum*, that *aion*—that lies between time and eternity. It was the gods who first taught us to speak of ourselves as the paradoxical and divided beings we are, at once part of nature but also somehow separated from it. They called to us out of the world's high and hidden places, and our response to that call was, for us, the beginning of self-knowledge. But then we progressively displaced them from the world they had so bountifully given us. From myth we passed over time wholly into history, and took to ourselves the glories that once belonged to them, and gradually dispensed with their mediations between us and the highest mystery of being. All of this was the fruit of that immemorial commerce of identities that once long ago existed between them and us.

Mortals and immortals, living one another's deaths, dying one another's lives.

Among us, of course, in these as in other lands, one god gradually displaced all others, and became God for us—jealously, cruelly, a deity of darkness and wrath—and then finally withdrew into the formlessness of the most inward sanctuary of all. In his place, and in the place of all the other gods, we took a man as our god. History and eternity became one for us, and as a result the realm of the gods—which is neither, which is nature in her endless cycles of abundance—was rendered vacant.

They are so distant now. But it is only so long as we remember the communion we enjoyed with them in that time before time—in that aeon of dreams—that our histories have any real meaning at all; it is only so long as we remember the gods, however fading the recollection, that we remain human.

Forgive me. I began to tell my story and all at once was diverted.

Let me say that I understood very little of any of this before the night when everything was altered for me. At least, I understood it at most as one might understand a curious fact of history, but not as I should have done: with an acute awareness of a terrible and catastrophic division that had opened up between our kind and the world about us, as well as between us and those from whom we came. I was, as I say, a student at Marburg, promising but by no means extraordinary among my peers. Though my prospects were not lofty, I had enough of an income from my father—and would in time have a greater one from my inheritance—that I could be assured of a comfortable life, even if I should become only a professor in my discipline, or only a writer. I had even contracted a betrothal with a parson's daughter—a lovely girl of seventeen—and her father had clearly considered it something of a triumph on his part when he granted me her hand. The world that I knew was an inviting place, one in which I was destined, I thought, to live out the life of a perfectly accommodated man.

It was, in fact, on a night when I had been visiting my fiancée and her father that the world was changed for me, and I was changed with it. The rectory where the two of them lived—he had been widowed when she was only three—was outside the purlieus, and between it and my rooms in the town the road ran clear but through a good three miles of forest and into another half mile of country lanes. I had come on foot and, forgetting that the days were growing shorter in the waning year, had departed after night had fallen. My prospective father-in-law had provided me with a lantern, and I my beloved with a parting kiss upon the cheek, and I was in good spirits as I made my way back homeward. Apart from a slight chill in the air, the night seemed clement; the sky was clear and half a waxing moon hung high in its sky. But I was only midway through the woods when a strong wind arose, positively moaning and sobbing through the bare branches of the trees and raising clouds of dust and dry leaves in the narrow horse path ahead. Quickly, too, the darkness deepened as clouds spread across the sky above. I had been caught in a storm before, of course. But there was something about the astonishing, unpresaged suddenness of this change in the weather—especially here, in the shadowy autumnal woods, with the stark outlines of the treetops beginning more and more to sway and then to heave against the lowering vault overhead—that felt altogether uncanny. I sensed a threat in the violence of the winds, in the soughing branches, in the cold. Not only a threat, in fact, but perhaps a kind of anger, inexplicably directed at me. And then the glow of lightning from the west flickered past me among the trunks, and a moment later the slow roar of distant thunder rolled after it. I told myself not to be superstitious, and reminded myself that I had only ever once heard of a man struck by lightning—and then not fatally—as I drew my now quite inadequate cloak more tightly about me, placed a hand atop my hat to hold it in place, and quickened my stride. Ahead the path was straight enough that the lines of trees on either side formed a succession of high ogival arches, like the interior of a Gothic cathedral, at the far end of which, beyond an open field, the ridge of a low hill was visible. And, as I hastened toward it, and toward the lanes I knew lay on its other side, a great vertical fulguration, descending all the way down to its crest, lit up the sky above it, and a second later there was a burst of thunder as tremendous as any I had ever heard. The nerves in my legs and arms reacted to the blast with a momentary but shocking throb of pain. I found myself uttering a startled cry, which quickly transformed itself into a few words of tremulous supplication. I started to run, though the wind and the cold made it hard to breathe very deeply, and I soon had to slow my steps again to a mere vigorous walking pace. Now I was terrified, truly, though at what I could not quite have said. It was certainly something more than the storm and the darkness.

And then it happened, all in an instant. Lightning broke out in the sky before me again, but nearer now, visibly striking the crown of a tree at the mouth of the path ahead, with a crash of thunder so loud—as well as the sound of a great bough being rent from its trunk and falling among the trees—that it was for a moment as if the pillars of the world were being fractured, and the heavens were beginning to fall. I halted, then stepped back, and felt a weakness pass through me that nearly brought me to my knees. And then I saw them. A series of flashes coursed along everything from overhead and, ringing out like clashing bronze amid the thunder, it was as if a great door had all at once been thrown open before me. I saw their terrifying greatness. I saw their forms in the fire of the sky, on the hillside beyond the trees, in the trees themselves: immense, implacable, surrounded by aureoles of lightning; and I knew that they had summoned the storm. They were glorious and monstrously great, beautiful and impassive, mighty and serene. They were immeasurably more alive than I. They were life itself, of which I was barely a vanishing shadow. Now I fell on my face, idiotically, so fiercely and convulsively that my mouth was for a moment filled with dust. Then, after nearly a minute of shaking upon the ground with my eyes closed, I raised my head and looked again. Once more, the lightning flashed. Still I saw them. But now I saw also that they were not at all mindful of me. My presence among them was as nothing to them. And then I grasped how great the gulf between us and them has grown.

Moments later, the vision had passed, between one flash of lightning and the next. Perhaps ten minutes after that, I was able to rise to my feet and, still frail and trembling, continue my journey. The wind and lightning accompanied me, but the rain never came in any great quantity; only a few drops struck my face or the brim of my hat; and by the time I was at the outskirts of the town the night was calm again, and the sky clear.

I knew that I had become someone—something—else.

I cannot say I have seen them reveal themselves so nakedly again. Only for that brief interval, on that one night, was I granted a direct vision of what lies within the holiest place within the sanctuary. And yet I have never since then ceased to see them. In the sunlight that falls across a field, I am conscious of their majestic, shining forms striding through the oblivious world. In the prospect of distant mountains, upon the ridgelines, massive and sometimes contending figures move against the sky, calling down its mists and rains and fire—especially when I see the flickering lightning spilling down glaciated slopes. Only yesterday, I saw a cloud of golden pollen raised by the wind, rolling across a meadow, sparkling, glowing, fecundating everything with its glory; and in it I saw the gods entwined in one another's limbs, and saw the tenderness and exuberance of their carnal embraces. How can I explain it, though? It is not as it was on the night. They do not step forth from behind the veil. Yet I am aware of them always. A slowly flowing river is a god's languor, a great tree a god's patient gaze, the night full of stars a god's detached pity.

I know now that in those times and places of meeting, the blessing and the curse were one and the same. Those who had eaten at the tables of the gods—under whose feet lay a worked paving as of sapphire or lapis lazuli, of the clarity of heaven itself—were conquered by their own delight. They gave everything for that precious moment of commerce with imperishable beauty. Thereafter, this world must have been for them only shadow—the richest wine indistinguishable from brackish water, the most sumptuous fare possessing no more savor than ashes or dust. But the terrifying memory was sweet enough to sustain them for the rest of their time. Or so I believe.

Why I have been granted this knowledge—I of all men—I cannot say. Certainly there is no intimacy between me and them—no commerce of understanding . . . no obvious bond of love. I have been granted no oracles to speak, no wisdom to share. Was I elected for some purpose, or did I like Actaeon merely happen upon a mystery that should never have been intruded on, but should instead have remained concealed in divine pudency? Perhaps it is only because of the distance that has grown up between us and them, to the point that we scarcely merit their notice, that I was not similarly destroyed. How irremediable a schism it has become, as if gods and mortals are so remote from one another now that our very worlds have grown apart, into separate histories that are only very occasionally visible to one another, and that perhaps diverge from one another ever more greatly as the years pass. I see them, even if not directly, but I do not know if they are aware of me—or aware of any of us—at all.

It was not long after that night that I confessed to my own heart that I was no longer capable of the life I had once envisaged for myself. I was no longer suited to the world that had once sheltered me. I belonged somewhere between it and an altogether other world, burdened by the terrible knowledge that in former days they had been one and the same. I knew I had no home in either.

I could not, of course, honorably rescind my betrothal, and was entirely resigned to becoming a husband and a father, even though I knew I should now fail in both roles. I confess, I found myself somewhat relieved when, during that same winter, not long into the new year, my fiancée contracted the fever that bore her away. I wept at her graveside, it is true; I made myself do so, for the comfort of her father and out of a genuine fondness for her and her gentleness. But I was secretly grateful to know that now I would not be the source of a lifetime of sadness for her, as I would have been had she not died.

There is no story to tell beyond that. I am simply someone who—out of time—came into one of the last remaining places where gods and mortals had in the past freely encountered one another, and where in former times it would perhaps have been possible to seek a blessing or a word. I imagine that very shortly no such places will be left. The gods are always now departing from us, I think; their world and ours will soon no longer meet at any point.

They are great and awful and beautiful, eternal and radiant and wise, and to have seen them is to have seen the beginning and the end of all we are and all we have ever been. And when at last they have truly gone, and they have ceased to be like us and we have ceased to be like them, will anything remain in us that still reflects that beauty, that eternity? I very much doubt it. And this is why I say I am no longer suited to life. For me, the night is always deepening, the world is always vanishing.

I visited my fiancée's grave again two days ago. It is almost eighteen years now since her death. I am still capable of that much faithfulness to her, at least. I take some comfort in this.

... et tous brillent les uns dans les autres et les uns à travers les autres, leur lumière se confondant et se réfractant ... une seule lumière se déversant à travers tous ces prismes, glissant à travers ces voiles ... car il n'y a qu'une seule grande œuvre qui passe par tous ses merveilleux changements dans toutes les œuvres créées par nos âmes ...

Acknowledgments

I imagine I owe a great many persons thanks in connection to this collection, but there are five in particular whose names occur to me. My nephew Addison M. Hart convinced me to restore a detail of the story "Zalmoxis" that I had removed out of an overly fastidious concern for historical plausibility. Henry Weinfield gave me a good piece of advice with regard to the opening pages of "Recognition," which I probably should have followed more than I did but which did nevertheless improve the text. Tariq Goddard offered sage counsel regarding where one of the stories should appear in the text. Salley Vickers forgave me for writing "Thresholds," even though she arraigned me on the charge of having raided her subconscious for several of its motifs and plot devices. And Trent Pomplun told me— and what a fool I was not to have seen it before he pointed it out—that, in the final scene in "*Ensō*," the tea the protagonist brews for himself should be *gyokuro* rather than *genmai*; perceptiveness that keen is no small endowment.

Three of these stories have been printed before, though all arrive here in slightly revised form. "The True Helen" appeared previously in my 2016 collection, *A Splendid Wickedness*, released by Wm. B. Eerdmans Publishing Co., and both "The Scholar and The Nymph" and "Dialogue on an Island" appeared in my 2017 collection, *The Dream-Child's Progress*, released by Angelico Press. My thanks to both houses for giving their blessing on the incorporation of these tales into this volume, which was always in fact the home for which they were intended.

Photo by Nicole Waldron

DAVID BENTLEY HART is a writer of fiction, religious studies scholar, philosopher, and cultural commentator. He is the author and translator of twenty-three books, including the award-winning *You Are Gods*.

www.ingramcontent.com/pod-product-compliance
Lightning Source LLC
Chambersburg PA
CBHW050344030726
47503CB00008B/2608